Praise for Jaci Burton's *Rescue Me*

5 Angels "...Rescue Me is a tremendously written contemporary romance set in the midst of a ranch and the wonderful Morgan family. Sabrina is a compassionate woman readers will instantly love. Her personality and excitement towards every detail of the Rocking M Ranch offers Kyle the chance to experience the joys of the ranch in a different light as well as provide readers the sensation of experiencing it themselves. Kyle is a dedicated brother, son, and man that any woman would be honored to have the opportunity to love as their own. Even though he has the tendency to let his pride get the best of him, deep down inside he is an amazing man. Jaci Burton did a superb job at creating a beautiful story. This is the first story that I have read by this author and I assure you that I am already looking for more by her."

~ Jessica, Fallen Angel Reviews

4 Red Hearts!"Jaci Burton has penned a very sizzling romance between a former beauty queen and a bad-ass cowboy. Her characters are interesting, lively, sassy, emotional and adorable. The secondary characters give depth and feeling to the story. The plot is entertaining. ...Both Kyle and Sabrina are multi-dimensional characters that will find a place in the reader's heart. Ms Burton is well known for giving her readers a sizzling tale and this story is no exception. There is plenty of heat as the sexual tension is electrifying and when these two lovestruck lovers finally give in to their passions, the reader will sigh along with them. Fans of Ms Burton will enjoy this story and will add it to their keeper cyber shelves along with all her other works."

~ Valerie, Love Romance

"The story of Kyle and Sabrina is sizzling with chemistry. It is a very sexy story about very sexy believable characters. Sabrina wants to work with the Morgans to make things better on the ranch. During the process she encounters a lot of bad behavior by Kyle. Kyle and Sabrina both have very specific plans for their futures...The characterizations of Kyle and Sabrina are beautifully written by Ms. Burton. This contemporary western is a keeper."

~ Ellen Bunch, The Road to Romance

4.5 Ribbons "RESCUE ME is a charming story that explores passion, deceit, and trust. I took great pleasure in reading this exhilarating novel. The sexual tension between Kyle and Sabrina ignited instantly and remained flaming-hot throughout the entire book. ...This is one sweet and spicy romance that is sure to please many western genre-type readers. So run, don't walk to purchase RESCUE ME by Jaci Burton!"

~ Contessa, Romance Junkies

"Rescue Me is a touching story about love and family that will leave you with a warm feeling and happy tears! ...Jaci Burton does a magnificent job in creating an engaging story with characters that take root in your heart! Kyle and Sabrina hold a special place in my heart(and on mybookshelf!), with the fiery, passionate energy between them, tempered by compassion. As it seems to be with all of Jaci's books, the main characters aren't the only ones I've fallen for! ...Definitely a book for multiple reads, and I'm hoping for a sequel!"

~ LindseyAnn Denson, Ecataromance.com

Rescue Me

Jaci Burton

A SAMHAIN PUBLISHING, LTD. publication

Samhain Publishing, Ltd.
PO Box 2206
Stow OH 44224

Rescue Me
Copyright © 2006 by Jaci Burton
Cover by Scott Carpenter
Print ISBN: 1-59998-94-0
Digital ISBN: 1-59998-029-0
www.samhainpublishing.com

First Samhain Publishing, Ltd. electronic publication: March 2006
First Samhain Publishing, Ltd. Print publication: June 2006

Rescue Me

Jaci Burton

Dedication

To my wonderful editor, Angela James, for your insights, for making me laugh, and for making Rescue Me a much better book. Love ya babe. You're a true BB in the best sense of the word.

To the BB's... I love you guys for being there for me every day in every way, despite my daily whining.

To Crissy, the Diva Queen. You're the bestest. Sending chocolate kisses.

And to Charlie, with all my love. Thank you for helping me along the way with this one as with every one. Thank you for your love, your support and for putting up with me, which takes the patience of a saint on a good day.

Chapter One

"I'm here to rescue you."

Kyle Morgan was so intent on what he was doing he thought the female voice above him was his sister Jenna, bugging him about coming in for lunch.

"I don't need rescuing right now. Get lost." Another turn of the wrench and he might actually be able to get the blasted oil pan loosened.

"That's not what this paper says."

Definitely not his sister's voice. Those weren't Jenna's legs either. But then he couldn't see much while lying in the dirt under the truck. He tilted his head sideways and saw red-painted toenails and slim, tanned ankles. Jenna wouldn't be caught dead in skimpy sandals like that. Definitely *not* his sister.

He slid out from underneath the truck and squinted in the midday sun to see who thought he needed rescuing. All he could make out was a vague shadow attached to very shapely legs.

"Are you going to lie there and stare at me all day?" Her voice was deep and sexy, like skinny-dipping at midnight. Risky, forbidden, yet irresistibly appealing.

He so didn't have time for this. But he was damn curious and needed a break anyway, so he grabbed his shirt off the hood of the old blue Chevy truck, wiping his hands and sweat-soaked, dirty face.

Blinking to clear the sunspots out of his eyes, Kyle got his first look at the woman attached to the voice.

Stunning, was his first thought as he gazed at her beautiful face. Golden blonde hair hung in cascading waves over her shoulders and rested just above her full, high breasts. Eyes the color of amber ale stared levelly at him as she licked her lips nervously.

"Are you Kyle Morgan?"

I don't know. Am I? He seemed unable to think about anything except the vision standing in front of him. "I guess I am." *Great answer, dumbass. Sunstroke, obviously. Normally he had a freakin' brain cell.*

"Then as I said before, I'm here to rescue you." A smile that could light up the entire state of Oklahoma graced her face as she held out her hand. "I'm Sabrina Daniels."

Kyle was dimly aware of her slim, warm hand in his as she shook it with fervor. Her skin was soft, like sliding his hand over silk sheets, making him wish he'd had a chance to wash the grime off his.

Suddenly the name sparked recognition. "You're Sabrina Daniels?" Shit. He sure hoped he heard that wrong.

She nodded enthusiastically. "Yes. I'm so glad to finally meet you, Kyle."

So this was the woman who was going to spend the next three months at the Rocking M Ranch. Three months, and he would have to work closely with her every day. He stifled a groan as his eyes washed over her cover-model looks and centerfold body, trying not to lick his lips at the way the blue silk dress hugged her womanly curves. Surely this woman was punishment for something bad he'd done in the past.

Maybe he should have asked for a picture first. She looked totally out of place and too damned distracting. Not good.

"I didn't expect you until tomorrow." Frankly he didn't expect her to show up at all. *Hoped* she wouldn't show was more like it.

"I know. I arrived this morning and thought about grabbing a hotel and waiting until tomorrow but I was so excited I decided to come out a day early. I didn't think you'd mind since we had an agreement and you were expecting me. You were expecting me right?" The woman waved her hands around as fast as she was talking. He was already getting a headache and watching her swat invisible flies in the air was making him dizzy to boot.

"At first I planned to call, and then I thought if I called you might not let me come today and I really wanted to, so I decided to just show up and throw myself at you and here I am." She inhaled a huge breath of air.

Trying hard to recall if he'd had any whiskey for breakfast that could possibly be screwing with his clarity, he remembered he'd had coffee. So the reason for his confusion had to be the five-foot-six fast talking tornado standing in front of him.

"Yes I can see you're here." She might be here, but he'd be damned if he was going to be pleasant. No matter how good-looking she was, or how her voice reminded him of sex and sin, or how her face showed the enthusiasm of a child. This wasn't his idea in the first place. "So now what?"

She tilted her head, showing off a creamy expanse of slender neck. Kyle inhaled sharply, trying to avoid thinking of her as a beautiful, desirable woman. He wanted to think of her as a nuisance. Which she was going to be for the next three months.

"Well, now I guess we can get started."

"Get started with what?" He must have had whiskey *with* his coffee this morning.

Sabrina smiled shyly. "With my training."

His thoughts strayed to the kind of training he'd like to give Sabrina Daniels. Damned if all the blood in his brain hadn't migrated toward baser pastures. His long dormant sex drive sure picked a fine time to spring to life again. Great—now he could add lack of sex to his already long list of frustrations.

Maybe if he thought about all the negative things her presence represented he could get his mind off the fact Sabrina Daniels was a damned attractive woman.

It wasn't working. His mind continued on its wayward sexual course, heating his blood and tightening the crotch of his jeans. Maybe it was the weather. It was damn hot outside, way too hot for late April. He was dirty and sweaty and felt like a pig while she looked fresh and clean and smelled like peaches. He shuddered to think what he must smell like, but it was probably closer to rotted fruit.

He looked her over from head to toe. She crossed her arms across her chest, obviously uncomfortable with his scrutiny. Good. "I hardly think you're dressed to begin anything, other than maybe hosting a cocktail party. And gee, you just missed the one we hosted last night. All the Dreamwater elite were here."

Sarcasm obviously wasn't lost on her as she tapped her sandaled foot in annoyance. Maybe she'd be so irritated she'd leave. He should be so lucky.

"Kyle. I'm hot, I'm thirsty, and I've driven a long way today. It's my understanding we had an agreement and you were expecting me. But if there's a problem with our contract we can discuss it. Is there some place out of the sun we could sit and talk?"

Well hell. If his mother were still alive she'd kick his ass for lack of manners. He finally noticed sheens of perspiration moistened her face, and the shadow between her breasts that kept drawing his eye was damp. She looked about ready to pass out.

"Sorry. Let's go inside where it's cooler."

She nodded gratefully and Kyle directed her toward the large brick ranch house, following behind her. Watching her perfect backside swaying as she walked, it became quite clear this bargain he and his family had struck was a huge mistake.

Kyle didn't want to do business with Sabrina Daniels, but couldn't pinpoint exactly why. Maybe it was the instant attraction he felt for her, bringing to life feelings long held in check. More likely it was because she now held a financial interest in his family's ranch. That meant an outsider owned a part of the Rocking M.

When his parents died and he and his younger brother and sister took over the Rocking M, they vowed the Morgan's would retain ownership. And despite everything they'd been through, that's the way it had remained. Until now. Now Sabrina Daniels owned a portion of their ranch. At least temporarily.

If they didn't need the money so damn bad, if he hadn't been forced to pay his cheating ex-wife all that cash in the divorce settlement, they wouldn't be in this predicament now. This was his fault and an investor was the only way to dig the Rocking M out of the deep financial hole he'd put it in.

The sooner he finished his business with Sabrina Daniels and got her off the Rocking M, the happier he'd be. No one was ever going to own this ranch but a Morgan.

Sabrina gladly accepted the glass of iced tea Kyle offered, and tried not to drink too greedily as the cold liquid slid down her parched throat. Standing outside in the hot sun almost had her swooning. Wouldn't that have made a great first impression? Here she was coming to Kyle Morgan's rescue, and he would have been the one picking her up off the ground when she passed out from heat exhaustion.

She stole glances at him while he fixed himself a drink. When she'd asked a ranch hand on her way up the drive where Kyle Morgan was, she had no idea she'd find the owner of the Rocking M lying in the dirt near the house, working under an old Chevy pickup truck.

Her first look as he pulled himself out from under the truck had almost knocked her off her feet. He was tall, a bit over six feet, his bare chest covered with grease and dust which did absolutely nothing to distract from his well-muscled body. The old jeans he wore tightly caressed his slim hips and powerful, muscular thighs.

He was the classic picture of a rugged cowboy—tough, sexy, and hard muscled. His short hair was golden, a bit more brown than blond. A shadow of a beard covered his lower face, lending a dangerous look to his chiseled features. And those eyes. A compelling green with flecks of gold shot through them.

Sabrina sighed with pure feminine delight at the handsome looks of her new partner.

When her attorney recommended the Rocking M as an investment opportunity, Sabrina was so excited she couldn't sleep for weeks. Everything she desired but had been denied was closer to realization than ever before.

And now she had three months. Three whole months on the Rocking M to learn ranching. Then she'd buy a spread and raise her own cattle and horses. A lifelong dream finally coming true. And this time no one was going to stop her, no one was going to tell her she couldn't do it.

Kyle sat next to her at the table. It was engulfed by the monstrous kitchen and looked straight out of the movie set of an old western. She could imagine the giant oak table crammed with ranch hands and family come mealtime, all hustling to grab a plate before the food was gone. As she traced her fingers over the worn grooves in the wood,

Sabrina felt the history of family. Something she'd never felt before, at least not in her own life.

In fact, the entire ranch was huge. As she'd approached the entrance gate to the Rocking M, the tall brick ranch house loomed above her at the top of the hill, reminding her of the sweeping panoramas of the Southfork Ranch in the old television show *Dallas*. Sabrina's expectation of a charming little four room ranch dwelling was blown away by a house the size of the mansion she used to live in.

Everything about the Rocking M was big. Including the man sitting next to her at the table with a big scowl on his face.

"I really appreciate you agreeing to my terms," she said.

"I didn't agree to your terms."

"Yes you did. I have the contract right here." She started to look through her briefcase but Kyle grabbed her hand and stopped her.

Sabrina looked down at her slim hand covered by his much larger one. He made no attempt to remove it, letting it rest on hers. Her eyes swept up and scanned his face, looking for a sign of his intent but unable to read what she saw there. She felt a jolt of awareness as he finally slid his palm away from her hand.

Whatever reaction Kyle had to that brief touch was masked by his irritated look. "I know what the agreement says. I signed it, remember?"

"Yes, I remember. That's why I don't understand what you're saying. You agreed to this. It was clear you didn't want an investor to have permanent ownership in your family's ranch. I don't want that either. We struck a bargain, signed a contract. So what's the problem?"

Kyle blew out a breath. "There isn't one. You're here, and we'll have to make the best of it. I'll go find Brady and Jenna and we'll get this over with."

She watched as he rose from the table and slammed out the back door, leaving her alone in the kitchen.

Well thank you so much for the warm welcome. This wasn't what she'd expected. Maybe she didn't need a big family greeting with open arms, but an attempt at making her feel comfortable would have been nice. Sabrina definitely didn't feel comfortable right now.

He was trying his best to annoy her. But why? Her attorney assured her the Rocking M was desperate for a capital infusion to avoid foreclosure. The death of Kyle's parents several years earlier along with Kyle's divorce and subsequent settlement payout placed the Rocking M in dire financial straits. The ranch was struggling to merely break even, despite its location on prime Oklahoma land with enormous cattle potential. Its plight had already raised the interest of several local buyers.

One of the things Sabrina knew about the Morgan family was their unwavering commitment to retaining ownership of the Rocking M. That's why they agreed to her offer. Actually it was one of the things that excited Sabrina the most. She could come to the Morgan family's rescue and take the first step toward her own independence at the same time.

Maybe she'd handled this all wrong. No, that was Mark talking. Mark's influence. That was one of the primary reasons why she divorced him. She'd finally had enough of him controlling her, telling her what to do, how to think, how to dress, how to act. Always making her feel like she'd made the wrong move or said the wrong thing.

No one ever built her confidence, told her she was worthwhile or competent. Not even her mother. But then neither Mark nor her mother had loved her. She was a pawn, both of them using her for their own selfish reasons. No love, no feeling of permanence. Never feeling at home.

And from the looks of things, she wasn't going to feel it at the Rocking M either. This wasn't her home. She didn't have one.

Oh get over yourself, Sabrina. You made this move for a damn good reason, and it was to grow a backbone. Feeling sorry for yourself isn't the way to do it. She wasn't here to win a popularity contest. If they didn't like her, tough. She was here, the contract was signed, and like it or not, she was going to stay and they were going to teach her to run a ranch.

The back door opened and Sabrina stood. She watched with increasing anxiety as Kyle came in with two other people. One was a slightly younger version of Kyle, the other a very obviously pregnant brunette.

"You must be Sabrina. I'm Brady, the good looking Morgan brother." Brady grabbed her hand, shaking it furiously. His easy grin was infectious, and Sabrina liked him immediately.

Brady was almost the spitting image of Kyle except his hair was darker and his eyes more bluish-green. And he smiled a lot more than Kyle did.

"Nice to meet you, Brady," Sabrina said, returning his smile.

"And I'm Jenna White, the sister and caretaker of these two cowboys. Welcome to our ranch." Jenna was as friendly as Brady, her hazel eyes sparkling.

"I'm pleased to meet you, Jenna." As Sabrina looked down at Jenna's swollen belly, she smiled. "Congratulations. When's your baby due?"

Jenna grinned like a kid in a candy store and rubbed her stomach. "Less than two months."

"Oh that's fairly soon, then." Sabrina was in awe of the happiness reflected in Jenna's eyes and wondered how it would feel to know you were carrying a new life inside you. That familiar ache of regret made her want to rub her own stomach. But she knew what she'd feel there. Emptiness. Knowing she'd never feel that life kicking inside her. She pushed those thoughts aside, burying them as always.

Jenna rolled her eyes. "Not soon enough for me," she answered as she grabbed a chair and sat down. Brushing her long brown hair behind her shoulders, she smiled at Sabrina. "Sorry. I've been shopping this morning by myself—big mistake in my condition, I know. Had to carry the damn bags too. My back is killing me and my legs are swelling up like tree trunks."

The woman was still quite slender, with a petite body that most women who weren't pregnant would envy. "You don't look swollen to me," Sabrina said. "You look great."

"Thanks. This unseasonably warm weather is doing a number on me, though. I'm puffing up like a balloon. By the time the baby comes I'll look like an orca." Jenna glared at her two brothers. "Don't say a word about me already looking like a beached whale or I swear I'll kick you both in the butt."

Apparently they decided discretion was the better part of valor, because neither brother uttered a word.

"Are we going to discuss babies all day or are we going to do some ranch work around here?"

"I'm sorry, I didn't mean to—"

Jenna waved her hand at Kyle. "Ignore him, Sabrina. He's always grumpy."

"I am not." Kyle glared at his sister. "I'm trying to run a ranch, not have social hour. Now let's discuss what we're going to do with our partner here."

She didn't care for the way he said partner, as if he was discussing dirty laundry instead of her. But she really was going to have to toughen up and not have her feelings hurt by every casual word or look. Damn Mark for what he'd done to her self-esteem.

"Seems pretty obvious to me," Brady answered with a casual shrug. "We agreed she could learn about ranching, so it's our job to teach her."

Kyle shot a curt look at his brother. "No, you and Jenna agreed to this. I didn't."

Well that explained a lot. No wonder Kyle wasn't receptive to her presence. His brother and sister had outvoted him. He didn't want Sabrina here at all, which made her feel even less welcome than before.

She watched as the three siblings glared at each other, feeling like she'd somehow disrupted their family. She wanted to go where she was welcome. The last thing she wanted right now was more turmoil.

"I had no idea this was going to be such a burden for you all. Perhaps I should reconsider this arrangement." She tried to keep the emotion out of her voice, but was near tears already. It had been a long day; she was tired and she needed a shower. Her excitement at this new phase of her life was losing its luster.

"Sabrina," Brady said. "We agreed to this deal as a family, and we all want you here."

"Brady's right. Please stay." Jenna's pleading look was genuine, which was more than she could say for Kyle, who leaned against the kitchen counter, arms crossed, his mouth tight and grim.

Sabrina sighed heavily, trying to quell the feeling of rejection. She'd spent too many years feeling rejected to go through this again for another three months. Ranch or no ranch, she wouldn't be abused again. "Look. I'm not sure if that's a good idea. I really thought this would work, but I'm not staying where I'm not wanted. If you agreed to this deal, fine. But if it's going to be a constant battle between us, then I'll pull the financing and you can find yourselves another investor." She looked to Kyle and waited for a response.

Brady and Jenna glared at their brother with looks that indicated he better say the right thing. Or else. A battle of wills ensued as he returned their looks with one equally as challenging.

He sighed and walked over to her. Their eyes met for a brief moment, and despite her worry that he was about to tell her the deal was off, she couldn't help but notice how beautiful and expressive his eyes were. Full of the emotion he seemed to be trying so hard to mask under a veil of indifference. But she could see the anger, frustration, and a spark of something else. Something dangerous, yet exciting.

"We made a deal. I signed a contract. You're here, and we're going to teach you how to be a rancher." He held out his hand to her. "Welcome to the Rocking M, Sabrina."

The tears welled as the full impact of his words sank in. Whatever momentary battle went on between the siblings had passed. She really was going to learn to run a ranch. The realization thrilled her so much she threw her arms around Kyle and hugged him, whispering in his ear. "Thank you, Kyle. You won't regret this."

She moved to draw away but Kyle wrapped his arms around her, pulling her closer. Sabrina couldn't think, couldn't breathe as his warm hands splayed against her back, holding her. Her breasts pressed against his chest, her nipples tingling with never before felt excitement. She leaned back to look at him, certain the surprise she felt showed on her face.

Was he holding her like this to try and embarrass her? It was working, as she felt her face flame. Or was the heat she felt from another source?

His golden green eyes darkened, burning her with intensity. His arms remained around her and Sabrina couldn't make herself break the contact, completely lost in the whirlwind of emotion reflected in his eyes.

"Hey, that's not in the contract." Brady's teasing voice broke the spell Kyle weaved over her senses. Embarrassed, she pulled away and turned to Brady and Jenna.

Before she could utter a word, Brady swooped her up in a huge hug, holding her so high she had to rest her hands on his shoulders to balance.

"Put her down, Brady," Kyle said sharply.

"Why?" Brady grinned at his brother. "*You* hugged her. Isn't this how we welcome partners?"

Sabrina was mortified and so shocked she couldn't speak. The look Kyle gave his brother should have frozen him on the spot, but Brady seemed oblivious to it.

"Um, excuse me." Sabrina smiled uneasily at Brady. "Could you put me down now?"

"Sure, honey," Brady said with a laugh as he set her feet on the floor, his eyes alive with mischief. "I for one am glad you're here. Now I'm not the financial whiz around here, seeing as I have more horse sense than dollar sense, but I know we have money problems and I know you coming along right now is perfect timing." He threw his arm casually around Sabrina's shoulders and looked over at his brother, smiling devilishly. "Like a dream come true, isn't she?"

Sabrina watched for Kyle's reaction. He grunted in response to his brother's comments, but said nothing.

"Well I'm in total agreement with Brady," Jenna said as she struggled to her feet. She held out a slim hand. "Welcome to our home and to the Morgan operation, Sabrina."

"Yeah, ditto. Welcome," Brady said exuberantly as he turned to Sabrina again, his arms spread out.

"Don't even think about it," Kyle interrupted. "You already about crushed her once with a hug. Just stick to a handshake this time."

Brady shook his head in disappointment. "Damn," he said with a twinkle in his eye as he held out his hand. "Guess a plain old handshake will have to do for now. Looks like the hugs are reserved for Kyle alone." He winked at her and turned innocent eyes on his brother.

"This is a business partnership, Brady, and nothing more." Kyle shot a warning look at his little brother.

"Uh huh. Whatever you say. Well, gotta go check the horses. Later," he said to Sabrina. He grinned at her and walked out the door.

Sabrina hoped Brady didn't think there was anything between her and Kyle. She had acted before thinking when she hugged Kyle, and now wished she could take it back. Where had that come from? She should know better than to make a spectacle of herself like that.

"Well, I need a nap. All this shopping has worn me out." Jenna rubbed her lower back.

Kyle gave his sister a hug and kissed her temple. "I'll bring your shopping bags over as soon as I've finished up with Sabrina."

Jenna nodded and turned to Sabrina. "If you want a tour, or if there's anything I can help you with, don't hesitate to ask. My husband, Luke, and I live in the small house next to this one, and the door's always open. It'll be nice to have a female around." Shooting a teasing look at her brother, she said, "Way too much testosterone on this ranch, if you ask me."

"Thank you, Jenna." Sabrina liked Jenna already. Friendly, with a great sense of humor and obviously loved both her brothers very much. Sabrina envied her in so many ways. She didn't have any brothers or sisters. Maybe if she had she wouldn't have felt so lonely all those years.

After Jenna left, Kyle turned to Sabrina. He stood at the doorway, leaning casually against the frame. Was there a move the man made that wasn't sexy? Even standing still he exuded a sexuality and heat she could feel from across the room. Maybe it was the smoldering look he gave her, like a banked flame waiting for a single spark to ignite it into a firestorm.

She cleared her throat. "I guess I should get my things out of the car and unpack. Where will I stay while I'm here?"

"You'll stay in the house, of course. Brady and I are the only ones here, though he's rarely around. He either hangs out in one of the cabins or in the bunkhouse with the hands, playing cards all night."

"Does anyone else live in the house?"

"No. Just Brady and me." His gaze wandered over her, a questioning look in his eyes. "Is that a problem?"

Just Kyle. Sabrina thought about being alone with him. Of course it was a huge house and it wasn't like they'd be sharing a bedroom. But still, they'd be alone. And Sabrina found him attractive, of that there was no doubt. But thinking about it and doing something about it were two different things. She'd let a man control her for too long, and that was something she'd never let happen again. It was time for independence and that meant no men, either. She had to stand alone for the first time in her life.

"No, that won't be a problem." She'd just have to forget she was sharing a house with a gorgeous, virile man. The thought both frightened and interested her at the same time. She *had* lived with a man before. She and Mark were married for almost eight years. But then again, she never felt a spark of attraction with Mark like she did with Kyle. Marrying Mark was more about escaping her mother than it was about love.

At eighteen, what had Sabrina known about love? For that matter, what did she know about it now? Not much.

"I hope you brought different clothes than what you're wearing," Kyle said as he looked her up and down. "Sexy little dresses aren't really the uniform of the day on a ranch."

Despite his attempt at insult, she couldn't help the ripple of awareness at his husky tone. He said her dress was sexy.

"Of course I have more appropriate clothes with me."

21

"Fine. Let's go grab your things and get you settled in."

Sabrina followed Kyle outside to her car. She surveyed the ranch with a renewed interest.

It may not be permanent, but at least temporarily she owned part of this beautiful ranch. She wanted to get out and explore the property, already anxious to see the barn and the animals, and of course to ride a horse. She'd finally learn to ride a horse. Sabrina was so excited she almost ran up to Kyle and hugged him again out of sheer gratitude, but held herself back.

Something felt so right when he wrapped his arms around her, his touch sparking a desire she'd never felt before. But Sabrina couldn't afford to be thinking that way, certainly not about her new partner. This was a business arrangement and that's the way their relationship would stay, despite these new feelings awakening inside her.

She'd worked hard to get here, and nothing was going to stand in the way of her goal.

Chapter Two

"There are five bedrooms upstairs," Kyle said, looking over his shoulder. "You can choose whichever one you like."

She tried to avert her eyes from the firm butt attached to the man ascending the stairs ahead of her. But it was hard not to appreciate such an incredible body encased in tight jeans. He was carrying the bulk of her luggage, which Sabrina knew was incredibly heavy. And he wasn't even slightly out of breath.

He waited for her at the top of the stairs, gesturing down the hall to a series of doors on each side of a long hallway. "Take your pick."

Sabrina walked past Kyle and peered into each of the rooms, then selected one at the end of the hall. It looked like a cheery bedroom, containing a large four-poster bed covered with a lavender and yellow flowered bedspread and matching decorative pillows. A huge dresser and mirror were placed against the wall across from the bed, and nightstands on either side held small purple lamps. Two large windows with sheer lace curtains bathed the room in light. The soft beige carpet felt thick and comfortable.

It was nothing like her former bedroom. With Mark, it was designer sheets, nothing frilly. Austere, sterile, no knick-knacks, and absolutely no plants. The hardwood floors were always cold. Art deco on the walls—only the best and most expensive, of course, even if it was ugly. Nothing out of place or sitting on top of the dresser. And definitely no color.

No color, no life, nothing cheery or happy. Strict, devoid of emotion, and empty. Sabrina thought wryly that the description not only matched her former bedroom, but also her former life.

Not anymore. This room was everything she had wanted before, but wasn't allowed to have. The splashes of flowery art on the walls and myriad plants interspersed throughout the room warmed Sabrina's heart in ways she couldn't have explained to Kyle.

"This room is fine, if that's okay." She turned to Kyle, who had been silently following her room to room. A slight frown formed at the corners of his mouth.

"It's all right with me," he said flatly, although he seemed disturbed by something.

"If you don't want me to stay in this room, any of the others would be more than acceptable."

Had she picked the wrong room, and if so then why hadn't he just chosen one for her?

"I said this room is fine." He carried the luggage through the door and placed it on the bed. "The bathroom is through the doorway to the left of the bed."

Sabrina followed behind him and peered with delight at the charming, oversized claw-footed tub and antique sink, their shiny brass fixtures a lovely complement to the pale cream of the porcelain. And more lush beige carpet, making Sabrina want to slip her shoes off and wiggle her toes through its depth.

It was definitely a woman's bathroom—with a matching cream vanity across from the tub, and an extra closet in the bathroom for towels and linens. The tub sat underneath a large bay window overflowing with flowering plants, and Sabrina could picture herself reading and enjoying the sunlight while bathing. It was perfect.

"It's a lovely room, Kyle. Thank you."

"You're welcome." His eyes were dark and unfathomable. She had sensed them on her, watching her as she walked around the room. But instead of making her feel uneasy or self-conscious as she always had when Mark had his eye on her, knowing Kyle was watching didn't bother her at all. In fact, she kind of liked it. How strange she should feel that way.

"Where is your room?"

With a slight smirk, he motioned for her to follow him. "This way, I'll show you."

But instead of walking out of her bedroom and back into the hall, Kyle led her to a door at the opposite end of her own room. He opened it and Sabrina realized why he had frowned when she chose this bedroom. It was an adjoining one to Kyle's.

She remembered looking at this room when she was choosing her own. A king sized bed of dark walnut dominated the room, and Sabrina thought the décor was quite masculine. She wondered why he hadn't told her it was his room. Then she wouldn't have picked the one right next to it.

And now, a single door separated her room from his. He leaned against that door as he smiled enigmatically at her.

"Why the adjoining rooms?" she asked.

"My room used to belong to my parents. The one you picked was my mother's sanctuary. When we were little she kept our cribs in there so she could hear us cry at night. After we got older she used it as a sewing and reading room, and kept an extra bed in there." Kyle smiled. "My dad used to snore and sometimes it was more than mom could handle."

The memories sailed unguarded across Kyle's face. Sabrina glimpsed fond recollection coupled with pain and loss.

She looked at Kyle uncertainly. "Would you like me to stay in a different bedroom?"

Kyle shrugged, once again masking his emotions. "Doesn't matter to me where you sleep. This room's as good as any other." As he headed out the door of her room, he added, "Go ahead and unpack. I've got some work to finish, so we'll meet later and take a tour of the rest of the house."

She watched him leave, then sat on the bed and opened her suitcases, still feeling a bit uneasy about her bedroom being so close to Kyle's. But why? Because it felt too intimate. Almost as if they were actually sharing a bedroom.

And you have way too vivid an imagination, Sabrina. About things she had no business imagining.

The afternoon sun peeked above the top of the windows, compelling her to look out through the gauzy haze of the sheer lace curtains. A calm settled over her as she viewed an incredibly lush green valley peppered with hills and tall trees. What it must be like to view land as far as the eye can see and know it belonged to you.

She just needed to relax, get acclimated, and blow away the incredible stress of the day. She began to unpack, and slowly that feeling of rightness came over her again as she took out her clothes and hung them in the closet. It was almost as if she belonged here.

But she didn't. She shook her head and mentally admonished herself for getting comfortable. It wasn't going to do her any good to feel at home here. This wasn't her place, and it never would be. It was nothing more than a temporary stop on her way to independence.

Then again, as she surveyed the cheery bedroom and felt the warm sunshine streaming in from the windows, for the time being, it was home.

∞ ∞ ∞

Kyle cursed as he crawled out from under the truck, finally finishing the task he'd begun earlier that day. If he could reach his own rear end with his foot, he'd kick himself in the ass for allowing Sabrina to choose her own bedroom. What the hell had possessed him to do that? He knew there was a possibility she'd choose the adjoining room to his.

And why *hadn't* he pointed out which room was his? She probably wouldn't have selected the one right next to him if he had.

Well it could have been worse. She could have chosen *his* room.

That idea conjured up all kinds of intimate thoughts. Kyle pictured her silky blonde hair spread out like a fan across his pillow, lying naked on his bed, her body gleaming in the moonlight shining in through the French doors of his bedroom. Her full breasts would be showcased in the light, nipples erect and begging for the touch of his tongue. Her feet flat on the bed, legs spread, moisture clinging to her pussy lips as she trailed a hand there, opening herself up to him, inviting him in. He felt the familiar tightening, visions of tangled limbs and sweat-soaked bodies heating his blood. His cock went rock hard in an instant, his balls aching for release.

Shit. This he didn't need right now.

After his divorce from Amanda two years ago, he had been too busy figuring out how to get the ranch out of debt to even think about the opposite sex. Coupled with the fact he was so damn pissed at Amanda and therefore any other member of her gender, sex had been the last thing on his mind. And he'd kept busy, working from sunrise to sundown trying to keep the ranch operating. Falling into bed exhausted each night was a perfect way to squelch any lustful thoughts.

Then Sabrina showed up with her warm, whiskey eyes and flowing blonde hair, not to mention the kind of body that made the strongest man weak in the knees. Suddenly his long dormant libido fired up like an old furnace cranking up its first heat of the winter.

When she threw her arms around him earlier he knew he was in trouble. Her body fit his like she had been created just for him. She enticed him with her soft skin, perfect curves and the sweet scent of peaches until his hands automatically wrapped around her.

When she whispered her thanks in his ear, her warm breath on his neck heated his body. Her full breasts pressed against his chest, forcing his body into awareness of how long it had been since he'd made love to a woman. And all she had done was give him a hug. Thank God Brady said something, reminding him they weren't alone. Otherwise Kyle might have been tempted to follow through on his desire to press his mouth to Sabrina's warm lips and see if she tasted as good as she felt.

And he wouldn't have stopped with just a kiss.

Damn. And now she was going to be sleeping in the room right next to his, with only a doorway separating them. He threw the wrench roughly into the toolbox and blew out a breath. He needed a shower again. A cold one this time. Or else he needed to jack off because he hadn't come in awhile. Maybe the cold shower and a damn good orgasm would do the trick and wipe sexual visions of Sabrina Daniels from his mind.

"Frustrating as hell, isn't she?" Brady smirked as he walked up to Kyle.

"Huh?"

"The Chevy. Changing the oil in that beast is one lesson in patience I don't ever care to repeat," his brother said, motioning to the old pickup Kyle had been trying to work on all day.

"Oh, that. Yeah, frustrating as hell."

Brady's amused grin did nothing to assuage Kyle's foul mood.

"What are you smiling about?"

"You."

"Why?"

Brady leaned casually against the truck. "I think you're digging yourself a big hole, brother."

"What are you talking about?"

"Sabrina."

"What about her?" Kyle wasn't in the mood to play guessing games with his brother. He was already behind on the day's work, and it was almost time for supper.

"You're interested in her." Brady raised his eyebrows in a *you know what I mean* look.

"You don't know what you're talking about," Kyle denied. Sabrina Daniels was a complication he didn't need in his life right now. Or ever.

"Don't I? How about that scene in the kitchen today? Sure looked like interest to me."

Kyle bent down and retrieved the tools he had thrown on the ground. "I didn't instigate that hug. Sabrina did, when I told her she could stay."

"Uh huh. And you pushed her away, didn't you? So far away your arms were wrapped around her waist and you two were shooting out flames that scorched me from across the room. Christ, that almost turned into an X-rated scene. My poor virgin eyes."

Kyle looked sharply at his brother. "You're full of shit and need to get your eyes examined. That's not the way it was at all."

Brady raised both hands in surrender. "Hey, I just call 'em like I see 'em. And what I saw was anything but the beginnings of a business partnership. Looked to me like the beginning of one hellacious love affair. Or some kind of affair, anyway."

"You're way off base on this, Brady. What I want from Sabrina Daniels is her money, to buy extra stock and get the Rocking M out of debt. And that's all. The last thing we need is to get personal in any way with her."

"We'll see, brother, we'll see. I'm going in the house to clean up. Later."

Kyle nodded absently to his brother and watched him walk toward the house. He most certainly did not want Sabrina. He wanted her money—her investment in the ranch, but that was it. Anything else would be a waste of his time, and hers, and would be disastrous for a partnership. They'd be working closely together for the next three months, and Kyle would make damn sure to keep it on a professional basis only.

He'd let one woman get under his skin, and she burned him so bad he almost lost his family's ranch. Never again.

Kyle wondered if there was any way he could put his libido on hold for the next few months. If not, he was at least glad the weather was warming because he could feel some very cold showers coming up.

ა ა ა

The afternoon sun brightened Sabrina's bedroom considerably. The light cast a warm blanket over her, making her reluctant to rise from the bed. Unable to clear the sleepy fog and open her eyes, she lay still, not fully certain of her whereabouts.

The sun was heating her—that must be why she felt so flushed. Or maybe it was the dream she'd been having. Water, warm and steamy, and a man. But where was the water coming from, and who was the man?

Then Sabrina heard water running, and finally realized where she was. In her bedroom on the Morgan ranch. The bedroom adjoining Kyle's. It was *his* shower she heard running. Not a dream at all.

The steady, rhythmic sound of the flowing water lulled Sabrina back into a half-awake, half-asleep mode. Unwarranted, visions of Kyle standing naked in his shower entered her mind. His tanned, muscular body lathered up with soap, water splashing over the top of his head, his eyes closed. And what a body. Definitely a man who used it for working. Lean and muscular in all the right places, he made her mouth water. God, he made her wet.

A fantasy. She was having an erotic fantasy. How strange, since she'd never had one before. But here she was, imagining opening the shower door and stepping inside. Kyle's emerald green eyes glowed with passion as he raked his gaze over her naked body. Her nipples tightened under his perusal, her breasts swelling as she eagerly moved toward him. As she took the soap from him, she lathered her hands and slid them slowly over his shoulders and across his chest, tangling her fingers in the crisp dark hair, feeling the strength of his muscles. Then her hands drifted lower, over the taut muscles of his abdomen to encircle the thick length of his cock. She shuddered at his heat, at the life in his shaft as she stroked him, keeping her gaze focused on his face as he thrust against her hand.

He moved his hands over her skin, soaping her breasts, lingering at her nipples. When he pinched them she cried out and squeezed his cock, stroking harder, needing more than this, needing him inside her.

Yet she couldn't say the words, lost in the sensations as his hand moved lower, over her belly, cupping her sex and circling her clit. He drove her mad then, sliding back and forth over the tiny bud until she squeezed her legs together, holding him there.

"Yes," was all she could manage when he found the spot that gave her the most pleasure.

"There?" he said, his breath a harsh whisper against her ear.

"God, Kyle. More."

He gave her more then, dipping down until his fingers rubbed her swollen pussy lips, parting the folds to slide inside her.

Oh, God. She'd never realized how empty she'd felt until his fingers filled her. He drove them deeper, using his thumb to circle her clit now. She was close, so close, and she lifted her hips toward him, driving toward the edge, knowing nothing would stop it.

"Come for me, Sabrina. Come on my hand."

And that was a command from a man she didn't mind obeying. She shuddered and cried out, biting her lip as her climax rocked her. She clutched his shoulders as she rode out the waves of ecstasy rolling over her.

"Now, baby, I'm going to fuck you," he murmured in a voice that was dark, seductive, driving her arousal to new heights.

"Yes. Fuck me. Do it now."

The sound of the shower being turned off jolted Sabrina from her fantasy. She sat bolt upright in her bed, shocked to find her hand between her legs, drenched in her own juices. Her body felt hot and she was breathing heavily. Oh, God. She'd just masturbated in her sleep. Had just had a most incredible orgasm, too. And she'd never done that before.

What was wrong with her? Sabrina never had fantasies about men.

Her only experience had been with Mark, and sex with Mark had been as austere and sterile as their bedroom decor. Don't move, don't breathe, don't initiate. Just lie there like a good wife. Sex was for men's pleasure only. She had learned the lessons well, and not once had she ever looked at, desired, or fantasized about a man. Until now.

Forcing away the erotic visions of her and Kyle in the shower, Sabrina rose from the bed, washed up and changed clothes. After donning shorts and a T-shirt, she opened the door to her room, intending to slip downstairs and wait for Kyle there.

Except Kyle's door opened at the same time Sabrina stepped out of her room. She was embarrassed, although she didn't know why. He obviously didn't know what she had been doing a few minutes ago. But looking at him now, his hair still wet from the shower and a damp sheen across his forearms, Sabrina's shower fantasy came back at her full force and she felt the warm flush heat her face and neck.

"How was your shower?"

"Cold," he answered curtly.

"Oh, that's nice," she replied absently. Mental images of Kyle's naked body, how he'd pleasured her, refused to leave her mind. Maybe it would help if she thought about something else, like ranching and cows and horses—anything but that shower scene playing over and over in her head.

They walked downstairs together into the kitchen. He showed her where everything was located, from the food in the refrigerator and pantries to the cooking appliances and cleaning products. Sabrina nodded, making a mental note of the location of everything in the kitchen so she wouldn't forget. Mark had always told her to pay attention. He hadn't liked explaining things more than once.

"You might as well start here," he said.

Sabrina was confused. "Start where?"

"Here. In the kitchen." He was looking at her like she was a moron. "You know, kitchen stuff. Cooking."

"Oh." Cooking. "Okay." Good Lord. Cooking?

Kyle leaned against the counter and crossed his arms. "Let me take a wild guess here. You don't know how to cook."

She shook her head, embarrassed for the umpteenth time today. Mark had never wanted his wife to do anything he thought was beneath her station. He thought cooking was for the servants, not for Sabrina, even though she had wanted to learn to cook for as long as she could remember. Not even her mother had allowed her to cook. Not that they ever could, considering they never spent more than a week in one place at a time. And her mother explained time and again that cooking would only ruin Sabrina's lovely hands.

After her divorce when she had the opportunity to live alone, she'd lacked an appetite for cooking. The best she could manage was microwave meals.

"Never mind. I'll do it." Kyle turned away and grabbed pots and pans from the cabinet next to the stove.

"Wait," she interrupted. He shot her an impatient look but stood still. She could feel the tears welling in her eyes, but forced them away. "Please. I can learn—I'd like to try. Do you have a cookbook or something?"

Kyle hesitated as if debating whether to put his family's stomachs in her untrained hands. "Fine. Cookbooks are in the drawer to the left of the sink. You've got about an hour until Brady, Luke and Jenna come in. I'll go see about the horses." He turned and left abruptly, leaving Sabrina alone in the kitchen.

Fine. She had to learn to cook—tonight. And not just for Kyle, but his entire family. Sabrina almost sat down in the middle of the kitchen floor and cried, but years of forcing her feelings aside prevented it. She had withstood much worse than this, and she wasn't an idiot. She was twenty-seven years old and it was way past time to learn some of the basic necessities of life. Cooking was as good a place to start as anywhere else.

Kyle inhaled, searching for the smell of burned food. Instead, a delicious aroma surrounded the kitchen. Fully expecting to see Jenna cooking instead of Sabrina, he was shocked to find Sabrina in there by herself. Covered in flour, her hair a tangled mess, half having come loose from her ponytail, but nevertheless both her and the kitchen still in one piece. And she wore the biggest grin he'd ever seen in his life.

She had set the table like she was giving an elegant dinner party. His mother's fine china adorned the large oak table, along with the good silverware and even wine glasses. And way too many utensils as far as Kyle was concerned. How many forks did a person eat with anyway?

"Smells great in here." Brady walked in grinning, then washed his hands and sat down at the table like a king expecting to be served. Kyle rolled his eyes as he walked to the sink.

Luke and Jenna came in and Jenna introduced him to Sabrina.

As was typical for most people meeting Luke White for the first time, Kyle watched Sabrina's look of surprise as she surveyed the six-foot-seven giant standing next to the petite, pregnant brunette.

"I'm pleased to meet you, Luke," she said.

"Likewise, Sabrina," Luke answered in his booming voice, then held out his hand to her. "Jenna's told me all about you. Welcome to the Rocking M."

Sabrina smiled and blushed as she shook Luke's hand, obviously embarrassed at having flour-caked hands.

Leaning against the sink as he dried his hands, Kyle couldn't believe how easily Sabrina had settled in with his family. They treated her like she was one of them, when she was nothing more than a business partner. For some reason that irritated him.

"What did you fix for dinner?" he asked as he sat at the table.

Sabrina beamed. "Salmon patties, almond rice and broccoli. We were going to have salmon steaks," she added nervously, "but they died a slow and painful death during my first try, so I ended up just opening up a couple cans of salmon and making patties." Sabrina smiled slightly at Jenna and added, "Thank heaven for cookbooks."

Jenna laughed and nodded. "Been there, done that. We all have to learn sometime."

"I hope you don't mind," Sabrina said to Kyle as she pointed to the bottle sitting in an ice bucket on the table. "I found some Chardonnay and thought you might like to have that with dinner."

"We don't drink wine with dinner, and this is private stock. You don't even know how much it cost, do you? This could be a vintage bottle we were saving for a special occasion."

Sabrina looked crestfallen. "I'm…I'm sorry, I didn't think it was, I mean I know wines pretty well and this one was—"

Jenna shot her brother an angry glare. "It's a cheap bottle of wine from the liquor store. Ignore him." Turning to Luke, she smiled sweetly. "Honey, would you open the wine?"

Kyle was still annoyed. This wasn't a banquet, it was dinner. And it was supposed to be simple. "And why did you put out my parents' good china and silverware? I showed you where the everyday dishes were."

Again that look from Jenna. "It's lovely, Sabrina," she said sweetly. "We haven't used these dishes in awhile. It's actually very nice to see them again. Thank you."

Sabrina nibbled on her lower lip as she set the food in the center of the table. Stealing glances every few minutes at Kyle, she looked like she might turn tail and run if he opened his mouth again. For some reason this whole dinner extravaganza annoyed the hell out of him. And why were Brady and Luke and Jenna being so goddamn accommodating? Sabrina had to be taught the right way and this sure as hell was not the right way.

Salmon. Of all things. Where was the steak and potatoes? And the bread for God's sake? This wasn't what they normally ate. "Usually we have red meat for dinner, not fish," Kyle said curtly as Sabrina sat down next to him at the table.

"Do me a favor, Kyle. Shut up and eat. If you can't do that, then leave." Jenna was beyond pissed, and by the tight tone of her voice, Kyle could tell she was heading for a tirade. Not wanting to upset his sister too much considering her condition, he sulked and scooped the food onto his plate.

Kyle watched out of the corner of his eye as his family started eating. Sabrina sat with her hands folded in her lap, and hadn't once taken up her fork to eat her own food. Probably poisoned, he thought. Or tasted like crap and she already knew it.

As he turned and surveyed the faces of his family, he was surprised to see their looks of pleasure.

"Sabrina, this is excellent," said Jenna. Luke agreed with his wife, pronouncing Sabrina a very good cook.

Apparently Brady thought so too. "Yeah. It's great, Sabrina. You did a damn fine job cooking. You can even take over my night to cook if you'd like."

Kyle watched as Sabrina relaxed, then tentatively tasted the food she had prepared. Although she didn't look up, she smiled. Finally, Kyle took a bite of the salmon patty. He had to admit, for a first time cook, it was pretty good.

Sabrina studied Kyle expectantly as he ate.

"Is it all right?"

He looked at his sister, giving him the official Morgan glare, and turned back to Sabrina. "It's fine." That was all she was going to get from him.

He continued to eat, but still something annoyed him. "But I'd rather have a steak or a hamburger."

"Dammit Kyle!" Jenna yelled.

"What? I said it was fine."

"If you'll excuse me, I'm a bit tired from the long drive today," Sabrina said quietly.

As she rose from the table, Kyle saw tears glistening in her eyes. He felt a momentary twinge of guilt but quickly pushed it aside.

"I'll clean up the dishes later," she added, her voice quaking.

"Don't worry about it." Brady shot his brother a *go to hell* look. "Kyle and I will take care of the dishes. You just get some rest."

Sabrina nodded without looking and walked out.

Kyle watched her leave and immediately felt pangs of remorse. What had come over him? He usually wasn't so rude, and he had no idea what compelled him to treat Sabrina so badly. Turning back to his family, he was greeted by three of the coldest stares he'd ever received.

The rest of their meal was spent in silence. When everyone was finished, Jenna, Luke and Brady rose from the table to clear the dishes. They talked amongst themselves, but for the most part ignored Kyle as he handed the dishes to Brady to load in the dishwasher. Jenna washed the pots and pans and Luke dried them.

Well, this was ridiculous. This was his family, not hers, and they had no reason to shut him out. And besides, she had done it all wrong, not the way it was usually done. She needed to learn about ranching, and it was his job to teach her. And part of that learning process was what to feed a ranching family. That's what she was investing her money for, and he would make sure she was got her money's worth.

His treatment of Sabrina certainly had nothing to do with how he felt about her being here in the first place, or how much his attraction to her annoyed him. And besides, the more distance Kyle placed between himself and Sabrina, the better it would be for him.

"So, what did you buy at the store today, Jenn?"

Instead of a sweet reply, Jenna mumbled something about *stuff* and ignored him.

Turning his attention to his brother, Kyle asked about one of the sick horses. Brady's only response was a comment that Kyle couldn't quite hear, but he was certain it contained the phrase *horse's ass*. And he didn't think it had anything to do with the rear anatomy of the animals in the corral.

"What's up with you two, anyway?" he asked.

Jenna whirled on him and pointed her finger at his chest. "You are the biggest jerk I've ever had the displeasure to be related to."

He held up his hands. "Whoa. What did I do?"

"You treated Sabrina terribly over dinner, and you know damn well you did. How could you, Kyle? You criticized everything she did."

Kyle shrugged, his defensive shield rising. "It *was* all wrong. She used mom's good dishes and silverware, for God's sake. Nobody's touched that stuff since they died. And what was with three forks anyway?"

"It was a nice meal. She's new here, and instead of gradually teaching her how to do things, you launch into her like she's incompetent hired help."

"I did not. She wanted to learn about ranching, and I'm teaching her. There's a right way and a wrong way to do things."

"That's a load of bull and you know it," Jenna said heatedly. "That meal she prepared tonight has nothing to do with ranching. And the way you treated her had nothing to do with teaching."

Kyle looked at Brady and Luke for help, but saw none forthcoming. As they sat at the table and let Jenna do the talking, it was clear whose side they were on.

"Let's go home, Luke. I've had enough of my brother's company for the evening." Jenna kissed Brady on the cheek and paused in front of Kyle, her look cold and hostile. "I'm ashamed to call you my brother, Kyle. You didn't act at all like a Morgan tonight."

They left, leaving Kyle with Brady.

Brady muttered under his breath and shook his head as he grabbed his cowboy hat off the peg at the back door. Placing the hat on his head, he turned to Kyle as if he wanted to say something, then thought better of it and slammed through the back door, leaving Kyle alone in the kitchen.

They were right. He had treated Sabrina badly. He knew she didn't know how to cook, and maybe he expected her to fail. And when she didn't, it irritated him. And now he felt shitty, and didn't really know what to do about it.

The problem was obvious. He didn't want her here in the first place. Sabrina represented his failure to make a profit off the ranch, and every time he looked at her he'd be reminded of that failure.

But there was something else. Kyle was attracted to Sabrina. Not just her beauty, but her vulnerability and spirit. She was putting everything she had on the line to start a new life, and he wanted to admire her for doing so. But the thought of finding anything appealing about Sabrina sent warning bells clanging in his head. So instead of complimenting her efforts at cooking, he had done his best to make her appear a failure. And all to protect himself.

Jenna was right to be ashamed of him. He was going to have to learn how to work around Sabrina and force his attraction to her aside. He considered going upstairs and apologizing, but thought better of it. She was pretty upset, and probably exhausted. It had been an eventful day for both of them. Better to let things settle, then he'd apologize tomorrow.

As he turned out the lights in the kitchen and headed down the hall into his office, Kyle knew he was being a coward. He was afraid to face her tonight after the way he acted. It wasn't like him at all. And now he'd have to figure out how to work around a woman he was attracted to, without making an ass of himself every time.

Chapter Three

Sabrina sat on the window seat in her bedroom, watching the first fiery rays of the sun lift slowly above the horizon. She sat with her knees to her chest, resting her chin on her forearms. And she was brooding.

Coward. She was angry with herself for her behavior last night at the dinner table. Had she so desperately wanted Kyle's approval that when his responses weren't exactly how she pictured, she had to run and hide in her room so he wouldn't see how much he upset her?

Old habits died hard. She swore after her divorce she was going to find her missing backbone and learn to stand up for herself. Wasn't that what independence was all about? She'd never be independent if she cried like a baby every time someone told her they didn't like the way she did something. That was how the old Sabrina would behave. Not the new and improved version.

So Kyle hadn't liked her dinner. Big deal. It was good, she knew it, and so had Jenna, Brady and Luke. If Kyle didn't, so what? But instead, he was the one whose approval she wanted. She wanted to prove she wouldn't be a burden to him or his family and had succeeded. Then he'd acted like a bully and told her it wasn't steak. Well he could just kiss her...salmon patties.

She stood and paced the room. A glance at the clock told her it was time to face the family. She'd gotten this far and wasn't going to stop now. With a new resolve and much more courage leaving the room than she had when she entered it last night, Sabrina headed downstairs, ready to go head-to-head with Kyle Morgan.

Just past dawn and already the kitchen was a bustle of activity. Sabrina almost lost her newfound courage and went back upstairs, but decided now was as good a time as any to prove she could hack it as a ranch owner. Inhaling deeply to quell the queasy feeling in her stomach, she stepped into the kitchen.

Jenna bid her a cheerful good morning. Sabrina put on her biggest smile and walked into the kitchen as if she lived there. Well, she *did* live there.

"Morning everyone." They were all there. Jenna and Luke, Brady, and of course, Kyle. Jenna and Luke were fixing breakfast and Brady was pouring coffee. Kyle sat at the table, going over some paperwork. He looked up when she entered and smiled slightly, but his eyes gave away nothing of what he was thinking. He simply nodded to her and returned to his paperwork.

"Morning, how about some coffee?" Brady smiled easily and poured some of the dark brew. "Cream or sugar?"

"Just cream please, but I can help myself."

Brady pointed to the pitcher of cream on the table. She picked it up and poured some into her cup, watching out of the corner of her eye for any reaction from Kyle. Nothing.

"What can I do to help?" Sabrina made a mental note to get up earlier tomorrow so she could help with breakfast. She'd have probably risen earlier had she gotten more than a couple hours sleep last night, but instead she lay awake, pondering her behavior at dinner and chiding herself for acting like a child.

"Not a thing," Jenna responded. "Breakfast is almost ready. Just grab a plate and get in line."

Jenna heaped Sabrina's plate full of eggs, bacon, pancakes, and biscuits. "I don't think I can eat this much food," she said, looking at the mound piled on top of her plate.

Jenna grinned at her. "Ranching works up an appetite. Trust me, you'll need it."

As they ate, Sabrina listened while Kyle spoke with Brady and Luke about the day's activities. Perfect—she had arrived before the spring roundup. Calves would need vaccinating, branding and castrating, the thought of which made Sabrina's nose wrinkle in distaste. They were going to wait awhile for the roundup, and instead prepare for the arrival of new stock, which would be purchased thanks to the influx of capital provided by Sabrina.

"What will I be doing today?" Sabrina asked as she helped clear the dishes from the table. Just listening to the activities of the day fired her excitement. She couldn't wait to roll up her sleeves and get involved.

"I need to go out to the east pasture today," Kyle said as he sipped his coffee. "You can ride out with me."

Ride? A horse? After all the years of wanting, yearning to do just that, it was going to happen. Today. "Really? We're riding today?" She tried to contain her enthusiasm, but couldn't. "Oh I'd love to. Will you teach me to ride, Kyle? I've never ridden a horse before. I won't be a burden, I swear, and I'm a really fast learner. Oh this is so exciting!"

Kyle's lips twitched and then he smiled. He rose from the table and grabbed his cowboy hat off the peg, sliding it onto his head as he turned to look at Sabrina. "Well then let's get started. You ready?"

Sabrina nodded as she quickly finished the dishes and followed Kyle outside. Her first day as a rancher was about to begin.

Kyle shook his head as he walked with Sabrina out to the horse barn. He must have been out of his mind when he agreed to teach her. The woman obviously didn't know the first thing about living or working on a ranch. The time involved would put him so far behind it would take him a year to get caught up.

At least she was dressed more appropriately today. Her hair was pulled back in a low ponytail, and she wore jeans and a long sleeved, blue cotton T-shirt. Kyle did his best to ignore the way her jeans molded to the curves of her hips and legs. That flimsy silk thing she wore yesterday was bad enough. Even worse was the denim she wore today, hugging her ass the way grass clung to the face of the land. It just wasn't fair.

He almost laughed as he thought about her reaction when he told her she could ride with him today. It was like watching the face of a child who had just been told they were going to the county fair. Her warm amber eyes glowed with pleasure and her voice rose with excitement. And even though he knew it would be work for him to teach her, he couldn't help but feel a tinge of her enthusiasm. It brought back memories of his father teaching him to ride when he was a young boy.

The horse barn was a short walk behind the ranch house. A penned area surrounded the front of the barn, and several horses were contained within the pen.

"Are these the horses we're going to ride?"

"Yeah." He watched her eyes widen as they drew closer to the pen. She stopped as they reached the gate and hooked her booted foot on the bottom rung of the fence, lifting herself higher so she could view the horses. Her face was flushed with excitement, her fingers flexing anxiously as if she were physically restraining herself from going over the fence and leaping on a horse.

Now that he'd like to watch.

"Sabrina."

She turned to look at him, a flash of uncertainty crossing her face. Did she think he'd deny a horse ride to her? Of course after his behavior last night he didn't know what she thought.

"Yes?"

"About last night, I...uh...want to apologize for the way I acted. I had no right to treat you that way. The meal was fine."

She said nothing for a minute, then a slight smile formed on her full lips. God she was beautiful when she smiled.

"You don't need to apologize, Kyle. If I'm going to pout like a child every time someone tries to teach me something, then I shouldn't be here. But I do appreciate the apology." She returned her focus to the horses.

That went better than he thought it would. He expected repercussions and reminders, and then constant browbeating about his attitude for at least a few days. Amanda would have done it that way. She'd have made him pay—over and over again.

Maybe Kyle was wrong about Sabrina.

"Let's go pick a horse."

Sabrina nodded as she surveyed the horses in the corral. "They're beautiful."

Kyle climbed up and over the fence, jumping down with a thud onto the dirt floor of the corral. He stood in front of her and held out his hands to help her down. She hesitated for a second, then slid her legs over the top of the fence, her bottom on the top rail, and rested her hands on his shoulders as he placed his around her waist. Lifting her easily, he held her up for a brief second, enjoying the feel of her, then placed her gently on the ground. Yet he couldn't seem to let go of her.

Their eyes met and Kyle was struck once again by her beauty and guileless eyes. She wore her emotions on her face, hiding nothing of what she was feeling. Right now her eyes shined with excitement and her whole face lit up with an excited innocence Kyle couldn't quite believe was real.

She made his heart pound and his palms sweat as they rested against the soft swell of her hips. How old was he anyway? Seventeen?

He turned abruptly and walked toward the horses. "Come on, I'll show you how to saddle your horse."

"Do you only use quarter horses?" she asked, walking quickly to keep up with him.

He nodded. She at least knew the breed. "I wouldn't own anything else."

"Why?"

"Because they're the best cutting horses around. They're quick and agile, good for short sprints and they have great cow sense."

"And a cutting horse would be good in order to cut off an errant cow or something?"

Kyle looked at Sabrina and smiled. "You've done your homework."

Sabrina shrugged. "I may not have been allowed to ride one, but I've studied horses my whole life."

Why wouldn't she have been allowed to ride a horse? He'd investigated Sabrina before they agreed to bring her on as an investor. He knew she'd recently divorced some rich guy in Dallas. He thought she could have done whatever she wanted then, including ride a horse. Guess he didn't know as much about her as he thought.

Did he want to? That was a question he wasn't prepared to answer right now. Better to concentrate on work, he reminded himself.

"Which one do you want?"

Sabrina looked them over, finally pointing to a chestnut mare.

Kyle nodded. She had selected one of the best horses in his stock. The chestnut was a good ranch horse. "Good choice. Let's get her to the barn and saddle her up."

It had been impossible for Sabrina to suppress her grin when Kyle told her she made a good choice of horses. Having Kyle's approval meant a lot to her. Not in the same way as having Mark's approval had been—that had been more to keep peace rather than a genuine desire to please him.

Now she was going to saddle her own horse. And a beautiful one too, with her reddish-brown coat and dark legs.

The mare was much taller than she imagined a horse would be. Trepidation mixed with excitement as she thought about climbing on and riding her.

The barn was a large wooden building located directly behind the corral. Sabrina wrinkled her nose as the smell of fresh hay coupled with the pungent odor of horse manure assailed her senses. She inhaled quickly, trying to adjust to the unfamiliar scents, not all of them pleasant. Ick. But if she was going to be a rancher she'd have to get used to these smells.

The thought thrilled her and scared her to death. Now she was going to find out how little she really knew about ranching.

Kyle explained that half the barn was designated for storing hay while the other half contained stalls for horses. There was also a workshop, a working area for horse shoeing and grooming, and a separate room off the barn to store saddles and other tack.

He led the horse to the work area and tethered it to a post, then motioned for her to join him. She'd researched enough to know horses had a tendency to be skittish around strangers, so she approached the mare from the front, slowly.

"Good. Let her get your scent. Put your hand near her nose and let her smell you."

"What's her name?" Sabrina asked as she placed her hand near the horse's nostrils and then giggled as the mare sniffed and licked her palm.

Kyle grunted and gathered the saddle and supplies. "Naming horses is something they only do in books and movies. In reality, we don't give them names."

"That doesn't make sense. How do you know which horse you're referring to?"

"We just do. We might call one the chestnut mare with the white star." Shrugging, he continued. "I don't know how we do, we just know."

"Well that's silly. I'm going to name her." Sabrina stroked the mare's nose and bridge, running her hands slowly over the horse's forehead. The mare snorted, remaining calm. "She looks like a Maggie to me."

He rolled his eyes at her. "Call her whatever you want. Let's get her saddled."

Kyle showed Sabrina how to lay the blanket on the horse's withers, then place the saddle over the blanket and cinch it into place. He went through the instructions so quickly she wished she had a notepad to write it all down. What was second nature to him was completely new to her. So she watched and took careful mental notes so the next time she'd be able to saddle the horse without help.

Once Maggie was saddled, Kyle leaned out the door of the barn and whistled. A beautiful Appaloosa trotted over to the gate leading to the barn entrance, and Kyle walked over to the rail. The horse held its head down so he could scratch it.

Sabrina watched, mesmerized, as Kyle opened the gate and the horse followed him into the barn without having to halter or lead it.

"That's amazing. How do you get him to do that?"

Kyle stroked the horse's muzzle. "We have an understanding. I feed him, and he pretty much does whatever I want him to."

Sabrina knew it was much more than that. Kyle obviously had a close relationship with his horse, but didn't want to appear as if he cared one way or another about the animal.

"I suppose he has no name either."

"You suppose right."

Sabrina studied the beautiful animal. It had a creamy beige coat and legs, with brown polka dots dappled all over its hindquarters. "Spot."

"Huh?"

"I'll call him Spot."

His incredulous look made Sabrina grin. "You're joking, right?"

"No, it's a sweet name and he does have spots after all. It's just logical."

Kyle laid a blanket over his horse's back, followed by a much larger saddle than he had put on Maggie. "Spot's a damn dog's name, not a horse's."

"So?"

He actually looked angry, but not in the same sense that her ex-husband would have. More a frustrated angry. Sabrina didn't feel threatened at all, in fact found it very amusing.

"Spot's not a horse's name."

"Well you said you don't name them anyway, so what difference does it make?"

"You're not naming my horse Spot!" He blew out a breath and turned away from Sabrina to continue saddling the gelding. "I don't know why I'm even having this conversation with you," he said, frustration ringing in his voice. "If you don't mind, I'd like to finish saddling Spot...dammit! Now you've got me calling him that stupid name."

Sabrina giggled, not at all upset by Kyle's sharp tone. In fact, she was having a wonderful time watching him finish saddling Spot. When both horses were ready, he grabbed their reins and led them outside the barn, tying them off to the corral post.

"Okay, get up."

She looked at Maggie and then at Kyle, who was waiting expectantly for her to mount. All she needed to do was place one foot in the stirrup, slide the other leg over and she'd be on. Of course, in the movies the horses didn't appear to be as big as they really are. And in the movies they hold still. Maggie was skittish.

"She senses your nervousness," Kyle explained. "Relax. Just hold the side of the saddle, then hook your left boot in the stirrup, stand up and grab the horn. Then when you get your balance, throw your other leg over and slide it into the stirrup. Once you're on I'll adjust them for you. It's easy."

Oh sure, easy for him. He'd been doing this for years.

Sabrina nodded and took a deep breath. The stirrup was about waist high, so she'd have to lift her foot up a good distance to slide her boot in. Now how was one supposed to do that? She looked at Kyle and hesitated until he sighed and walked over toward her.

"Let me help you." He instructed her to slide her foot in the stirrup and as she did he grabbed her hips and lifted her into a standing position.

Sabrina balanced precariously with one foot in the stirrup, but fortunately Kyle was still holding on to her legs or she would have surely fallen on her butt.

"Now grab the saddle horn and swing your other leg over, then settle in on the saddle."

She'd done it! She looked at Kyle triumphantly, expecting praise for her ability to get it on the first try. Only he didn't appear to be nearly as excited as Sabrina was. In fact, he seemed completely oblivious to the fact she had just mounted her very first horse. Instead, he was bent over, measuring Sabrina's foot in the stirrup.

"Your knee's bent too much, I need to lengthen the stirrups." He held on to her ankle, instructing her to sit still.

Kyle ran his hands up her ankles and calves, insuring she was relaxing her foot. His hand was warm as he grasped her calf, and Sabrina looked down to watch. The sight of his hand running up and down her leg unnerved her. Her traitorous body was having the wrong kind of reaction to a non-intimate act. Something about his touch caused her entire respiratory system to go haywire.

"How does that feel?" he asked as he finished his adjustment and looked up at her with questioning eyes. His hand still rested on her leg, lightly flexing his fingers on her calf muscle.

"Very nice," she said softly. Their eyes remained locked, his intense gaze compelling and magnetic until she realized that several seconds had passed and neither of them had spoken. Good Lord she was gawking at him like a schoolgirl. She averted her eyes and looked straight ahead. "Uh, the fit's fine, thanks."

He walked around and adjusted the other stirrup. Then he headed over to his horse and grabbed Spot's reins. With quick, agile moves he mounted the horse and walked it over to hers. He was so fluid, the way he slid onto the horse as if he were merely getting on a bike. How she wished she'd be able to do that, to make it look as easy as Kyle did.

He spent a few minutes instructing her on the basic movement commands, like laying the right rein on the side of Maggie's neck to make her turn left, and vice versa. He taught her to give the physical commands gently, and not to pull or tug on the reins. Although he went through them all, Sabrina wasn't really interested in the commands to gallop or run, figuring she'd be happy enough right now with walking and being able to stay astride the horse without falling.

"We'll start out slow. Just ride alongside me so I can watch and help you if you need it." Kyle turned Spot and they headed around the corral. Sabrina followed with Maggie, pleased when the horse followed her commands.

They headed out of the barn, passing pens, corrals and multiple buildings. Kyle pointed out each building as they went by and explained what it was used for. Sabrina was surprised at how much went into working a ranch. And she had so many questions, which she asked Kyle as they approached each building or structure.

Buildings were needed to store feed as well as house equipment and perform maintenance. She knew when she investigated the ranch it was large, around three thousand acres, but she had no idea how big it really was. And she'd only seen a small portion of the ranch so far.

After they cleared the buildings they rode in silence for awhile. Sabrina marveled at the changes in landscape, from flatlands of small sage and grasses to tall birch and sycamore trees as their elevation increased. In between scanning the scenery and trying to control Maggie, Sabrina watched the way Kyle rode his horse, as if the two were of one mind and body. He sat comfortably on Spot, his body moving in time to his horse, whereas every joint in Sabrina's body jolted with each step Maggie took.

"How long have you been riding a horse?" Sabrina asked as she pulled alongside Kyle.

He turned to her, cowboy hat pulled low over his eyes to shield them from the bright sun. She'd never seen anything sexier in her entire life. How could a hat make a man look so wickedly desirable?

"As long as I can remember. Dad put us all on the back of a horse as soon as we were old enough to hang on by ourselves."

What it must have been like to grow up on a ranch. Sabrina wished she'd have had the same experiences. "You must have had a wonderful childhood."

Kyle smiled. "Yeah, I did."

And when he smiled, dimples appeared on either side of his mouth. It should be illegal to look as good as this man did. Sabrina warmed and unfastened the top button of her shirt, hoping the cool morning air would provide relief.

"You miss them, don't you?"

"Who?"

"Your parents."

"Yeah, I miss them." His soft tone spoke volumes. She heard the pain in his voice.

"What about *your* parents?" he asked, obviously trying to change the subject.

"Not much to tell really. My dad and mom divorced when I was very little. My father never wanted kids, so when I came along he split."

"Do you ever see him?"

Sabrina shook her head. "No. My mother tried to track him down for child support, but he'd quit a job and move every time they found him to garnish his wages. Finally, she just gave up and found another way to make extra money."

"What way?"

"Beauty contests."

Kyle reined in Spot. "Your mom entered beauty contests?"

Sabrina pulled on Maggie's reins, and the horse stopped immediately. "No, she entered *me* in them. From the time I was a toddler until I was an adult."

"Why?"

"Because she thought I was a pretty baby, I guess, and then when I won a couple, she realized prize money and maybe a modeling contract would follow, so she continued to enter me in them."

"And you kept on winning."

How would he know that? "Yeah, I kept on winning."

"That doesn't surprise me."

Her eyes met his in question. "What do you mean?"

"You're beautiful now, you must have been equally as beautiful as a child."

This wasn't the first time someone had told Sabrina she was beautiful. She had heard it for years, but to her it had been empty compliments that she ignored. The matter-of-fact way Kyle said it made it different. He wasn't trying to get anything out of her, or to fuss over her appearance or praise her for some sort of performance. For the first time it meant something.

"Thank you." She could feel herself blushing. The last time she blushed was when she met Mark, and fell for his lines about what a difference he could make in her life. How naïve she had been to believe anything he said. Although he *had* changed her life, in so many ways. None of them good.

"So you were a beauty queen."

She nodded. "The reason for my existence my entire childhood."

Kyle started them riding again, but stayed closer to Sabrina so they could continue talking.

"You didn't like beauty contests?"

"No. I hated them."

"Why?"

The images returned, contest after contest, month after month, year after year. So many of them she couldn't recall the number of places she'd been, how many contests she had won, or how often she begged her mother to let her quit competing. But her mother told her that her beauty was supporting them, that someday she'd thank her because this was going to be the way for Sabrina to become rich and famous.

"I didn't want to be on display. I hated dressing up in those stupid frilly dresses, having to strut and sing and dance on stage and have my hair and makeup done."

"What did you want, then?"

"A normal childhood. I wanted to go to school like everyone else instead of relying on tutors because we traveled so much. I wanted to have friends. Childhood friends who would be with me to adulthood." She laughed then, at the memories of her childhood dreams. "And mostly, I wanted to be a cowgirl. Wear jeans, get dirty, and never wear makeup or have to curl my hair. I wanted to ride horses and live on a ranch."

His mouth formed a crooked grin. "Did you ever tell your mother what you wanted?"

"Yes. All the time. She said I was too young to know what I wanted, and it was up to her to guide me, teach me and make sure I got everything I deserved. That she knew better than I did what was best for me."

"And beauty contests were the best thing for you, in her opinion."

"Yes." After all, how was Sabrina going to catch a rich husband if she lived on a ranch? And that, in a nutshell, was what her mother had wanted. A rich husband to take care of her, as well as her mother.

"Is that how you met your ex-husband?"

She nodded. "He was a judge at the Miss Dallas competition. Mother arranged an introduction after the contest was over."

"Did you win?"

"Yeah, I did. But I never went on to compete any further because Mark and I got married and I relinquished my crown to the runner-up."

"So love won over career, huh?"

Her response tasted of the bitterness she felt over Mark's betrayal. "He never loved me. And I only thought I was in love with him. I was eighteen, had never been allowed to date, and Mark was the first man who ever showed an interest in me. At least, the first man mother let get near me. One date and I was hooked. Signed, sealed and delivered into the hands of the devil himself."

Why had she said all that? She finally realized Kyle had stopped, having been so lost in her thoughts she hadn't paid any attention to him riding beside her. Now, she turned around to see him looking at her, gentle compassion in his eyes.

Embarrassed at having revealed so much, she turned in her saddle and stared straight ahead, hoping Kyle would take up riding again and not mention anything about what she had just told him.

Fortunately he started moving, and they rode in silence. Why had she told him about her past? It seemed so easy to talk to him about her childhood, her mother's wishes for her, and how she felt when she met and married Mark. Sabrina never told anyone those stories before. With Kyle they just slipped out as if telling him about her life was as natural as breathing.

Eventually they reached a pasture. A herd of cattle grazed on the lush green grasses, and Sabrina marveled at the landscape. It was almost noon, and the sun shone brightly over a brilliantly colored meadow of green grasses and tall, shady oak trees. Interspersed throughout the fields were wildflowers, stunning in their purples and yellows.

Sabrina inhaled the sweet scent of jasmine, thoroughly enjoying the exhilarating feeling of being outdoors in the warm sunshine, the cool spring breeze caressing her face. She took a deep breath and could actually smell summer approaching.

"Oh Kyle, it's so beautiful here."

He dismounted, and Sabrina followed suit. Kyle looked over the pasture as he tethered the horses to a nearby tree. "It's always nicest in the spring. Wait until summer when there's no rain and everything turns brown and dry like the desert. Then it won't be so beautiful."

"Yes it will." The whole ranch atmosphere was like a living dream to her. Having lived most of her life in hotels, moving from town to town to compete in the next beauty contest, the idea of wide open spaces and owning land as far as the eye could see was overwhelming. She wouldn't care if the land looked like a razed shopping mall after a wicked tornado.

"Here, hold on to these and follow me." He handed Sabrina two pairs of work gloves. Grabbing what looked like a large spool of wire and a compact tool kit from his saddlebag, he motioned for her to follow him as they headed toward the fences.

"Put these gloves on. I'll need you to help me hold these posts together while I string the wire." Sabrina did as she was told, putting on the leather gloves that were way too large for her, and held on to the spool as Kyle unwound a length of wire and snipped it off with the cutters.

"What are we doing?" she asked.

"We're rewiring the gate." The gate was in actuality nothing more than two large posts at the tail end of the fence, leaning against each other and obviously meant to be closed by wire loops. Sabrina watched as Kyle expertly wound the wire over the top of the two posts, securing them together.

"That ought to keep the critters in the pasture now."

"Critters?"

Kyle managed a quick grin. "Cows. The gate loops came loose, and sometimes the cows wander off onto a neighboring rancher's land. And sometimes someone comes along and removes the wires purposely in order to let the cows loose."

Sabrina watched his eyes harden like glass as he surveyed the land on the other side of the gate.

"Who would do that? Vandals?"

"Yeah, something like that."

"So the land on the other side belongs to your neighbor?"

Kyle snorted. "Yeah. Jackson Dent."

"And you don't like him?"

"No, I don't like him."

"Why not?"

He shot a smoldering glare at her. "You sure ask a lot of questions."

"I'm just curious why you don't like your neighbor. Aren't neighboring ranchers typically friendly?"

"Some are."

"But you and Jackson Dent aren't because…"

"Just leave it alone, Sabrina."

Oh sure, he asked all kinds of questions about her life, which she willingly volunteered, but then one simple question and he clammed up on her.

"I just wanted to know if…"

"I said I don't want to talk about it!" Kyle all but shouted his response to her.

She didn't flinch. She'd been yelled at too many times over the years to let a slightly raised voice unnerve her. But this time, it wasn't her husband yelling at her, it was her partner. And this time, she vowed things would be different.

"I was just asking a simple question. It's not necessary to bite my head off over it. How am I going to learn about ranching if you don't tell me everything?"

"You don't need to know about this."

"Why not?"

"Dammit, Sabrina! I said leave it alone and I meant it!" Kyle stormed off toward the horses.

She ran after him and grabbed his arm. His eyes were molten green fire, shooting sparks of anger at her. "Stop yelling at me!"

"Then stop asking stupid questions!"

"It's your job to teach me, and that means if I have a question then you need to answer it. That's why I invested my money with you, so I could learn something!" She was shouting as loud as he was, a fact that wasn't lost on her. Never had she raised her voice to Mark—not after the first time she'd tried to argue with him. She had known better after that.

"I agreed to teach you about ranching, and that's what I'm going to do. My relationship with Jackson Dent is none of your business, and has nothing to do with the ranch." He stepped closer, his expression intense and angry. She felt the anger radiating from him, yet refused to step back.

"Don't interfere in my personal life, Sabrina. You and I have a business relationship, and nothing more."

She refused to be dismissed. This was a two-way street, and she'd already walked down one side of it. Now it was his turn. "Then why did you ask me questions about my childhood? Why did I give you so much personal information?"

He smirked at her. "Because, as is typical for a woman, I ask one simple question and I get an hour-long dissertation on your life. I didn't have to pull the information out of you, honey, you volunteered every last sordid morsel."

"You bastard." They were practically nose-to-nose, both breathing heavily, so close Sabrina could feel Kyle's breath on her cheek. Her heart pounded as she remembered what happened the first time she raised her voice to her ex-husband. Oh, he hadn't struck her—Mark punished her in more subtle ways. Belittling her, making her feel small and worthless. Sabrina almost retreated, but held her ground. She was so scared her knees were shaking, but she would not back down. Not this time, never again.

This was a different type of argument. He was clearly angry at her, and she at him, but a current of something else ran between them, stoking the fires, flaming the argument, making her aware of him as a man, and herself as a woman.

Sabrina noted Kyle's hands clenched into fists at his sides, and he glared at her, unmoving, unspeaking. The two of them stared at each other, an argumentative dance, a stand off. And yet, in the back of her mind, something else.

A spark that had nothing to do with a fiery argument.

Finally he spoke, his voice low and simmering with anger. "Let's go. It's getting late and we need to go back." He turned abruptly and stomped over toward the horses, leaving Sabrina standing in the field alone.

She took a couple deep breaths to quell the seething emotions she felt all the way to the pit of her stomach. Her heart was racing with the heat of battle. As she headed toward the horses, she realized something new had just happened.

She'd had an argument. With a man. Had actually yelled at him and held her own while he yelled back. Kyle even insulted her, but Sabrina didn't cry, and didn't back away. And she had survived it.

Not only that, she felt something that passed between them, something elemental and passionate. Beyond anger, yet an equally fierce emotion. But she couldn't pinpoint what it was.

What she could admit was that she'd fought, and stood her ground. For the first time in her life.

Maybe she'd finally found her long-missing backbone.

Chapter Four

They rode back in virtual silence, lost in their own thoughts. Sabrina felt good despite the uncomfortable lack of conversation between her and Kyle. Her first day as a rancher, and she had learned to saddle and ride a horse, fix a fence, and argue with her partner without fear of retribution. All in all, a pretty darn good day.

When they finally reached the barn she was grateful. Although she thoroughly enjoyed riding Maggie, after a few hours on a horse she was starting to feel a little sore. Okay, maybe a lot sore. Her legs ached, her back was stiff and her butt muscles were screaming. Not that she'd complain to Kyle. Sabrina would never let him know she was hurting, or give him any signs to think she couldn't cut it as a rancher.

"You need to take her saddle off then brush her down before you cut her loose," Kyle instructed.

Sabrina nodded and watched him remove Spot's saddle and grab a brush. She undid the saddle cinch but struggled with lifting it off. The horse was too tall, and she didn't have the strength to lift the heavy saddle. But she'd figure out how to do it somehow. No way was she going to ask Kyle for help.

Apparently he noticed her difficulty and silently moved behind her, lifting the saddle easily off Maggie and walking away without a word. Sabrina sighed in frustration and grabbed a brush, busying herself with grooming her horse and trying not to think about anything at all.

After the horses were cleaned and penned, she followed Kyle as he headed toward the ranch house. Jenna sat in the swing on the front porch, sipping tea and reading a book.

"How did it go today?" Jenna asked.

"Fine."

Kyle's one syllable answer made Sabrina grin. He was still angry with her. But today it didn't bother her. Today was the best day she'd ever had, and nothing, not even Kyle's foul mood, was going to spoil it. He walked past his sister without another word and entered the house. Sabrina sat on the large wooden chair across from Jenna.

Okay, muscles were definitely sore. And a wood chair was not the prime choice at this moment.

"How about some tea?" Jenna asked.

"That sounds great. I'll get it." Without letting Jenna know how much it hurt, Sabrina got up and poured her own glass before Jenna could maneuver out of the porch swing.

"Thanks. Seems to get harder and harder every day to get up once I've sat down. By this time of the day, I'm pretty much done for." Jenna sipped her tea and ran her hand in circles around her swollen belly.

Sabrina knew all about *done for*. She was cooked and ready to be served. "Do you know the baby's sex yet?"

"No, Luke and I decided we wanted to be surprised. I realize it's easier to know as far as decorating and buying clothes, but it just seemed like it would be more fun if we found out whenever he or she pops out."

Sabrina laughed. "I'll bet you can't wait for that to happen."

She rolled her eyes. "You have no idea. I am so ready to get this baby out of me." Jenna inclined her head toward the empty front door

Kyle had stormed through a few minutes earlier. "What's up with him?"

"We had an argument."

"Really." Her brows wrinkled as she leaned forward in the swing. "About what? Was he picking on you again? I swear I'll kick his butt if he was."

That brought a grin from Sabrina, imagining all five foot two of Jenna in her last trimester of pregnancy taking on six feet of lean, muscled, Kyle. But then again, judging from the fierce expression on Jenna's face, Sabrina didn't doubt who the winner would be.

"No, he wasn't picking on me. I asked him about his neighbor, and he didn't want to tell me anything about their relationship."

"Oh, him." Jenna leaned back in the swing. "Jackson Dent is a major thorn in the Morgan family's side."

"Why, if I might ask?" Maybe Jackson Dent was a subject that was off-limits to all the Morgans.

"For a lot of reasons. Jackson and Kyle have always had an animosity toward each other, from the time they were kids."

"How come they didn't like each other?"

"Kyle was always better looking, smarter, more popular. You know how it is with kids. Plus Kyle rode a horse like he'd been born on one. And Jackson tried and failed every time he and Kyle competed, both on and off horses. It's kind of sad, actually."

"Why is that?"

"Dent's a smart guy, but I think his father always pushed him to be better than Kyle. He tried, but failed miserably. So not only was he humiliated every time he went up against Kyle, but then he had to face his father's disappointment."

"That is sad when a parent tries to compare you to someone else." Sabrina knew all about not being good enough, not measuring up. First with her mother, then with Mark.

Jenna nodded. "Dent inherited the Double J Ranch from his parents after they died, and he's been trying to one-up the Morgans ever since. Couple that with the fact that Kyle's ex-wife Amanda cheated on him with Dent and you can figure out why he doesn't even like the mention of the man's name."

No wonder Kyle was so upset when Sabrina wanted to talk about Dent. He must have felt completely betrayed by his wife. Her heart went out to him as she thought of how much that must have hurt.

"Oh, I didn't know that. I'm sorry."

Jenna shrugged. "All water under the bridge now. Except Dent can't keep himself from reminding Kyle whose bed his former wife is warming every time they run in to each other. That's the only area, in Dent's mind, where he bested Kyle."

Sabrina's eyes widened. "You mean she's still with him?"

Jenna nodded. "Jackson and Amanda got married last year, so Kyle's ex-wife is now married to his biggest enemy. And don't think Jackson ever lets Kyle forget it either."

How awful. Not only to have his wife cheat on him, but then to be faced with it on an almost daily basis, knowing the woman he once loved lived on the neighboring ranch and slept with the man he hated the most. Sabrina wouldn't be able to tolerate living so close to Mark. That's one of the reasons she came to Oklahoma, and when she bought her own ranch she'd make sure it was as far away from Dallas and her ex-husband as she could get.

"Well I see now why he was so angry at me for wanting to know more about his neighbor."

"Don't take it personally, Sabrina. He gets like that whenever Dent's name is brought up, no matter who says it."

"He must have loved his wife a lot. How sad she would do something like that to him."

Jenna laughed. "Loved her? I don't think so. She was a useless piece of trash from the day she said *I do.* Pretty much every day after that it was *I don't, I won't* and *I hate you.*"

"Was she always that unpleasant?" Sabrina couldn't imagine him wanting to be with a woman like that.

"I don't know what he was thinking when he married her. She made promises to him about what a great wife and partner she'd be, when all she was really interested in was being the wife of a rodeo star. When Kyle had to quit competing and work the ranch after our parents died, Amanda was livid. Then she found out that as a rancher's wife she'd actually have to do some work. After that, being Mrs. Kyle Morgan no longer interested her."

Sabrina knew all about Kyle. Her attorney had given her a family bio when Sabrina expressed interest in investing. Kyle was a rodeo star with a bright future, but had given it up when his parents died in the plane crash. He took over managing the Rocking M, and subsequently went through an ugly divorce which cost the ranch almost one-third of its value.

"Then why would she marry Jackson Dent? He's a rancher too."

Jenna smiled. "Oh, but Jackson is a rich rancher. Big difference. As his wife, Amanda can spend all her time hosting parties and playing tennis at the country club in town. Sure a lot different than what she had to do around here. Amanda made life pretty miserable for Kyle. That's why he paid her so well, even though her settlement request was ridiculous. He'd have paid any amount to get her off the Rocking M and away from him and everyone else."

Sabrina couldn't imagine what Kyle went through being married to Amanda. But then again, she'd had dreams of what marriage was going to be like, and her dreams had been shattered too. They had much more in common than she realized.

With a huge effort Jenna rose from the porch swing, then stretched her back. "It's my night to cook dinner, so I'd better get started."

"Please let me help you with dinner."

"It's not necessary. I can do it."

"Don't be silly. You need to rest and not spend so much time on your feet. Besides, since I'm such a novice in the kitchen, I can stand to learn a lot more about cooking, and I'd really like to help."

"Okay, then. Thanks, Sabrina. I appreciate it. It's been a long time since I've had a friend around here. I'm glad you came."

As Sabrina followed Jenna into the house, she mentally added another plus to her already great day. She had a friend.

ৎ ৎ ৎ

After helping Jenna get dinner started and into the oven, Sabrina headed upstairs to change. She felt dusty and dirty from riding all day, and couldn't wait to put on some clean clothes and freshen up. She slipped on shorts and a tank top, then brushed out her hair and wound it up in a clip on top of her head. Later she'd take a nice long bath in that gorgeous tub.

On her way back down, she felt aches and twinges she hadn't felt earlier. Every part of the lower half of her body hurt. The simple act of walking down the stairs caused the muscles in her rear end to announce their overuse. She was hurting, and had a feeling it was only going to get worse as the evening wore on.

Jenna was setting the table. Earlier, Sabrina had insisted Jenna sit and give instructions on how to fix the roast, so she could rest while Sabrina did the cooking. With a modest amount of protest, Jenna agreed. They had a great time, laughing about Sabrina's inability to cook at the tender age of twenty-seven. Jenna had the capacity to make the things most embarrassing for Sabrina seem inconsequential, and for that she'd be forever grateful.

"The roast smells wonderful. You did a superb job. But then again, you had an impeccable teacher." Jenna winked at her.

Sabrina laughed as she helped Jenna finish setting the table. Her muscles were aching more and more by the minute, but she tried her best to hide it. By the time Kyle and Luke came in, she had the roast and vegetables on the table ready to serve. But she was almost too tired and too sore to eat.

"Where's Brady?" Jenna asked.

Kyle shrugged as he washed up and sat at the table. "Said something about a hot card game in town tonight. Doubtful we'll see him again until morning."

"Dinner smells great honey," Luke said as he sat next to his wife and placed a soft kiss on her mouth.

"Don't thank me, Sabrina made it," Jenna answered at the same time she shot Kyle a *don't even think about saying a word* look.

"With Jenna's expert help," Sabrina added, smiling at her friend.

"You didn't need my help. You're a natural in the kitchen. But I really appreciate that you did the cooking. My back was hurting and I want to drag Luke crib shopping in town tonight, so the rest was helpful."

"Oh, crib shopping. I can't wait," Luke said, tongue-in-cheek. At her affronted look he grinned, his brown eyes twinkling. "Anything for you, princess." Luke pressed a kiss to Jenna's temple, and Sabrina was in awe of the loving looks that passed between them. It was clearly obvious they cared deeply for each other. She wondered what that kind of love would feel like.

The meal once again turned out edible. Actually, it was very good. And although she tried not to pay attention to Kyle, she watched out of the corner of her eye for his reaction. He ate in silence, but Sabrina noticed with some satisfaction he had two helpings.

Take that one and shove it down your palate, Mr. Morgan. Yet another triumph for Sabrina, another test passed—at least to her own satisfaction.

Now if only she could quit squirming in her chair. Sabrina counted the minutes until dinner was over so she could limp up to her room for a hot bath to ease her sore muscles.

ဏ ဏ ဏ

Kyle had to admit the meal was good. Great in fact, as good as anything Jenna ever cooked. If nothing else, Sabrina was a fast learner. At least in the kitchen. The rest still remained to be seen.

He watched her as she finished cleaning the kitchen. The two of them were alone now, as Sabrina had shooed Jenna and Luke off right after dinner so they could get to town and do their shopping. She rinsed the dishes and washed the pots while Kyle wiped up the kitchen table and dried the pots and pans.

As the last of the dishes were loaded into the dishwasher, Kyle watched Sabrina grab her lower back and stretch. She absently ran a hand over her butt, and Kyle could guess what the problem was. He suppressed a grin as he imagined how sore she must be from her first ride today.

"Feel okay?"

"Fine," she said tightly.

It was obvious she wasn't. In fact, he could tell every movement was painful for her. Okay, so maybe he had taken her out too far today considering it was her first time on a horse. He hadn't thought about the soreness that resulted from being bounced around. Riding was as natural to Kyle as breathing, and he'd never experienced an ache from spending hours on end in the saddle. But Sabrina wasn't accustomed to being on a horse.

"You're sore aren't you?"

Sabrina whirled around, then winced at the sudden movement. "Sore? No, I'm feeling great."

She was a terrible liar. Pain showed all over her face. Her expression was drawn and tight, and Kyle wagered she'd fall in a heap and cry if given an opportunity.

He shook his head and walked over to her. "Come on, it's time for you to go upstairs. You need a hot bath and then you need to rub some liniment on your...uh sore spots."

"No, really, I'm fine. Just a little tired."

Kyle put his hands on her shoulders, forcing her to look up at him. Her amber eyes were shimmering pools of pain. "Sabrina. Listen to me. It's not a sign of weakness to be sore from your first ride. I shouldn't have let you ride so long today. Now you need to go soak in a hot bath and rub some liniment on. Trust me, it'll help."

She nodded and headed toward the stairs. He followed behind her, intending to take a hot shower himself.

But watching her attempt to take the stairs was a lesson in frustration. First of all, he was behind her. Her skimpy shorts stretched tight against her ass as she agonizingly lifted each foot slowly to ascend the stairs. His jeans were going to get tight, too, if he didn't hurry this along. Finally, he had enough and told her to stop. As soon as she did, he swooped her up in his arms.

"Kyle! What are you doing?" Her expression registered shock as he adjusted her against his chest. He tried to ignore how perfect she felt in his arms.

"I'm carrying you up the stairs so it doesn't take me, or you, twenty minutes to get there." She was light as a feather and he took the stairs two at a time, not stopping until he gently deposited Sabrina on her bed. He watched as she sat immobile, either unable or unwilling to move.

"I'm going to run your bath for you."

Sabrina nodded, exhaustion clearly showing on her face. Purple shadows darkened under her eyes and every movement caused her forehead to crease. She didn't even try to argue with him when he told her he'd run her bath for her.

After filling her tub, Kyle went into his bathroom and found something he wanted to pour into her bath water. When he came back, Sabrina was still sitting on the bed, her legs dangling over the side, head bent to her chest. Was she asleep sitting up? He shook his head, damning himself for being stupid enough to take a greenhorn out riding for six hours on her first day.

He prepared her bath and bent down on one knee to look at her. "Are you going to live?"

She lifted her head and nodded, making a pathetic attempt at a smile. "Just tired I think."

"Go take your bath, then, before you fall asleep."

Sabrina started to get up, then winced in pain when she put her feet on the ground. "I think I should just go to bed."

Kyle knew she was too sore to think about getting into the bathtub, but he also knew if she didn't relax those muscles tonight they would be even worse tomorrow. "Come on, I'll help you."

Apparently she wasn't so tired that she didn't guess the implication of his words. "I don't think so," she said with eyes wide.

"Look, you're in tremendous pain, and it's obvious if I don't help you're never going to get into the tub. I have no desire to ravage you, I just want to get you from here into the bathroom. Now will you let me help?"

Weakly, she nodded. He helped her stand and walk slowly into the bathroom, then stood her in front of the tub. "What do you need me to help you with?"

"Nothing."

He started to leave, but she didn't move, just stood where he left her.

"Do you need me to help you undress?"

Sabrina's head whipped up, shock registering on her face. "I don't think so!"

Still he waited to see if any movement was forthcoming. Nothing. Not an inch.

"Let me help you. You're obviously hurting and can't even get your clothes off."

"No, really, I'm fine, see? I can do it myself." She grabbed the hem of her shirt and started to lift it up, then grimaced as she dipped from the waist.

"Fine my ass," he answered. "Are you going to stand here all night like this, or are you planning to bathe fully clothed?"

Sabrina paused as if actually considering the idea. "I guess not."

"Then let me help you."

She chewed her lower lip indecisively. "If you could help me get this T-shirt over my head, I'm sure I can manage the rest. The shorts should just fall off after I unbutton them."

Kyle tried his best to force aside the image of Sabrina's shorts pooling at her feet. Instead, he helped her raise her arms, and without looking any more than necessary, lifted the shirt over her head and tossed it on the floor.

The good news was she had a bra on. The bad news was it was low-cut, white, lacy, and practically see through. Her full breasts damn near poured over the top of the tiny bits of material, and Kyle could just make out rosy pink nipples through the sheer lacy cloth. Nipples that hardened as he looked at them. He raised his eyes to her face. She was watching him. And she was blushing.

He shrugged and grinned. "Sorry, couldn't help it. I said I wouldn't ravage you, I didn't say I wouldn't look."

She managed an exhausted smile as he turned to leave.

"If you need anything, just yell. I'll be in my room and I'll leave the door open in case you need help." She nodded and he made his escape.

He entered his room, stripped off his clothes and turned on the shower. Damned if it wasn't going to have to be another cold one.

He paced, the cold shower having done nothing to lift his mood, which grew darker by the minute. The sounds of Sabrina in the bathtub conjured up all kinds of images he really didn't want to see. Then it got quiet. Too quiet. He worried she might fall asleep in there and drown.

He listened for sounds of activity coming from the bathroom as he stood in the doorway between their rooms. Nothing. Finally, he could stand it no longer.

"Sabrina?"

No answer.

"Sabrina." This time a little louder.

At last, a weak answer. "Yes?"

Relief flooded Kyle's mind. At least she wasn't dead.

"Are you doing okay in there?"

"Um, sorta."

What did that mean? "What do you mean, *sorta*?"

"I have a slight problem."

"What?"

"I can't get up."

Damn. He knew what that meant. He walked into Sabrina's bedroom, stopping at the doorway to her bathroom. "You need me to help you?"

No answer.

"Sabrina."

"Yeah?"

"Do you need me to help you get out of the tub?"

"No! I can do it!"

"Then do it." Kyle leaned against the doorjamb, waiting.

Silence. Then he heard a slight splash and a groan, followed by a heavy sigh of frustration. She couldn't do it.

"Sabrina."

"What?"

"Let me help you get out."

"I don't think so."

"You obviously can't do it yourself, I can help."

Kyle waited while she thought it over.

"Kyle?" Sabrina's voice was quiet, almost a whisper.

"Yes?"

"I'm naked in here."

Didn't he know it. Already, visions of Sabrina in the tub were arousing everything male in him. So much for the cold shower. His cock was hard and clamoring for attention. Any kind of attention, but preferably Sabrina's.

"I'm aware of that fact. But it seems to me you have two choices. Stay in there until your muscles start to work, which could be tomorrow, or let me help you get out."

No answer.

"Sabrina!"

"Um, I guess so. I'm sorry, I tried, but my muscles are so stiff they're not cooperating."

Great. *This is your punishment Kyle. You have no one to blame but yourself. You did this to her, now you have to suffer because of it.* Glumly, he wondered if eternity in hell wouldn't be a better penalty than what he was about to face.

"All right, I'm coming in."

Without looking in the direction of the tub, Kyle entered the bathroom and stared at the opposite wall. "I'm going to grab a towel. Then I'll lift you out of the tub, and we'll get the towel around you, okay?"

"Yes."

Weak, pitiful response. She must really be hurting to allow a man she barely knew into her bathroom while she was sitting naked in the tub. "I promise, Sabrina, I won't look."

Then she giggled softly. Of all things. "I'm not worried, Kyle. I trust you."

Well that was the biggest mistake she could ever make. He was hard already and he hadn't seen or touched her yet. Foolish woman.

Grabbing a towel from the linen closet and slinging it over his shoulder, Kyle backed up to the bathtub, then closed his eyes and turned to face her.

"You're going to have to help me. Reach out and grab my arms so I know where you are." Sabrina did as she was instructed, and Kyle felt warm, wet hands grabbing his arms. He hadn't bothered to put on a shirt after his shower, and her slippery skin glided over his forearms.

She giggled again, a low throaty sound that was driving him crazy. "You look silly with your eyes all scrunched tight like that."

Kyle grunted. At least she was looking at his face. If her gaze traveled south she'd see something that wasn't silly at all. At least not to him. His erection was dead serious about straining against his jeans. "Put your arms around my shoulders, I'm going to lift you up."

He bent over and slid his arms under Sabrina's so he could get a grip on her, then lifted her to a standing position. She grunted in pain at the change of position.

The scent of lavender filled the air. God. Warm, wet, sweet-smelling naked woman. He heaved a sigh and pulled the towel off his shoulder.

His blindness hindered him, and while trying to wrap the towel around her he brushed his hand against a full, warm breast. A breast whose nipple puckered and hardened the second his hand touched it. Kyle heard Sabrina's sharp intake of breath. It took every ounce of willpower he could muster not to slide his palm over her breast again, to feel its fullness and weight in his hand, to lower his mouth and taste her.

"Sorry." No he wasn't. It had been like touching a slice of heaven.

A moment of silence passed before she answered. "It's all right."

Kyle needed to get out of there, and fast. He fastened the towel between her breasts, feeling them rise and swell against his knuckles as he tucked one end of the towel into the deep valley between them. God help him, this was the worst form of torture he'd ever endured. Placing one arm behind her back and the other under her thighs, he lifted Sabrina out of the tub and set her on the floor.

He finally opened his eyes and looked at her. She was far sexier in that towel than he ever could have imagined. Flushed from the hot bath, her hair was swept up on top of her head and the tired look in her eyes only made her more desirable. It wasn't fair.

"Are you okay now?"

"Uh huh."

"Fine. Just put that salve on and by tomorrow you'll be good as new."

"Umm…"

Good Lord, now what? "What?"

"I can't reach."

Of course he hadn't thought about that. The most tender spots would be her upper thighs and rear end, and she wouldn't be able to reach them in her current condition.

"I'll get Jenna. Maybe she's home by now."

"Thanks," Sabrina answered weakly.

Kyle went to his room and dialed Jenna's number. No answer. Dammit. He walked to the French doors and looked out. No lights. They hadn't returned from shopping.

"She's not back yet," Kyle said as he stood in the doorway to Sabrina's room.

"I can do without the salve."

Hell and damnation. No she couldn't. The salve needed to be applied while the muscles were softened by the warm bath or it wouldn't be as effective.

"I'll do it."

"No!" Sabrina said sharply.

"Sabrina, I thought you said you trusted me."

"Yeah, I trusted you not to look. This would require…touching."

He was goddamn well aware of what it would require. Every part of his male anatomy was screaming for him to run like hell. He was hot, aching, and hard as stone. And he'd damn well better earn heaven points for doing this.

"You need to have this done, and since I'm the only one around, it'll have to be me."

"Kyle, I can't let you do that. It's…inappropriate."

"Hell, Sabrina, I have a little sister. I've seen her naked butt more times than I care to." Of course he didn't mention that Jenna was four years old at the time.

"Still, it wouldn't be right."

He raked his hands through his hair in frustration. It wasn't as if he was dying to touch her. Not in a medicinal way anyway. But he needed to convince her the salve was necessary.

"Do you want to be able to get back on that horse again tomorrow?"

"Of course I do."

Finally he was getting somewhere. "If I don't rub this salve on you, you'll be so sore tomorrow you won't be able to ride for days." Now for the clincher. "You have a lot to learn in three short months, and you can't afford to waste a day. Now are you going to stand here and waste my time arguing or are we going to get to it?"

He watched Sabrina's face. She chewed her lower lip as she considered his words. Then she looked at him, as if deciding whether she could trust him with her body. If Sabrina was as smart as he thought she was, she wouldn't trust him at all.

"Okay," she said finally. "What should I do?"

What should she do? It would be great if she'd remove her towel, lie down on her back on the bed, and let him make love to her. Then he could relieve both their aches.

"Lie down on the bed on your stomach, and I'll rub this salve on your as—uhh, bottom and legs. It will only take a few minutes, then I'll get out of here so you can get some rest."

And he'd go back to his room and jack off. His balls were quivering, goddammit.

She regarded him warily, with a mixture of innocence and uncertainty. Eventually pain won out over modesty, because she turned and gingerly lowered herself face down on the bed.

Kyle stood there for a moment, transfixed and unable to move. The towel barely covered her upper thighs, and Sabrina had untied it from her breasts when she lay down. Spread out over her, it was the only thing hiding her body from his view.

His breathing came in rasps as he struggled for oxygen to fuel his brain. All the blood in his body rushed to his dick and was now working overtime, causing him an incredible amount of discomfort.

This was surely going to kill him.

"Um…Kyle?"

"Yeah?" For some reason he couldn't move.

"Are you going to start soon?"

Oh, he certainly hoped so. Very, very soon.

"Huh?"

"The massage."

Oh that. "Yeah, right now. Are you ready?" He certainly was. More than ready. Ready, willing, and excruciatingly able.

Sabrina mumbled something that sounded more like *mmhmm* than anything intelligible, but Kyle wasn't sure since her face was buried in her arms.

"This will be a little cold at first." Kyle applied the salve to his hands, then started at the lower half of her thighs. Sabrina winced and tightened when he first applied pressure to her legs, but then relaxed as he softly kneaded the muscles. Her legs were firm and muscular, which worked in her favor. She'd recover more quickly since she was already in shape.

Kyle forced himself to think of what he was doing as an act of mercy. Sabrina was in pain, and he was helping her. That was it, nothing more. The sooner he finished the job, the quicker he'd be able to extricate himself from this tortuous task. Wryly he wondered where the mercy for his condition was.

He moved further up her thighs, lightly sliding his hands under the towel. Sabrina sighed and instinctively parted her legs to allow him better access to her inner thighs.

Agony. Torture. This was horrible. Sabrina had the softest, most perfect skin he had ever felt. Coupled with the fact he could touch but not see, his tactile senses were working overtime. Every stroke of his hands on her body, every one of her quiet moans in response to the pressure on her muscles, caused Kyle's breath to catch. He wanted to moan like Sabrina, but for a completely different reason.

He used light pressure to massage her inner thighs, taking great care not to touch her intimately. But he wanted to. God how he wanted to. Kyle had reached the point where he was certain his physical pain was much worse than Sabrina's.

Now for her rear end. He doubted it could get any worse. Kyle poured more salve on his hands, then reached further under the towel, searching for the twin globes. When he felt the rise of her buttocks at the back of her thighs, he gently began massaging in a circular motion. Then Kyle realized he had been right. It *was* worse.

Sabrina's ass was soft as satin, yet firm. Kyle felt her muscles relax under his ministrations, but still he kept on, mesmerized. He could do this all night long. Actually, there were other things he'd like to do with Sabrina all night long. Visuals of pulling her to the end of the bed, parting her thighs further and sinking between her pussy lips had his cock lurching against his jeans.

A man shouldn't be tormented like this. It would be so easy to cup her sex and bring her relief from the tension soaring through her body. Then, when he had her fully relaxed, he'd unzip his jeans and drive his cock into her hot pussy, relieving the pounding ache that he'd been living with since she first stepped foot on the ranch yesterday.

But as he worked, he heard unmistakable sounds. Not the slight moans he had heard earlier, but even, steady breathing, followed by a soft, incredibly girly snore. He leaned over to look at her face.

She was asleep. Deeply, soundly, asleep. Kyle was aroused to the point of wanting to howl at the moon, and she had been completely unaffected by the whole thing. In fact, he had put her out like a boxer cold-cocking his opponent.

So much for his seduction skills. Kyle pulled back the covers on Sabrina's bed, and gently turned her so he could wrap them around her. She didn't budge an inch.

He walked to the doorway to his room, looked longingly at the beautiful woman slumbering peacefully under the covers, and turned out the light. Sleep would be the best thing for her.

But sleep wouldn't come for him tonight. Not yet. He was too wound up, too agitated. Too damned aroused to even think about sleeping.

No cold shower was going to quell the heat he was feeling right now.

Chapter Five

New horses and cattle were arriving. Sabrina watched from the porch as the deliveries were made. Mother cows and their babies marched out of the loading truck in pairs like the survivors from Noah's Ark. Men on horseback shouted and whistled, driving the cattle into a nearby pen. They'd be taken out to the grazing pasture along with the Rocking M's existing cattle.

The horses had arrived a couple days ago. Twenty beautiful quarter horses had been bought at auction earlier in the week. According to Kyle, Brady had done a good job selecting the new stock and they'd be invaluable working animals for the ranch.

Sabrina watched the whole process in awe. Between the new horses and cattle, the ranch was hopping. A multitude of activities occurred simultaneously. Each hand knew their job and did it without hesitation or question. In the middle of it all, shouting orders and organizing, was Kyle.

The mere thought of their intimate, if innocent, encounter the other evening had her body heating all over. Gentleman that he was, he never brought it up in the days following, but Sabrina remembered.

She had been hurting, that much was certain. Thank heavens Kyle had the wherewithal to know what needed to be done to alleviate the pain. When she woke the next morning, she had been a bit sore, but it could have been worse if Kyle hadn't attended to her.

The night he took care of her, Kyle had been tender and compassionate, never once asking for anything in return. He didn't berate her or make her feel foolish like her ex-husband would have. Mark would have used her pain as an opportunity to make her feel stupid, until she'd end up apologizing for her own pain.

She could still remember the feel of Kyle's hands on her. Yes, she'd been in pain, almost unbearable, and exhaustion had set in to the point where sleeping was a needed and wanted relief. But through the haze she was aware of Kyle's strong, capable hands sliding over her body—gently pressing into her aching muscles. Sabrina wondered how those hands would feel if he had been touching her as a lover. The thought made her ache all over, an urgent, spreading need that both pained and thrilled her at the same time.

Heat flowed through her at the thought of Kyle as a lover. What would it be like to have someone actually make love to her, instead of the way it had always been with Mark? Mark had used her body in the same way he had used her heart. Calculating, cold and controlling, he'd never once allowed her to participate—instead, told her what to do, how to do it, and she knew better than to deviate from his instructions. Lovemaking was not what she had done with her ex-husband. In truth, Sabrina had never really made love. Or been made love to.

"You ready?" Kyle's deep voice jolted Sabrina into the present. She turned and saw him leaning casually against the railing.

He certainly made jeans and a shirt look sexy. The worn denim hugged his body, and Sabrina marveled over the strong thighs encased within them. He had discarded his long sleeve shirt, and wore only a navy blue T-shirt that tautly outlined his muscled chest and wide shoulders.

"Ready for what?"

Kyle's eyebrows lifted and he smiled at her obvious forgetfulness. "To go to town. Remember? We talked about getting supplies a couple days ago."

"Oh yeah. Sure, I'd love to." They had talked about Sabrina accompanying Kyle into town to purchase supplies, something she'd need to know how to do as a ranch owner.

"I'll bring the truck around. Be ready in about five minutes."

She went inside to grab her purse and sunglasses. Pausing to apply some lipstick, she glanced at her reflection in the hall mirror, and smiled as she thought about how different she looked now. Before, Mark had required her to have her makeup on, hair done and dressed up at all times. That usually meant skirts or dresses, and always heels. Mark didn't like her to wear flats or tennis shoes.

But she was no longer someone's dress-up doll. Today she wore a pink cotton T-shirt under a denim jacket, blue jeans and tennis shoes. Very little makeup adorned her face, just a touch of mascara and lipstick. And she was starting to tan from being outside. Not really dark, just enough to add some color to her face.

Her hair wasn't curled, wasn't teased, and wasn't perfectly combed. She'd left it straight and in a high ponytail on top of her head. She smirked at her reflection in the mirror as she tucked her lipstick away in her purse. Mark would probably have a stroke if he could see her now.

The drive into town took about forty-five minutes, and gave her an opportunity to look at the scenery as Kyle pointed out the land markings where the Rocking M property began and ended. From the main highway, Sabrina could see green sloping hills and scatterings of oak, blackjack and sycamore trees, providing ample shade for the cattle. Before they turned off the highway away from the Rocking M, she saw hundreds of cattle grazing in a green grassy meadow at the far end of the ranch property.

"Impressive ranch," she said to Kyle, who had been mostly silent since they left the house. His dark sunglasses made him look like a sexy movie star rather than a rancher. He certainly had the looks of one. His light brown hair wasn't combed since it was short enough not to require it. He had a couple days growth of beard, which by now Sabrina had noticed was fairly typical for Kyle. All in all, he looked sexy, rugged and utterly masculine. And every day she was around him, Sabrina grew more aware of that potent masculinity.

"Thanks."

"It's fairly large by most ranch standards, isn't it?"

Kyle shrugged. "Not really. The Rocking M is bigger than some, smaller than some. There are ranches that encompass hundreds of thousands of acres."

Sabrina's eyes widened. "Really? I can't imagine one that large." She didn't want to own a ranch that would be more than she could handle. Just a small one she could manage herself, but large enough to generate a profit. The thought of being responsible for her own operation made Sabrina's stomach lurch. She wasn't ready—not yet. There was so much yet to learn, and in addition to what she'd learned already it made her head spin.

"What are we shopping for today?"

Kyle handed Sabrina a list he had made. "Groceries, supplies, and I need to make arrangements for the vet to visit and check out the new stock. Plus most of the cows have dropped their calves by now, and when we round them up I want vet services around."

Sabrina nodded, making mental notes as she perused the list Kyle gave her. "That's a lot of groceries."

Kyle smiled and glanced at Sabrina. "When you have to take an hour and a half out of your day to drive into town, you better buy enough supplies for a month, and you better make damn sure you don't forget anything. The trip's too long to go back the next day because you forgot to buy something."

Good point. Sabrina hadn't thought about that. Of course she hadn't shopped for groceries or anything normal for a very long time. While married to Mark, the house staff handled all the shopping, and Sabrina was only allowed to shop for clothes if Mark accompanied her and chose the outfits he wanted her to wear.

They arrived in Dreamwater and Kyle parked at the local grocery store's lot. Kyle told her they'd go see the veterinarian first, so they started walking. Sabrina marveled at the quaint, small-town life. A typical main street lined with local merchant's shops centered Dreamwater. Actually, every store seemed locally owned. No national retail chains or fast-food restaurants spoiled the ambience of a slice of life that, to most people nowadays, was either unheard of or long forgotten.

A sign on one of the buildings was emblazoned with *Sheriff, Jail, Courthouse and Post Office.*

"All of those are in that tiny little building?"

Kyle nodded. "Don't have much crime in these parts. Usually one of the local kids will get in trouble or a fight will break out at the bar, but that's about it. The sheriff can take care of everything right in one building."

She thought it was the most charming thing she had ever seen. Sabrina fondly remembered watching reruns of *The Andy Griffith Show*, and Dreamwater's Main Street reminded her of that.

"I'll bet everybody knows everybody else in this town," she remarked as they made their way past Dolittle's Clothing Store, Aunt Mary's Coffee Shop, Susie's Sewing and Fabrics and Dreamwater Mercantile. Brightly striped green and white awnings provided ample shade for window shoppers looking for bargains.

"You got that right. And they know too much, sometimes." She glanced at Kyle's expressionless face and wondered what he meant by that.

They arrived at Dr. Emma Steven's clinic. Inside, the clinic was spacious and clean, smelling of disinfectant and all the scents associated with animals. As she turned to take a seat in the waiting room, Sabrina was shocked to see a man, obviously a farmer, sitting in one of the chairs with a tiny pink pig at the end of a leash. She'd never seen a pig before in her life.

She took a seat next to the farmer. He looked up at her with sharp brown eyes and long graying hair partially hid under a green John Deere ball cap. He wore overalls and a red and white flannel shirt. And she was fairly certain the man had no teeth whatsoever, but he did seem to be chewing something. It didn't take her long to figure out, after she watched him spit out a long stream of brown liquid into a cup in his hand, that he was chewing tobacco. She tried not to grimace.

"Is that your pet?"

The farmer turned to her but didn't smile. "Nuh uh. Pain in the butt is what she is. I'm hoping the doc will take her off my hands."

"Why don't you want to keep her?"

"Don't have no use for a pig on my farm. Got sheep, goats, cows, horses, cats and dogs. Damn daughter-in-law got it for my birthday."

Obviously a gift he didn't want. "Well that's a nice gift, isn't it?" She watched the pig walk as far as the leash would allow, and then sit like a well-behaved dog. It was the most adorable creature she'd ever seen.

She'd never been allowed a pet before. Not a dog, a cat, or even a bird. Her mother said they couldn't care for a pet since they were on the road all the time. Then after she'd married Mark, pets were out of the question. They were dirty, after all.

"So why don't you sell her?"

"Hoping the doc will trade her for some medicines I need for my stock."

Sabrina considered the pig for a moment. She glanced over at Kyle who was watching her exchange with the farmer, his emerald eyes shining with amusement. When she shot him a hopeful expression, his smile died.

"Don't even think about it," he whispered in her ear. "We're not buying a pig."

She'd been turned down way too many times in her life, and Kyle's immediate refusal got her dander up. "No, *we're* not, but I might."

Before he could respond, she turned to the farmer and smiled at him. "I would like to buy your pig. How much?"

"Sabrina," Kyle warned, his voice low.

The farmer watched the interplay between the two. "A hundred dollars ought to do her."

"No." Kyle said forcefully. "That's too much money for a damn pig, anyway."

"Sold," she countered quickly. She paid the farmer and he handed the leash to her and headed to the counter to buy medicines. He made his purchase and headed to the front door.

"Wait," Sabrina called to the man, who turned and paused. "Does the pig have a name?"

The farmer finally cracked an all but toothless smile. "Now darlin', who in their right mind would name a pig?"

Sabrina looked down at her new pig and smiled like a proud parent. The pig looked up expectantly, and as she bent down to pet it, it snorted lightly and rubbed its snout against her hand, making her giggle.

She turned to look at Kyle. His arms were folded across his chest and he shook his head as he looked down at her. He obviously wasn't happy she bought the pig. Tough. She was free and independent now, and she'd be damned if she'd ever let another man tell her what she could or couldn't do.

"I've never had a pet," she said defiantly.

Kyle shrugged and rose as the receptionist called his name. Sabrina and her pig followed him into the doctor's office.

They headed down the back hallway of the large medical facility. She was amazed at how well the pig followed on the leash. She smiled down at the little pink wonder and verbally praised it, then looked at Kyle who rolled his eyes and did his best to ignore them both.

As they entered the doctor's office, Sabrina was surprised to find a young, very attractive woman sitting behind the desk. Vivid blue eyes graced a heart-shaped face, and her shoulder-length auburn hair perfectly complemented her creamy skin. The doctor smiled brightly at Kyle and hugged him. Sabrina felt a sharp twinge of jealousy as Kyle returned the hug and beamed at Dr. Emma Stevens.

Feeling forgotten, Sabrina lightly cleared her throat. Kyle turned to her and introduced her as his new partner.

Emma's eyebrows lifted as she smiled at Sabrina and shook her hand. Glancing at Kyle, she said "Partner?"

Kyle nodded as he and Sabrina took a seat. "Business partner. Sabrina invested some capital in the ranch on a temporary basis, and in return I'm teaching her about ranching."

She didn't want to like Emma for some reason. But she didn't understand why. Just because Emma Stevens and Kyle seemed friendly, or for that matter even if they were dating, it shouldn't affect Sabrina one way or the other. But it did. And she didn't care for this feeling she was having. Suddenly she felt—competitive.

But Emma was charming, gracious, and very friendly.

"So you want to be a rancher?"

Sabrina nodded. "Yes I do."

"Did you grow up on a ranch?"

"No. Actually, I've never set foot on one before." Even as she said it she knew it sounded ridiculous, and for some reason felt the necessity to explain. "I know it seems silly to want to do something you have absolutely no experience with..."

Emma waved her hand and grinned. "Don't be ridiculous. Of course it's not silly. You're chasing your dream. Nothing wrong with that. So did I. That's why I became a vet."

The women talked for awhile longer about making one's dreams come true. Well, so much for first impressions. Sabrina found she really liked Emma Stevens. She was around her own age, and had worked her way through veterinary school by herself since her family couldn't afford it. Dr. Jacob Lewis, the former town veterinarian, had planned for years to retire and was just waiting for Emma to graduate so she could take over.

Emma had been working at the clinic since she was a child. She even interned with Dr. Lewis while she was in vet school. Not long after she graduated, she took over the practice and had been providing animal care services to the town and neighboring farms and ranches for the past two years.

As Emma and Kyle talked about his veterinary needs, Sabrina observed how comfortable the two were with each other. There always seemed to be tension between her and Kyle, but with Emma he was completely relaxed, even laughing and cracking jokes. Maybe they had something going on. That would certainly explain the ease of their relationship.

As they completed their business, Emma rose and walked around the desk to Sabrina. She smiled at the pig.

"This your pig?"

Sabrina nodded, smiling. "Actually, I bought it from a farmer sitting in your waiting room when we came in. He was going to ask you for a trade for medicines."

Emma rolled her eyes. "I'm so grateful. Bob Hanson wants to trade every stray animal that shows up on his farm for some goods or services. For some reason he thinks I'm in the animal broker business. Thanks for giving me a break on this one."

Emma bent down and picked up the pig, cradling it in her arms. "Would you like me to examine and inoculate her?"

She nodded. "That would be great, thanks."

The doctor buzzed for one of her technicians, and she was instructed to follow the tech into a waiting room while Emma finished her business with Kyle. A young girl came in and Sabrina and her pig were taken to a small exam room, where the technician weighed her, started a chart, and then left to obtain the necessary inoculations.

The pig was thoroughly examined, poked, prodded, given her shots and pronounced healthy as a…pig. Emma told her what to feed it, how to care for it and then asked her the animal's name so she could add it to her chart.

Sabrina looked down at the pink squirming bundle in her arms and smiled.

"Petunia."

Emma laughed. "Perfect."

They walked out of the exam room and back to the front desk where Kyle was paying for his supplies. When he finished, she paid for Petunia's checkup and shots and turned to Emma.

"Thank you, Emma, it was a pleasure to meet you."

The doctor smiled brightly at her. "It was great to meet you too, Sabrina. Now if you have any questions about Petunia, just give me a call, any time of the day or night." Emma removed a business card from her pocket and handed it to Sabrina. "I'm on call all the time anyway."

Turning to Kyle, Emma hugged him. "And don't forget what we talked about. I want to talk about this some more, okay?"

Kyle nodded and they left. Sabrina wondered what Emma wanted to talk to him about, but it sounded personal and she didn't want to ask. Probably something they would discuss on their next date. And then she had that feeling again as she pondered Kyle with Emma. She couldn't be jealous. She and Kyle had a professional relationship, and that's where it ended.

After they left the vet's office, they dropped their supplies at the truck.

Kyle motioned to the pig at her feet. "Throw her in the back."

"I don't think so." She picked up Petunia and held her to her breast as if protecting a child. "I really don't want to leave her in the truck. What if someone steals her?"

Kyle rolled his eyes. "This is Dreamwater, not Los Angeles. If it were that easy to get rid of the pig, Bob would have left her in his own pickup, hoping someone would take her. Believe me, no one will steal your pig."

"I don't care," she said, lifting her chin. "She's coming with me."

His eyes narrowed and she braced for an argument. Then he surprised her.

"Fine," he said tightly. "Let's go."

They entered the small grocery store and Kyle grabbed a cart. She held the list as Kyle pushed the cart up and down the aisles. Petunia strutted proudly at Sabrina's side, pausing now and then to sniff something on the bottom shelf of the racks.

Kyle was right. Everybody knew everybody in this town. He had to greet someone he knew in almost every aisle, and then introduce Sabrina. She thought people would be surprised he had taken on a partner, but he was correct about small towns. Most people already knew all about her, when she had arrived, why she was there and how long she was staying. Small town grapevines were definitely the most amazing thing she had ever encountered.

But everyone was friendly, welcomed her to Dreamwater, praised Kyle and his ranch and told her she couldn't have picked a better one to learn on.

And almost everyone commented about Petunia.

Nice pig.

Every time someone said it Sabrina grinned. Nice pig. Her pig. Her first pet.

"Petunia, huh?" Kyle looked down at her pet, currently rolling around on her little pink back at his feet.

Grinning, Sabrina nodded. "Yeah."

He bent down and picked up Petunia with one hand, cradled her on her back in the crook of his arm and absently rubbed her fat pink belly while they walked. Sabrina pushed the cart and placed a few items in it as they strolled along.

Petunia seemed perfectly content being held in his strong arms. So content, in fact, that as he stroked her belly, she eventually went to sleep. Sabrina smiled, remembering drifting off to sleep herself when Kyle gave her the massage that night. Suddenly the thought of his hands on her sent her mind reeling into non-grocery-like thoughts. She wanted to be the one being held in his arms, his hands absently running over her body, not stirring her into sleep this time, but awakening her to passion.

But he had a woman already, or at least she thought so. And besides, she had to keep reminding herself that involvement with Kyle Morgan was not in her grand plan. He wasn't even interested in her.

"What are you thinking about?" Kyle's deep voice penetrated the haze surrounding her mind. She realized she was wandering aimlessly down the aisle, and hadn't once checked the grocery list to see if anything in that aisle was on the list.

She stopped pushing the cart and turned to him, hoping her face didn't betray her thoughts. "Um...nothing. Sorry, my mind was wandering." *To you, your hands, how they'd feel on me. Wondering how your mouth would taste on mine, where you'd kiss and touch me if I gave myself to you.*

"Wandering where?" He raised his eyebrows in curiosity.

"Why do you want to know?"

Awareness flickered in his sparkling green eyes. "Something about the expression on your face. You looked, I don't know, pained, but also happy. I can't explain it, I just found it...intriguing. I'd like to know what you were thinking about."

Oh God, he knew. Warmth spread over her face as she thought about having to tell Kyle exactly what she had been thinking. Not a chance.

"My future," she lied. "I was thinking about what I was going to do when I left the Rocking M."

"I see." From the disbelieving look and slight smile showing at the corners of his mouth, she knew he didn't believe her explanation. "Come to any conclusions about that?"

Great. Now she'd have to make up a pack of lies. And she was a terrible liar.

"Not yet."

"Can't wait to leave though, can you?" Kyle still held a sleeping Petunia in his arms. She was certain the pig was snoring. He shot her a teasing grin.

"Oh yes, I can wait," she answered without thinking. "I'm not ready to leave you."

She didn't mean to say it that way. The way it sounded, so personal, like it was Kyle she didn't want to leave. She meant to say the ranch. She didn't want to leave the ranch. Oh damn. She sucked at lying.

The smile died on his face, and his expression grew serious. The heat in his eyes ignited the flame she had fired up earlier with thoughts of him. Something passed between them, a spark completely elemental and powerful. Kyle took a step toward her, closing the short distance between them.

Words were unnecessary and she couldn't have spoken them had she tried. An awareness of him unlike anything she ever experienced before settled over her. Her senses went into overdrive, heightening everything around her, making her more cognizant of everything male about him. Surprisingly, the fact they were in the middle of aisle twelve at the grocery store didn't even seem to matter.

She inhaled his scent, so powerful and masculine. Her heart rammed against her chest as he rested his hand on her neck. She could feel her own pulse beating erratically against the palm of his hand. He leaned his head toward her, his mouth a mere inch away.

He was going to kiss her. God almighty, right here in the middle of the grocery store, he was going to kiss her. And she never wanted anything more in her entire life.

"Well isn't this a cozy little scene?"

His eyes lingered on hers for the briefest of seconds, and she swore regret reflected in them. They turned at the same time to see a very tall, thin man in dark jeans and a gray shirt.

She'd been around enough moneymen to know this one was loaded. He looked expensive, from his handmade, snakeskin Justin cowboy boots to his top-of-the-line Stetson hat, both of which she had seen her ex-husband wear. Several diamond rings, all worth a fortune, adorned his long, slender fingers. The man wore enough silver and gold around his neck and wrists to add fifteen pounds to his lanky frame.

But what really bothered Sabrina was the look this stranger gave Kyle. Dislike was too light a word to use for the expression on the man's face. It was more like hatred.

She turned to Kyle and immediately knew who the man was before he could say a word. He handed Petunia to her and turned to face his nemesis.

"Jackson Dent. Out slumming in the grocery stores today? Thought you had *people* to handle the menial tasks like this."

Dent smirked. "Nah, just taking the little woman out for a little shopping today and I needed a pack of cigarettes. It's the least I can do for the light of my life." He looked behind Kyle and Sabrina, and suddenly broke out into a huge smile. "There you are, darlin'. Was wondering where you'd wandered off to."

A dynamic looking woman with shoulder-length, dark hair strolled past Kyle and Sabrina. She was very attractive and wore enough jewelry to ring bells like a Salvation Army volunteer at Christmas. And she reeked of expensive perfume. Sabrina wrinkled her nose and coughed at the overpowering scent. She heard Kyle's quiet chuckle.

The woman sidled next to Dent, kissing him on the cheek and smiling. "Just wandering around, honey." She turned and looked at Sabrina, disdain apparent in her eyes as she checked Sabrina out from head to toe. A smirk formed on her mouth as if to say Sabrina wasn't worth the visual tour. Then she turned to Kyle. Something flashed in the woman's dark eyes, but Sabrina couldn't quite pinpoint the emotion. Anger? Jealousy? The woman's smirk died, and a straight line formed on her full, blood-red painted lips.

"Kyle," the woman said flatly.

"Amanda." No emotion sprang from Kyle's lips as he answered the woman in a monotone voice, barely acknowledging her presence.

Amanda Morgan Dent. Kyle's former wife, and Jackson Dent's current one. Sabrina sensed trouble brewing.

Chapter Six

"Well, well, well. Isn't this interesting?"

Sabrina didn't find it interesting at all, and wished she and Kyle were anywhere else but here right now. Dent's comments only fueled Kyle's anger, which she could feel growing as he stood rigid next to her.

"Kyle, darling, it's been so long since I've seen you," Amanda said as she dramatically flipped her hair away from her face. "Of course you know I've been so busy these days, what with chairing the charity gala at the country club, and all the tennis I'm playing now. And of course Jackson keeps me busy in other ways too," she said as she winked at her husband.

Ouch. Sabrina bet that one hurt.

She turned and watched for Kyle's response. He merely arched an eyebrow. "Really. Can't imagine he'd even be interested. It's not like you really have that much to offer." With a yawn, he added, "And I'd know. It was all I could do to stay awake during most of it."

Yes! A big zinger in Amanda's direction. Sabrina secretly cheered Kyle on, her dislike for his ex-wife growing by the minute.

Undaunted, Amanda had a comeback ready. "Oh come on now, Kyle, I know better than that. I'll bet you're real lonely these days without me."

He threw his head back and laughed. "Actually, I'm not lonely at all now that you're gone, Amanda. Your departure was like spring cleaning at the ranch. I only wish I had booted your butt off the Rocking M a lot sooner."

It was all Sabrina could do not to jump up and down and cheer out loud for Kyle. He really let Amanda have it, but good. Instead she smiled pleasantly and didn't say a word.

"Well!" Amanda appeared at a loss for words. "So what are you looking for in this little hovel today?"

Kyle crossed his arms and smiled. "Well, it isn't aspirin because the previous cause of all my headaches married someone else."

Sabrina couldn't help it. The laugh just fell out of her mouth before she could do anything to stop it.

"You low-life, snake-in-the-grass bastard." Amanda shot her response at Kyle as she lunged at him.

Jackson wrapped his arms around his seething wife and glared at Kyle. "Don't fret, honey, he's just jealous that I have the prize of Dreamwater and he doesn't." Ignoring Kyle's snort, Dent continued. "Besides, it won't be long before he and all the Morgans get what they deserve. I'm gonna break them down and cast them out. Then the Rocking M will become Dent property, like I always said it would."

"Over my dead body, Dent," Kyle said as he crossed his arms, prepared for battle.

Sabrina hoped he was as good with the shots to Dent as he'd been with Amanda.

Dent laughed. "Won't matter to me one way or the other whether you're dead or alive. Either way, I aim to take the ranch out from under you, Morgan. Get ready for it."

"You'll never take the Rocking M away from my family, Dent. I'll sell it outright to someone else before I ever let you get your hands on our property."

"Well see, Morgan, won't we?" Turning toward Sabrina, Dent smiled, his crooked teeth gleaming in the harsh light of the grocery store. "You lined yourself up with the wrong man, honey. You're about to lose everything you invested on this piss-poor ranch manager here," Dent said as he pointed to Kyle. "Should have put your money with a winner, like me. I'd have shown you how to run a ranch the right way."

Sabrina's back stiffened. How Kyle could avoid knocking the man on his ass was beyond her. "No, Mr. Dent, I put my money exactly where I wanted it. Kyle's a smart rancher, with a good operation and a bright future." She sniffed and raised her chin. "It's doubtful you have anything to teach me that I'd be interested in learning. I have everything I need right here."

Dent laughed and tipped his hat to Sabrina. "Some women just don't ever learn." Turning to Amanda he said, "Let's go, honey, I feel like buying you something pretty and expensive today. Something you never got while married to poor, broke Kyle Morgan." Amanda threw a smirk at Kyle, ignored Sabrina completely and walked away with her husband.

The tension was palpable. Kyle stood in the center of the aisle watching Jackson and Amanda Dent retreat. Sabrina put the now-awake Petunia down on the floor.

"I'm so sorry," she said as she laid her hand on his arm. His forearm was stiff as a board, tension emanating from his body. "What an evil man."

Kyle stared straight ahead, refusing to meet her eyes. "Let's go," he said tersely. Sabrina followed him as they checked out and headed toward the truck.

The ride home was conducted in almost complete silence, except for Petunia's occasional snorting. Sabrina sat the pig on her lap, stroking her ears and rubbing her back. Petunia finally settled in and took another nap, apparently unbothered by the tension in the truck.

"Are you okay?" she asked, finally unable to bear the silence.

"I'm fine."

"You are not. And it's understandable that you'd be upset after that altercation with Dent and his wife. The man's pure evil, and Amanda is...well, she's..." Sabrina was unable to finish the sentence, not wanting to be rude considering Kyle used to be married to her.

"A raving bitch from hell?" he finished for her.

She laughed. "That certainly works."

The corners of Kyle's mouth lifted in a slight grin. "I have more I could say about her, if you'd like to hear it. How sensitive are your ears?"

"Go right ahead and vent. I'd agree with whatever you have to say about her." She could feel the tension melt away as Kyle visibly relaxed his shoulders and leaned back in the seat of the truck.

"She's not worth the breath. If nothing else, the exchange was fun," he said with a grin.

"I'll say. You really let her have it."

"Too much?" he asked as he glanced at her with curiosity.

Sabrina shook her head. "Not enough, in my opinion. She deserved much worse."

"Her own fault. She cast her lot with Dent, and it will ruin her some day. But she'll get what she deserves, married to that arrogant bastard."

"Does he really want to take your ranch?"

Kyle nodded. "He's wanted it for years, but even more so after my parents died. He showed up at their funeral and made remarks about me not being able to keep the ranch up and offering to buy it."

"That's terrible." She couldn't imagine someone being so insensitive as to mention a business deal during a time of incredible grief.

"Not surprising though. That's pretty much the way Dent has always operated. Any way he wants to, thinking money forgives all sins."

"Like someone else I know," she added. Just like Mark. Money could buy all kinds of things, in his opinion. Loyalty, business, forgiveness, and love.

Kyle glanced over at her. "Your ex-husband?"

She nodded. "Only worse."

"Why did you marry him, then?"

"Because I was young, eighteen years old. I had never been allowed to even talk to a man by myself, let alone date one." At Kyle's shocked expression, Sabrina smiled. "My mother kept a very tight rein on me. She didn't want her meal ticket to end up pregnant or running off with a boyfriend."

"Kind of overprotective?"

"Not in a loving kind of way. More like protecting her asset." Love hadn't entered the picture when Sabrina's mother was involved. Sabrina had been a marketing tool, a way to make money, and that was all.

"So tell me about your ex."

Sabrina stared ahead at the road, visual images of the past ten years sailing across her eyes. "I met him at the Miss Dallas contest, like I mentioned before. I was floored because Mother actually introduced me to a man, and then left so I could speak to him alone. That had never happened before—she guarded me so fiercely."

"And you liked him?"

She nodded. "What wasn't there to like? At least on the surface. He was good-looking, educated, charming and he showed an interest in me. For someone who had been sheltered her whole life, I was in heaven. Fell head over heels for him in the first five minutes."

"And then?"

"We dated for six months, married in an incredibly elaborate ceremony, reception at the country club and all. After the honeymoon, I moved into his mansion. Then the whole Pygmalion thing started."

"Huh?" Kyle glanced at her, a look of confusion on his face.

"Pygmalion? My Fair Lady? You know, turning the sow's ear into a silk purse?"

"Oh. Okay, gotcha." He smiled. "He thought you needed polishing, did he?"

Sabrina looked down at the sleeping pig in her lap. "He thought I needed everything. Nothing I did or said satisfied him."

Kyle's smile faded. "It must have been hard for you."

"It was. Well not at first. I was so in love and wanted to please him I'd have done anything he asked. And I worked very hard. I went to college, learned about running a large household, took tennis and golf lessons at the country club and was taught how to dress the way he liked. Everything."

"But that wasn't good enough for him?"

"No, it wasn't. Nothing I ever did was. He always seemed displeased with me, no matter how hard I tried. And when he was unhappy he made sure I knew about it."

"Sabrina, did he abuse you?" Kyle asked, his voice low and soft as he glanced over at her, a concerned look on his face.

She bent her head, busying her hands by petting the sleeping pig. "No. Not physically. His abuse was verbal. Belittling, making me feel worthless no matter what I did. Very subtle, but there nonetheless. And I guess I was weak, because I let him."

Kyle laid his hand on her shoulder. "I'm sorry."

"It's okay." She looked up at him and smiled. "It wasn't that bad. I got a college education out of it, and I learned how to play a decent game of tennis and a really lousy game of golf."

Kyle laughed. "I play neither, so I guess I won't get to find out."

"Good. I hate both of them. I'd rather ride a horse any day of the week than play tennis or golf."

"You'll get plenty of that at the Rocking M. Enough to make your butt sore." His eyes gleamed mischievously as he glanced at her. "But then you already know that, don't you?"

It embarrassed her to be reminded of her first day riding, and what Kyle had done for her. "I guess we never talked about that night, did we?"

He turned his eyes back on the road and shrugged nonchalantly. "Nothing to discuss, really."

"But I never thanked you for what you did."

His voice deepened, seducing her with its low and husky tones. "Believe me, Sabrina, the pleasure was all mine."

She felt a jolt of female awareness all the way to her toes, melting her like frozen butter in the hot sun.

Well, she'd brought it up, hadn't she? Kyle was obviously never going to mention it, but she couldn't leave it alone. His voice slid into her senses, making her want things she'd never wanted before. Maybe it was just the word, the way he said it. Pleasure.

She didn't speak of it again, or much of anything else, on the remainder of the ride back to the ranch. Kyle was thankfully silent also, apparently lost in his own thoughts and content not to pursue the conversation about massaging her sore muscles.

It was mid-afternoon by the time they got back. No one was in sight as Kyle pulled the truck around the back of the house and let her out with the groceries, then went to park the truck and find Brady.

Sabrina took Petunia and headed into the kitchen. Jenna sat at the table peeling potatoes, and smiled as Sabrina entered.

"How did the trip go today?"

"Well it was interesting to say the least," Sabrina replied as she put the groceries away. She wondered if it would be appropriate to tell Jenna about the episode with Jackson Dent, or if Kyle wouldn't even want to bring it up.

Jenna looked down at Petunia and grinned at Sabrina. "I guess so. I take it you got a pig?"

"Yeah, isn't she adorable? Her name is Petunia and I bought her at the vet's office from some farmer who wanted to trade her for supplies."

Jenna bent down and scratched Petunia's ears, and was rewarded with a happy snort. "She's very cute. Bet Kyle was thrilled," she said, rolling her eyes.

Sabrina sat at the table next to Jenna. "No, he wasn't exactly overjoyed at the idea, but I didn't really give him a say so in the matter. I wanted her, so I bought her."

"Good for you." Jenna beamed. "Never let a man tell you what to do. God knows I never have."

Laughing, Sabrina nodded. "I've done that already, and won't ever do it again."

Ex-husband a control freak?"

It was always difficult to talk about Mark without feeling stupid. Now that Sabrina had left him, it embarrassed her to admit she had allowed him to run her life for so long.

"You could say that," Sabrina said.

Jenna placed her hand on Sabrina's arm. "Hey, I'm sorry. I didn't mean to pry and you don't have to talk about him if you don't want to. I'm just too nosy for my own good sometimes."

She looked up at Jenna and smiled ruefully. "I don't mind, really. Sometimes I just feel stupid when I have to explain how I let the man abuse me for so many years." Sabrina relayed the same story as she had earlier to Kyle, from her first meeting with Mark through her decision to leave and divorce him.

Jenna's faint smile held compassion as she squeezed Sabrina's hand. "I'm glad you left him. You're much too intelligent a woman to have put up with that for long."

Sabrina nodded, grateful to have a friend to confide in. "I feel like I wasted so much time, though. I stayed with him much longer than I should have."

Jenna sat back in the chair. "Give yourself some credit Sabrina. Many women live with abuse their entire lives and never get away. You're one of the smart ones."

She'd never thought of that before. Had always thought she was stupid for enduring it as long as she had, but Jenna was right. She *had* left him, by her choice and of her own free will. And now she had a chance at a new life—a chance to do what she'd always wanted to do.

"Thank you, Jenna. I feel better."

Jenna's eyes sparkled. "I'm glad."

Kyle opened the back door and came in, Brady following close behind. From the angry look on Brady's face, Kyle must have told him about their run-in with Dent.

Brady opened the refrigerator and grabbed two cold beers, throwing one to Kyle across the kitchen, then looked in Sabrina's direction. "Sabrina? A cold one?"

A cold beer. Not a martini or a cosmopolitan. Nothing fussy, not like Mark used to make her drink. *Only cheap trash drink beer, Sabrina.* "I'd love one."

"What's up with you two? A horse kick you or did the truck die again?" Jenna grinned at her two brothers.

"You didn't tell her?" Kyle looked at Sabrina as he popped the top on his beer then leaned over and opened hers.

She shook her head. "No I didn't. I didn't think it was my place to tell her."

"Tell me what?" Jenna looked between Kyle and Sabrina, confusion furrowing her brow.

"Kyle and Sabrina met up with Jackson and Amanda at the Dreamwater Grocery," Brady said.

"And?"

Kyle shrugged. "Same old thing. He said he was going to take the ranch."

"Well that shouldn't surprise you. He always says that."

"This time it was different."

Jenna and Brady looked at each other. Brady asked the question. "How different?"

"I don't know. More sure of himself I guess. Like he had a plan."

Jenna halted her potato peeling. "That's a scary thought. Jackson Dent with a plan."

"Exactly. He's up to something."

"So what do you want to do?" Brady trailed his finger over the top of his beer can and looked over at his brother.

"I have an idea, but we need to vote on it."

Sabrina took that as her cue to leave. She rose from the table and excused herself, but Kyle reached out and gently grabbed her arm.

"Where are you going?"

"I…this is a family meeting. I didn't want to intrude."

"Sit down," he said. "You're an investor, your money is at stake here as much as ours. Besides, we can use an extra head for ideas."

He had asked her to stay. To join in, to participate. A rush of excitement swept through her at the feeling of belonging. "All right," she said and returned to her seat.

"Now, here's my idea. Sabrina's investment gave us the needed capital to pay the past due mortgage payments and buy additional stock. But we won't realize a profit until late fall."

"That's when you sell the cattle?" Sabrina had an understanding of how a cattle ranch worked, but wanted to make sure she was clear on when the money came in.

Kyle nodded. "Right. But this is April, and if Dent has something up his sleeve, you can bet we won't be able to outsmart him without additional money."

"I have more money I could invest," Sabrina added.

Kyle's gaze turned sharply in her direction. "Absolutely not. You've invested enough as it is. I don't want any more of your money."

Sabrina took a deep breath to argue, but something in the look Jenna gave silenced her.

"So where do we get additional money?" Brady asked.

Kyle stood and grabbed another beer from the refrigerator. Leaning against the kitchen counter, he said, "Weekend ropings."

Jenna and Brady's eyes lit up at Kyle's suggestion.

"Really? Oh, Kyle, that would be wonderful." Jenna looked excited as a child. "We haven't had ropings around here since before you entered professional rodeo."

Brady nodded in agreement. "About damn time you brought those back. I've been wanting to do that for years now."

"I hate to show my ignorance here, but what exactly does that mean?" She knew what roping meant—it was a rodeo term. But how did one happen on a ranch?

"Calf roping. You invite wranglers from around the area to participate on the weekends. Then you lease your own cattle and horses to the ropers, and bring in some extra cash."

A light shone in Kyle's eyes, something Sabrina hadn't seen since she'd been at the Rocking M. It was like a sudden interest sparked within him, an enthusiasm that hadn't been present before.

"And if it all goes well, I think we should have a rodeo this summer. Lease the horses and cattle and get the Rocking M on the rodeo circuit list."

"A rodeo? That would be great. I'd love it." Jenna was beaming.

"I think it's a good idea. I'm all for it," Brady seconded.

A rodeo. Jolts of excitement thrilled through Sabrina's body. To be a part of a rodeo event was more than she expected. "I have a question or two," Sabrina said.

"Go ahead." Kyle sat down at the table and turned his chair to face her.

"How much money do weekend ropings bring in? And don't you have to pay the ropers some kind of prize money? How much do you charge for leasing cattle and horses? Are the rates different for each one? Do the rates vary depending on the quality of the animal? And what about other ways to make money? Do you offer food and drink to the ropers? Do their families come along with them? Surely they get hungry, or are they allowed to bring their own food? Just how big an event is this?"

Kyle, Jenna and Brady all looked at Sabrina and then at each other and smiled.

"She's got a sharp head for business," Brady said as he smiled at her.

"Sure does," Jenna added. "We can use your help, Sabrina, if you're game."

She wasn't sure what she said, but apparently it was something good. "Well of course, I'd love to help any way I can."

Kyle folded his arms across his chest and leaned back in the chair, smiling at Sabrina. His sharp gaze was open and inviting. "Any other questions?"

"Probably, but at the moment I just had those few."

He laughed then. "A few huh? I'd hate to see what your long list looks like."

She smiled. "Sorry, I was always told I asked too many questions."

"Whoever told you that was wrong. Only an intelligent person asks questions. And you have some great ideas. Why don't you draw up a list and we'll go over them after dinner?"

As Sabrina cleaned up for dinner, she thought about today's events. She was thrilled at Kyle's compliment and excited to be a part of planning an event for the ranch. Each day the Rocking M was feeling more like home to her. She even started to think of the Morgans as family. Jenna and Brady were almost like having a brother and sister.

Kyle was different, though. She didn't have sisterly feelings for him. No, she definitely didn't think of Kyle as a brother. He had almost kissed her in the middle of the grocery store today. She couldn't help but regret their interruption. Admittedly she wanted to have his lips on hers, wanted to taste him, touch him, lean into him and see where it led.

And those were dangerous feelings for someone embarking on the road to independence. Soon she'd leave the Morgan Ranch to start a life of her own. Feelings for Kyle would only get in the way. Besides, he probably already had a girlfriend in Emma Stevens, and she'd never get in the middle of that.

But oh, how she wanted him to kiss her.

Kyle dried his hands and looked at his reflection in the bathroom mirror. What a day it had been. First the trip to the vet's office and then Emma's weird suggestion that he had feelings for Sabrina.

But when he'd denied any sort of involvement, Emma had called him a liar and told him to look in the mirror and face the truth.

Now how could Emma see something like that in the short time she had been around them today? He'd known Emma her whole life, ever since she was a kid, hanging around the Rocking M and riding the horses, playing with Jenna and annoying Brady until he pulled her pigtails and sent her crying to Kyle's mother.

Emma was like another little sister, the same age as Jenna. And she was just as big a busybody as Jenna. And just as damned observant as his sister, too.

Sexual attraction to Sabrina? Yeah, he'd admit that. But feelings? No. No feelings.

There was that almost-kiss at the grocery store. God he had wanted to kiss her today, more than he wanted to admit. Holding her against him, his heart pounding, her lips only inches away. Tempting. Damn tempting. If Dent hadn't interrupted them he would have swept Sabrina in his arms and tasted that sweet mouth like he'd been longing to do since...

Yeah, he wanted her all right. And if Kyle read Sabrina's expressions and body language right, she wanted that kiss today as much as he did.

Kyle was in over his head with financial problems and Jackson Dent, and the last thing he needed was an attraction to Sabrina Daniels. He'd sworn off women after Amanda, and so far had done a damn fine job of keeping that vow. Until Sabrina showed up at the Rocking M, blowing his self-imposed sexual exile to hell.

And she might be sweet and vulnerable and cute as hell walking around with that pig, but he damn well didn't have any feelings for her.

He'd just have to shore up his intentions and make it very clear to Sabrina their relationship was strictly business. And while he was convincing her, maybe he could convince himself.

Chapter Seven

"The ropings each weekend will bring in a good sum of money and should help us out a lot." Kyle leaned forward on one of the sofas in the family room. "But getting authorized to host a rodeo circuit event will make even more, both now and in the future."

"What about leasing part of the land?" Luke asked.

"No way," Kyle responded. "Our parents never had to lease out part of the Rocking M no matter how bad things got. And we aren't either."

Luke was silent for a moment. "Okay, then what about hunting?"

Kyle thought about it for a moment. "We could do that. If we get four or five hunters on a weekend in here, provide them a couple meals and give them access to prime game, we could bring in several thousand each weekend."

Sabrina was shocked. "You're kidding. That much money to hunt?"

Kyle nodded. "Yeah, you'd be surprised what they'd pay to hunt game like we have on the Rocking M. There are plenty of sections in the outer land portion to set up a blind and campsites. With a little bit of monitoring it could work."

She made quick notes as the brainstorming session continued. After dinner they all moved into the family room to discuss their income generating ideas.

"How about selling a portion of the hay we make, and put the cattle on feed instead?"

"That's like robbing Peter to pay Paul," Kyle said to her. "It's a good idea if you have extraordinary hay, but not really practical. Feed costs a lot. Hay is free if you grow it, but definitely cheaper than feed to buy."

"I think your original suggestion is still the best idea, Kyle," Brady said as he propped his feet up on the coffee table in front of the sofa. "Ropings will bring in the biggest crowds and the most money. And with your background in rodeo, people will come just to see you ride."

"I agree," said Jenna. "You're quite an attraction to up-and-coming rodeo competitors as well as crowds that miss seeing you ride."

Sabrina watched the interplay. It was clear Jenna and Brady had the ultimate confidence in their brother's rodeo acuity. She was touched by their loyalty. Apparently, so was Kyle, even though he looked a bit embarrassed by all the praise.

Brady threw in another thought. "Because we have Brahmans, if leasing our stock works out during the ropings and the rodeo, we could get our name out there to the professional rodeo and really make some money leasing the bulls as well as the steers."

"I agree with Brady," Jenna added. "I also like Sabrina's ideas about selling food and drink at the ropings and the rodeo. Some of the wranglers won't bring their wives or girlfriends and would have no food with them. We could make money selling our own."

Sabrina chimed in. "If we had a barbecue we could produce a volume of food and charge so much per plate. Easy enough to add side dishes like potato salad and corn on the cob."

Kyle smiled. "That works. God knows we have enough beef around here."

"We could also sell baked goods likes rolls and muffins and cakes and cookies," Jenna added. "You know I love to bake."

"And you do it so well too," Luke said. They sat close together on the loveseat, Luke absently stroking his wife's arm. Sabrina couldn't help but sigh at the contented looks on their faces. Truly they were a couple in love.

"How soon can we be ready for this?" Sabrina was already calculating costs in her head and couldn't wait to get on the computer and run a spreadsheet.

"Probably a couple weeks," said Kyle. "We need to get the word out. The sooner we get started, the sooner we can promote the rodeo too."

"I'm going to a horse auction this weekend, I can start spreading the word there," Brady offered.

"I can make up flyers on the computer. Then we could ask the store merchants in town and the surrounding communities to post them in their windows." Sabrina was so glad her business skills were finally showing some usefulness.

"Oh that's good, Sabrina. I can take the flyers with me when I go to my obstetrician appointment next week." Jenna smiled as Luke rubbed her stomach.

Brady stood up and stretched. "I'll take some to Emma. She travels to the neighboring towns when she does her mobile-vet thing. She'll convince folks to post them. Actually she'll browbeat them until they do," he added with a grin.

Sabrina nodded. "Okay, I'll work on those right away and have a draft printed out for you to look at by tomorrow."

ઇ ઇ ઇ

Later that evening Sabrina sat in Kyle's office running numbers through the spreadsheet in the main computer. She'd already created the draft of the flyer, and was printing it for Kyle to review.

"Working late?" Kyle's deep voice startled her and she whirled around in the chair, her heart pounding.

"I didn't hear you come in. You scared me to death." She watched as he rounded the desk and stood behind her.

His full lips turned upward. "Oh I hope not. We need you around here."

He needed her. No, *they* needed her. The family did. Either way, she couldn't help but smile. It was nice to feel like a part of things.

"What are you working on?" He looked over her shoulder at the numbers on the screen.

"The cost-benefit analysis we talked about earlier. As well as some preliminary profit expectations and pricing considerations for leasing the stock."

He scanned the information on the monitor. She could feel the heat of his body even though they weren't touching. His warm breath caressed the top of her head, sending shivers down her spine.

She tried to avoid looking up at him, uncertain what she'd find, or feel, if she did. "Would you like to sit here, or did you want me to print this out?" His nearness was driving her crazy. Every nerve fiber in her body was alive and wanting to gravitate toward his warmth. It was proving to be difficult to concentrate with him so close. His deep voice was more than enough distraction.

"No, I can see fine from here. Unless my looking over your shoulder bothers you."

Everything about you bothers me. Your looks, your smile, the way you smell, the way I feel when you touch me. Yeah, you bother me all right. "It doesn't bother me at all." Was that her voice wavering? Her hand trembling as she smoothed away the tendrils of hair sliding over her cheek?

For a few moments he didn't speak, just continued to lean over her while reading the spreadsheet. She tried to concentrate, but it wasn't working. Her senses were tuned to Kyle, his every breath, every move awakening desire in her.

"May I?" he said as he indicated the computer mouse. His chest rubbed against her shoulder as he moved in closer.

Taking a shaky breath, Sabrina tried to ignore the fact that Kyle was all but laying over her back. "G...Go ahead."

"Thanks."

But before she could remove her hand from the mouse, Kyle laid his on top of hers. The jolt of electricity from the touch of his hand almost sent her shooting out of the chair. His breath blew wisps of loose hair against her cheek as he slowly maneuvered the mouse through the spreadsheets.

His cheek touched her face, his breath waking every sensual nerve ending in her body. The day's growth of beard on his jaw lightly scraped Sabrina's neck, causing chills of desire to course through her. Each time he glided the mouse around on the pad, his arm brushed her shoulder and his chest pressed against her back. Sabrina tried to breathe quietly so Kyle wouldn't notice she was all but panting.

"This is good," he said, his voice deep and sensual against her ear. "Very good."

Yes it was, Sabrina thought. So good she didn't want him to stop, in fact wanted to go further. Take that next step. Right here and right now. For the first time in her life, she desired a man. Really and truly wanted him. And she had no idea what to do about it. She'd never taken the first step before, had never been allowed to with Mark. So how was she going to deal with her feelings for Kyle?

"Why don't you print these out and I'll take a look at them tomorrow?" Kyle moved away from the desk. Sabrina did her best to ignore the disappointment she felt at his departure.

"I'll do that," she said, barely able to form a coherent sentence. Images of what would have happened if she had faced him flooded her mind.

"It's late. You should get some sleep."

She turned in the chair to look at him. He stood in the open doorway, one arm resting on either side of the frame. His eyes glowed with emerald heat as they roamed over her. She felt it from across the room, bathing her body in the warmth of desire.

"So should you," she finally managed.

"I have more work to do yet."

"What work? Anything I can help with?"

His expression was unreadable, but then he smiled. "Sure. Come on."

Sabrina slipped on her tennis shoes and followed Kyle outside. She was glad she still wore her jeans and T-shirt as the late evening wind had picked up, chilling the air. Wishing she had thrown on a sweater, she hugged her arms as they headed across the dirt road toward the barn. By the time they got there she was freezing.

"Are you cold?"

"A little." He didn't seem to feel the cold at all. He also wore a short-sleeved shirt and jeans, but despite the spring chill wasn't shivering like she was.

Kyle grabbed a long-sleeved denim shirt from the hook inside the door of the barn. "Put this on," he said as he held it out for her.

She turned her back to him and slid her arms into the shirt. He pulled it up over her shoulders then rested his hands there.

"You're shivering." Instead of letting her loose he wrapped his arms under her chest and pulled her against him. He held her there for a moment, the heat of his body warming her much more than the shirt. She didn't want to move, to break the contact of his body against hers. She felt the rhythmic beating of his heart against her back and struggled to keep her breathing normal.

The steady drumming of Kyle's heart quickened as he held her, causing her own heart to race in kind. He didn't seem to be in a hurry to let her go, and she felt no compulsion to ask him to.

Holding a death grip on the shirt he gave her, she pressed it close to her chest. Kyle wrapped his arms tighter around hers, laying his hands across her forearms. With every deep breath she took, her breasts rubbed against his hands. Her nipples had hardened to pinpoints against her bra, the sensitive buds scraping against the silky fabric. Her butt was nestled against his crotch and she could feel his ever-growing erection. She might be a puddle of arousal, but what excited her even more was that he was turned on too.

He wanted her. God, what a heady thing that was. Even more thrilling was him holding her there, without words, wondering what he was thinking. Was he thinking about fucking her right there in the barn? What would she do if he turned her and kissed her, pulled her into the hay and started undressing her?

She knew what she'd do. She'd been ready for it for days, weeks now. Her throat tightened and she shuddered against him. Lightheaded like this was not a good thing. It was quite possible she might actually pass out from the sheer pleasure of it if she didn't move away soon. She had to get her bearings about her before this went any further. It was all moving too quickly.

"So—what can I help you with?" Gently breaking the contact, she stepped away and turned to face him. Thinking the separation of their bodies would remove the torturous need she felt, Sabrina was shocked to her toes at the expression on Kyle's face.

In the dim light of the barn his features looked harsh. Shadows crossed his face, but she could still clearly see the fierce longing in his eyes. A fire burned deep within her as she saw need equaling her own. His breathing was ragged as he dragged his hand through his hair.

How easy it would be to step back into his arms and see where their mutual desire led.

"Right. Work." He blew out a forceful breath and turned toward the corral. "Let's give the horses some feed."

Grateful for anything to break the web Kyle wove over her senses, Sabrina helped him fill the feeders.

They worked in silence, broken only when he told her what to do next. Finally, all the horses were fed and she helped him tidy up the work area of the barn.

She leaned on the rake she was using to gather the hay. "Do you really think the ropings and rodeo will bring in enough money to help?"

"Yeah I do, once the word gets out we're having them."

Kyle picked up a few discarded bridles and stretched to hang them. Sabrina sighed with elemental feminine approval at the play of muscles under his tight-fitting shirt. She could stand there for hours and simply watch him move. His biceps bulged as he lifted a heavy saddle onto his shoulder to carry it in the tack room. And all she could do was lean on the rake, and sigh. Pathetic.

"You'd be surprised how far cowboys will come to participate in a roping and being a sanctioned circuit event will bring in a lot of the region's competitors, all paying an entry fee. Which means a lot of spectators spending money to get in and buy food and drinks. Plus, leasing our bulls, cattle and horses to the participants will provide even more capital."

"But what if it isn't enough money? Then what?"

"Then we'll figure out something else." He gathered grooming supplies from the floor and tossed them in a nearby bucket, then finished brushing down a saddle.

"I'd be more than happy to invest more funds in the ranch." She still had plenty of money. And right now it was doing nothing but sitting at the bank. Earning interest, yes, but Sabrina thought it would be of more use invested in the ranch.

Kyle stood there with saddle in hand, determination on his handsome face. "I told you, I don't want any more of your money. You've done enough."

"I don't mind, really, and the money I have—"

Determination turned to anger. "No more. Do you understand? I can do this myself. You've already done more than I wanted you to."

Why did that sound like an accusation rather than a thank you for saving the ranch? For a brief second the timid woman who let her ex-husband browbeat her at every turn surfaced, and she was silent. But irritation drove her. She wasn't the same woman she used to be. She wouldn't allow herself to be. "What does that mean?"

He muttered a curse and dropped the saddle, quickly bridging the distance between them. "It's pretty clear don't you think? It means I didn't want you to rescue this ranch in the first place. I didn't want any outsiders here. It's bad enough I had to take the money you did invest. I certainly don't want to owe you any more."

Boy, his moods sure turned sharply. He was angry. At her, but not for something she did. This was about his pride. Why did men let pride stand in the way of common sense? Mark had done it all the time.

"That's ridiculous. It's good business sense to take investment money when it's offered."

An angry tic formed at the side of Kyle's mouth. His face was grim, his ire barely controlled. And yet Sabrina didn't feel an ounce of trepidation. Fleetingly she wondered why she'd feel safe with a man she barely knew, when an expression like that on her ex-husband's face would have sent her into hiding.

Kyle grabbed her arms and pulled her toward him, his hands rough but controlled. "Let me say this as clearly as I can. One last time. I don't want any more of your money. Got it?"

Wrenching her arms away from his hold, she held her ground and looked him in the eye. No one was going to treat her like she was stupid. Never again. "I'm not a child you know. I do understand simple English, so don't treat me like an idiot. I was only trying to help."

"Don't help me. I don't need you." He turned and headed toward the tack room, grabbing the previously discarded saddle on the way.

Sabrina followed him in. She stepped in front of him, forcing him to look at her. "You need me now just like you needed me when I made my original investment. You could show a little appreciation instead of making me feel like I've done something wrong for helping you out. Why don't you act like a man instead of a spoiled little boy who didn't get his own way?"

His emerald eyes darkened. "Be careful, Sabrina."

She glared right back at him, her confidence soaring with every angry word. She was angry, she was letting it show, and Kyle wasn't doing anything to harm her. She didn't know whether she wanted to slap him or kiss him right now.

Probably both.

"I don't have to be careful. I'm right, you're wrong, and you know it as well as I do. You're just not man enough to admit that you needed a woman's help to bail your ass out of financial trouble."

"I don't need a woman's help with anything. And your sex has nothing to do with investing in this ranch. Maybe if you weren't so hung up on being a woman trying to enter a man's world it wouldn't be an issue to you. Because it sure isn't to me."

Her heart raced with anger and frustration as she poked a finger at his chest. "My being a woman has nothing to do with this. You're the only one hung up on the fact that I'm a woman."

He laughed at her. "I hardly noticed."

She laughed back at him. "Right. That's why you were all over me in the office, why you put your arms around me here in the barn. Because you didn't notice I was a woman."

His eyebrows lifted. "I was all over you in the office? Honey, you were breathing so heavily in there you steamed up the computer monitor. I think it's you that wants me."

"Who said anything about wanting you? I don't want you at all." Her voice was high, higher than normal as she shouted her denial loud enough to maybe convince herself.

He stepped closer, his eyes darkening, a sardonic, self-righteous sneer plastered to his face. "Right. Well I'm glad you cleared that up. I don't want you either."

She didn't move away, but stood nose to nose with him, hands on her hips. "Good. I don't want you to want me."

They glared at each other, her heart beating powerfully with an adrenaline rush fueled by their passionate argument. Neither moved, neither spoke. Finally, the corners of Kyle's mouth lifted in a slight smile.

"Liar," he said softly as he took one step closer and pulled her in to his chest. "We're both liars." He slipped his hand under her hair, holding it gently against her neck as he tilted her head up and claimed her mouth.

The kiss was devastating. Gentle at first, he slid his lips across hers, barely grazing her trembling mouth. Sabrina parted her lips in a sigh as his tongue slid inside, searching for hers. A delightful warmth spread through her as Kyle wove a magical spell around her senses.

This is what she wanted, what she'd been dreaming of since the first moment she saw him. She couldn't recall ever wanting anything more in her life as much as she wanted Kyle's lips on hers.

His other hand wrapped around her waist and pulled her even closer to his hard, muscled body. She moaned as he molded against her. Their earlier rush of anger was forgotten as they moved against each other, so close not even air could slide between.

It was all she could do to breathe in shallow gasps as his mouth continued its tormenting attack. Kyle's tongue probed incessantly and she met it with hers, the contact electric, providing dizzying heights of sensation she'd never felt before.

This was what it was like to be kissed by someone you truly desired. It was a heady feeling, like too many turns on a rapidly spinning carnival ride. She felt giddy and nauseous at the same time. Overwhelmed, but unwilling to stop lest the incredible feelings stop.

His hands roamed over her as he continued to ravage her mouth with his kisses. Incapable of clear thought, she could only gasp as he massaged her shoulders, her back, kneading her hips and pressing his hands against her ass to draw her closer. He brushed against her thighs, his cock hard and insistent, and she could have wept at the sheer pleasure of the sensation.

She was completely lost in him.

Finally he tore his mouth from hers. She tried to grab his head to pull him back for another kiss, but he held her shoulders until she looked up.

Desire burned brightly in the emerald flames of his eyes. His lips were wet from her kisses, his hair tangled from her hands sliding in to hold his head to her. He didn't smile, in fact looked quite pained.

"Sabrina, we have to stop."

She didn't want to stop. "Why?"

He took a ragged breath and laughed lightly, a husky tone that spoke of sensual delights to be shared. "Because if we don't I'm going to fuck you right here in this barn."

Oh God he wanted to make love to her. The words were glorious, thrilling and exciting her with a promise of further exploration. She smiled back at him, her desire for him so fierce it wiped out any hesitation she might have felt. "I don't mind doing it in the barn."

"Jesus, woman, do you know what you do to me?"

She hoped it was exactly the same thing he was doing to her. Making her want him. Desire him. Even here, in the barn.

"But we can't." He held her close, laying his chin on top of her head. "We can't do this."

Coldness crept into her bones where a few seconds ago she was boiling with heat and desire. She leaned away from the comfort of his chest to look at him. "What do you mean?"

"Think about it. Neither one of us is looking for a permanent relationship. What we have together is business, and that's all it should be. I'm not ready for something as complicated as this, and I don't think you are either."

His words were like a splash of cold water, dousing the fire she'd felt only seconds ago. "I see." She pulled completely away, embarrassed that he was the one to stop things, when she knew better. She should have never let it start.

"No, I don't think you do see."

She nodded, willing the tears away. She was mortified enough that he turned her down, there was no way she'd let him see her cry. "Yes, I do. We both just got carried away. It's no big deal."

"Sabrina, I—"

"Please don't. I...I'm tired Kyle. It's been a long day and I think I'll head to bed." Her voice wavered and she knew it but could do nothing to stop it. "I have to go. Goodnight." With as much dignity as she could muster, she quickly fled the barn and headed to the house.

Once in the safety of her room, she let the tears fall. How could she be so stupid and naive? Would she never learn?

God only knows what he must think of her. She practically threw herself at him and then nearly begged him to make love to her. Until he put a stop to things. Kyle was the sensible one, while she ran on pure emotion and desire. He probably thought she was like this all the time.

But he didn't know she'd never been like this before. With any man.

As she started to undress for bed, she realized she was still wearing Kyle's shirt. She removed it and held it to her face.

What she'd felt earlier hadn't faded. The lingering scent of him, earthy and sensuous, clung to the garment, threading desire through her that was stronger than ever.

What a mess she'd made of things now.

Chapter Eight

The cattle roundup kept everyone at the ranch busy for the next several days. And Kyle was the busiest of all.

His job was to supervise the entire process, as well as make sure the calves got separated, and all were marked, castrated and vaccinated. Typically he also entered the details on each calf into the laptop, but this year Sabrina was going to do it.

He watched as she stared, mesmerized, at the wranglers assembling the cattle in the huge compartmentalized pen. She was standing on the outside of the corral, her chin resting on top of the steel bars, one booted foot slung casually over the bottom rung. Her eyes were like a child's, full of awe and wonder at experiencing something completely fresh and new.

Watching the process through her gave Kyle a new enthusiasm for ranching, made him remember why he loved it. His frustration at the cards dealt to him in life faded slightly as he remembered the thrill of rounding up cattle, cutting the calves from the herd and getting them through the chute in order to complete the process. For the first time in years, he looked forward to the day's events.

She glanced over and caught him staring at her, then turned her head away. She hadn't spoken more than three words to him in the days following their kiss in the barn and had done her best to avoid him completely. Either she was busy doing something with Jenna or working with Brady or Luke and the horses.

It was all his fault. He had handled the other night badly. First he practically seduced her in the office, all but threw her down on the floor of the barn to make love to her, and then he put a halt to things as if kissing and touching her meant nothing to him at all.

Nothing at all. That was a laugh.

He'd been suffering a constant state of hard-on-it is since the night he found her laboring at his desk. A goddess with a head for finance. She looked so beautiful, completely engrossed in her work on the computer and oblivious to the fact he'd stood in the doorway for nearly five minutes watching her.

Her hair had been swept off her shoulders, but some of the curling tendrils framed her face. Her look of intense concentration made Kyle yearn for her to give him the same kind of attention.

And then he made the mistake of leaning over and touching her. She smelled of peaches and summertime. And when she smiled at him, her amber eyes so innocent and full of sensual curiosity, Kyle wanted to gather her up in his arms and kiss her senseless. Then drop where they stood and pound his cock inside her until the need for her went away.

His attention diverted back to his job when a couple of daring steers attempted an escape from the gate. "Brady! Get Tom and Jody to sweep around the left and cut off those two critters trying to back out of the gate." Brady nodded and spurred his horse into a gallop and headed off after the escapees.

Once the animals were cornered he turned back to Sabrina and found her watching him this time.

He ached at her look of pain and confusion as their eyes met. He could swear he saw tears, but was too far away to tell for sure. Maybe it was just the sun glinting off her eyes. Either way, it was clear she was hurting, and Kyle knew damn well he was the one who caused her pain.

"You should go talk to her." Jenna's voice startled him as she placed her hand on his shoulder.

"I didn't hear you come up. Talk to who?"

"You know who. Sabrina."

"Why do I need to talk to her?" He turned to look at his sister.

"I don't know. Why don't you tell me?" Jenna had that look about her again, the one that said he did something wrong and better make it right.

"I don't know what you're talking about," he lied.

Her lips formed a straight line and her eyes shot a *don't give me that* look. God, she always looked like Mom when she glared at him that way.

"She's upset. What did you do?"

Leave it to Jenna to assume he was the one at fault. Well this time at least, she was right. "I didn't do anything."

When he would have turned away she held his arm. "She's falling in love with you, you know."

Kyle's mouth hung open in shock. "She's what?" He glanced at Sabrina and back at Jenna. "You're blind. She is not."

Jenna nodded. "Yes, dumbass, she is. With you." She added a teasing grin as she said, "Why, I have no idea, but she is."

"Why would you think that? Did she say something to you?"

"No, she doesn't need to. I'm a woman in case you've forgotten. I know that look."

That obviously meant since he was a man he was clueless. "What look?"

She sighed in frustration then began to explain with a back and forth tilt of her head. Like she was lecturing a five-year-old, for God's sake. "The one a woman gives a man when she's in love with him. I can't explain it. It's kind of a dreamy-eyed, lost in thought, head-a-million-miles-away kind of look. And she gets that way when she's looking at you. Why are men so dense?"

No, Jenna had to be wrong. Sabrina couldn't stand the sight of him right now. There was no way she was in love with him.

"Kyle," Jenna said softly. "Are you falling in love with Sabrina?"

Well wasn't that the damndest question he'd ever heard? "Me? In love with—well hell." He hung his head and stared at his boots, the same way he used to when he was a kid and in trouble with his mother. "I don't know, Jenn. To be honest, I don't know."

Jenna stepped into her brother's arms and hugged him. "Think about it then," she said against his chest. "And be careful with Sabrina's heart while you're thinking. She's vulnerable and susceptible to being hurt. I don't want you to be the one who hurts her. And I don't want to see you hurt again either." She reached up, kissed her brother's cheek and walked away to watch the roundup with Sabrina.

He couldn't believe that was his sweet baby sister, so grown up now she was giving her brother romantic advice. It used to be the other way around.

If what Jenna said was right, if Sabrina was in love with him, then what he had done the other night was even worse than he thought.

He didn't want his heart stomped all over again any more than Sabrina did. They needed to talk. After the roundup, after he sorted through his own feelings.

৩ ৩ ৩

Kyle mounted his horse and joined the cowboys working the cattle into the pen.

Sabrina's gaze was glued to Kyle's every move as he kicked his horse into a fast gallop and tore after running calves, neatly cutting them away from the adults and herding them into the secondary pen attached to the long metal chute. The hooves of his horse kicked up mounds of dust behind him.

She surreptitiously stole glances at his handsome face and lithe body as he yelled directions to the wranglers, only half listening as Jenna explained the roundup process.

"He's good isn't he?" Jenna said.

She nodded. "Yes, very good." It was clear who the best rider was in the group, although Brady was almost as good as Kyle. They both rode as if they and their mounts were one being instead of separate rider and horse, leaning easily from one side to the other as the horses made sharp turns and stops.

"He could have won everything if he'd continued to compete."

"He was that good?" Sabrina turned reluctantly from watching Kyle to question Jenna.

"The best out there. It was a given he'd win the All Around Champion the year he quit." Jenna sighed in obvious frustration for her brother. "But now we'll never know."

To be that good, to know he could have been the top winner, and still he walked away from it all—he gave it all up to help his family save the ranch. Sabrina wished she could tell Kyle how much she admired his courage and dedication to his family. But she couldn't.

She hadn't been able to face him. Not since the night she completely embarrassed herself. They hadn't had more than a few seconds of conversation, although he had tried to talk to her. She just couldn't. Not yet. She was still mortified at her own behavior and was afraid she'd burst into tears or humiliate herself in some other way if he so much as looked at her cross-eyed.

Get Kyle off your mind, Sabrina. Concentrate on the roundup. "They're cutting the calves and penning them separately to do all the vaccinating and castrating and tagging, right?"

Jenna nodded. "Then they'll force the calves into the chute, and two cowboys will set up on either side. One will tag and vaccinate, the other will castrate."

"Yuck." Sabrina didn't really want to watch that part, but if she was going to own a ranch she'd better get used to it.

Jenna laughed. "Yuck is right. I never much cared for it myself, but it's a necessity. More than one bull in a pasture is a dangerous thing."

"I suppose you're right, but it just seems so inhumane."

Sabrina smiled a greeting as Emma Stevens walked up and stood next to Jenna. "It's not really. They only feel the sting for a few minutes and then it's over. And like Jenna said, too many bulls and you have some way overworked heifers."

Even dressed down in worn jeans and a denim shirt, Emma was lovely. Her hair was pulled up in a ponytail and she looked like a young girl instead of a grown woman.

"Ever hear of Rocky Mountain Oysters?" Emma's wicked grin told Sabrina she wasn't talking about the ocean kind.

"No. Do I want to know about them?"

"No, you don't," Jenna said.

"Now I'm really curious. Tell me."

Emma and Jenna looked at each other. Jenna just shook her head and shrugged as if to tell Sabrina she had given her fair warning.

"Well they have to do something with the leftovers from the castration. It's a cowboy thing. Something about proving their manhood by frying and eating them. I've heard they're a real delicacy, but have to admit I don't have the stomach to try." Emma shuddered as she finished her explanation.

Sabrina stuck out her tongue in distaste. "That's disgusting."

Jenna laughed. "You can say that again."

The women spent a few minutes in entertaining conversation about cowboys and oysters.

"How's Petunia?" Emma asked.

"She's doing great. Getting bigger and plumper every day," Sabrina answered. "She's penned up in back of the house today so she doesn't get trampled. And not one bit happy about it either."

"I'll be she isn't," Emma replied with a grin.

With a cloud of dust trailing behind him, Brady approached the edge of the corral on his horse. Tipping his hat to the women, he addressed Emma.

"Kyle wants you over at the back end of the chute to check the vaccination supply, Em."

Emma nodded. "I'll head on over there."

Brady held out his hand. "C'mon, I'll give you a ride."

One side of her mouth lifted in a wry grin. "Think you can handle me and that horse at the same time?"

"I can handle you and ten horses, darlin," he answered with a smirk. "Let's go."

Without hesitation, Emma slid her booted foot on the stirrup and grabbed Brady's hand. He easily slung her onto his lap in one fluid motion.

"See you later," Emma said and waved as Brady wrapped an arm around her and urged the horse forward in a quick gallop.

"Those two will get married some day, mark my words," Jenna said.

"Emma and Brady?" Sabrina hoped the surprise she felt didn't show on her face.

"They've been antagonizing each other since they were kids. You'd think they hated each other, but they don't. They say there's a fine line between love and hate you know."

Sabrina watched as Brady halted the horse at the entrance to the chute, and jumped down, Emma still in his arms. He held her for a couple seconds longer than seemed necessary, their eyes locked on nothing and no one but each other, until Emma abruptly shoved him back, straightened her shirt and stomped away. Brady stood there for a few seconds laughing at her, then climbed on his horse and rode off.

"Well I was totally wrong then."

Jenna turned her attention to Sabrina. "About what?"

"I thought Emma had something going with Kyle."

Her eyes widened and she laughed out loud. "With Kyle? No way. He's like Emma's big brother. He's been playing peacemaker between her and Brady for as long as I can remember. There's never been anything between the two of them."

"I see." At least she felt a little better about kissing Kyle. The last thing she wanted was to come between a couple.

"Besides, Kyle's interested in *you*, not Emma."

Jenna had spoken so matter-of-factly Sabrina wasn't certain she'd heard her right. "Me? No he's not."

"Please, I'm not blind. And I know my brother."

"Well I can guarantee he isn't interested in me."

"How do you know that?"

Should she say anything about that night? God it was embarrassing enough to think about what happened, let alone share it with anyone. Especially Jenna. She didn't want Jenna to think badly of her.

Jenna turned, her hand lightly grasping Sabrina's arm. "Hey, you can tell me. What is it?"

She desperately needed someone to confide in. Her emotions were a jumbled mess of contradictions and uncertainties, and a sounding board would be helpful. So she took a deep breath and spit it out before she changed her mind. "The other night in the barn Kyle and I kissed."

"Really?" Jenna's eyebrows lifted in interest. "Tell me more."

She stared ahead at the cattle, watching as three wranglers worked the pen, cutting the calves out of the herd and separating them. "Nothing much to tell. We kissed and he stopped it from going any further."

"Kyle stopped it? Why?"

"Because he's not interested. That's why I say you're wrong."

"Hmmmm."

Sabrina looked at Jenna. "What does that mean?"

"When he kissed you, how did it feel?"

Sabrina was taken aback. "You're kidding, right? You want me to tell you how it felt to kiss your brother?"

Laughing, Jenna nodded. "Yeah. How did it feel? Was it a short kiss, a long one, did you both laugh, was it awkward?"

"No. It was perfect." She couldn't believe she was having this conversation with Kyle's sister.

"Ah. And did he seem as if he wasn't enjoying it?"

She could still remember every detail of their kiss. Kyle held her like he never wanted to let go. He kissed her thoroughly, passionately, pouring desire and longing into each brush of his lips against hers. Or so she thought until he pushed her away and said he wasn't interested.

"No, he seemed to enjoy it." She was *not* going to tell Jenna about Kyle's erection. She drew the line there.

A self-satisfied smile on her face, Jenna rested her forearms on the corral rung. "He's interested." She turned her head and grinned at Sabrina. "He's a man, Sabrina. Don't ever forget that. And he has conflicting emotions too, just like women do."

"I guess so." She had thought only of her own feelings and emotions about that night. Never about Kyle and what he might have felt.

"Amanda burned him bad. And since the divorce he hasn't wanted a woman, hasn't dated one, phoned one, barely even talked to one. But with you—he watches you, all the time, finds ways to talk to you, even irritates you in an effort to protect himself. Remember what I said about Emma and Brady? How there's a fine line between love and hate?"

Sabrina nodded.

"Same thing with Kyle. He irritates you, tries to get you angry with him. Love and hate are very powerful emotions. If he was indifferent then you could rest assured he didn't care. He's not indifferent to you. He's interested, for sure."

"Well it seemed that way at first, when he kissed me," she explained. "But then he stopped and said we couldn't. He couldn't. He wasn't ready."

"That doesn't surprise me. Kyle's always been cautious about everything. He takes nothing lightly, and after Amanda he's going to tread softly where another woman is concerned."

"Doesn't matter anyway." Sabrina shrugged, trying to show Jenna she didn't care. "Even if there was something there, we can never be. I'm leaving in a while and he values his independence too much to want a relationship. I can see that and so can he. I think we're being very smart about this and not letting things get out of hand."

Jenna laughed. "Love rarely fits into a neat organizational plan. When it happens, it's never expected. Like a powerful Oklahoma twister, it blindsides you, takes your whole world and tumbles it around, and you're never the same again."

Jenna's words echoed in Sabrina's mind as she trudged, laptop in hand, toward the end of the portable chute attached to the calves' pen. There she set up to enter data on each of the calves as they were tagged. This allowed ranchers to keep track of their inventory in a much more modern way than riding out to the grazing areas and counting heads.

As each of the calves was loaded into the chute to be what Sabrina squeamishly referred to as folded, spindled and mutilated, she entered their description and tag numbers into the stock inventory database. She tried not to listen to the incessant bawling of the calves as one by one they were led into the narrow chute and literally manhandled at both ends.

"Trust me, it's all for dramatic effect. They bawl like that if you pull their tails too, which doesn't hurt them at all." Kyle stood behind her, his voice resonating, instantly reminding her of the night they kissed, of the feelings he stirred.

"It's not bothering me at all, really," she answered as she added another inventory number to the database.

"That's why you're sitting here with your cute little nose wrinkled in distaste and all but shuddering every time one of them squalls like a baby, right?" He grabbed a chair and pulled it close to hers, peering over her shoulder at the growing list of numbers on the inventory sheet.

Why did he have to sit so close? She scooted her body in the opposite direction trying not to appear as if she was avoiding him.

"You're going to fall off the chair if you keep sliding your butt to the other side to get away from me." The obvious humor in his voice revealed her subtle attempts weren't so subtle after all.

"I wasn't trying to get away from you," she said as she continued to stare at the monitor, ignoring him. "I was merely shifting in my seat to get more comfortable."

"So when you fall off the chair, the hard, dry dirt will be more comfortable than the chair, then?"

God, the man was annoying. Why couldn't he just leave?

She looked at him, noting the way the dimple in his right cheek showed more prominently when his lips were curved in a genuine smile. She sighed, her frequent self-reminder that there was no magic between her and Kyle immediately banished. As soon as she gazed into the depths of his warm green eyes she was hopelessly lost.

"We need to talk."

"About what?" She knew about what, and didn't want to talk about it with him. Ever.

"About what happened the other night."

She turned back to the monitor, hoping for one of those squealing calves to come flying through the chute so she could look busy again. "There's nothing to talk about. It happened, it was a mistake, it won't happen again."

"Is that how you really feel?" His fingers tucked under her chin as he turned her face toward him. "Is it?"

What was she supposed to tell him? The truth? He pushed her away last time. She wasn't going to let it happen again. No matter how much she longed to feel his lips on hers again, or how fast her heart beat at his nearness. Even if the warmth of his fingers resting at her neck caused her pulse to beat so hard she could feel the rapid throb against her throat, she was stronger than her desires. It wasn't going to happen, and that was that.

"I...I don't want to discuss this any more." She turned her head away and Kyle dropped his hand.

"This is going to stay between us until we talk it out, Sabrina." His voice was low and quiet, but the underlying emotion was evident.

She just didn't want to believe he felt anything. It was safer that way.

"I really don't want to talk about it Kyle. Please."

Silence followed her plea until she turned her head to look at him. His lips were tight, his emotions once again masked.

"Fine. But we do need to discuss the inventory you're adding. Let's meet in my office tonight after dinner to go over the figures."

Damn. She could turn him down all she wanted when it came to personal matters, but this was business, and she was here to learn. She'd have to meet him.

"Fine. I'll see you then."

Kyle stood, moved the chair and walked away without another word.

Why did she feel as if she'd just hurt him? He'd have to care to be hurt, and he made it quite clear the other night he had no feelings for her.

Kyle's interested in you. Jenna's words came back to haunt her, making her doubt, making her want. If only that were true, but it wasn't. No matter how much she wanted it to be, it wasn't.

Jenna was way off base on her assessment of Kyle's feelings. He didn't care for her at all.

Kyle strode toward his horse, swung up into the saddle and took off in a gallop, hoping to ride off some of his frustration.

Why wouldn't Sabrina talk to him about the other night? How was he supposed to find out how she really felt if she continued to refuse to have a conversation with him?

She had already written off their encounter and the kiss they shared, making it clear she had no interest in discussing it further.

Why? Because he hurt her the other night? He was experienced, more experienced than Sabrina. Her innocence made her vulnerable, and he had taken advantage of that. Then, when she responded like he wanted her to, he shut her down and told her he wasn't ready.

And they called women teases? He was worse than any high school girl who offered it up then pulled it away at the critical moment.

No wonder she didn't want to talk about it. Not only had he fired her up, he'd also shut off the flame he ignited in her. With a snap of his fingers he doused her fire, as if her desire meant nothing to him.

And now that she agreed to forget about it, he was the one wanting to bring it up again. And all because Jenna thought she saw something there.

Maybe it had been there before, but he'd done a damn good job of pushing it away. And it appeared Sabrina was happy with the way things were now, and didn't want to take a step backward and dredge it all up again.

So why did she keep looking at him like she wanted to devour him on the spot? Like she wanted him so badly she could barely stand it.

It always gave him a headache when he tried to figure out what women were thinking. Why even bother?

Jenna didn't know what she was talking about. Sabrina was innocent and inexperienced, and Kyle had confused the hell out her. And now that he made it clear he wasn't going to pursue her, she didn't want him at all. Which suited him just fine.

Didn't it?

Chapter Nine

The calves bawled nervously in the metal pen adjacent to the long, rectangular corral. Crowds had begun to gather, many since early this morning.

Sabrina was so busy she didn't have time to watch the preparations for their first weekend roping. She had been working steadily, preparing the food and drink for the early morning arrivals. The tables were set up near the spectator's area, and already people were clamoring for coffee and pastries.

Participants in the roping were the first to arrive. They hung around the tables, thirsty for a cup of liquid caffeine to accompany the adrenaline already coursing through their veins at the thought of competition. Once they smelled the fresh baked pastries most decided they were hungry too.

Sabrina was thrilled at the turnout. There were at least twenty cowboys milling about, all talking about the roping. When the flyers were handed out announcing the ranch would be hosting a rodeo circuit event in four weeks, their talk grew more animated as excited whispers reverberated throughout the crowd.

"I can't believe it. A rodeo in our little town."

Sabrina smiled as a woman introduced herself as Lula Welton, wife of one of the ropers. A pretty young woman in her mid-twenties with a cherub face and short, curly blonde hair, Lula bobbed her head around excitedly.

"When Bobby told me the Rocking M was having a roping, I was so excited I couldn't stand it. Ropings are hard to find around here—usually we have to travel more than fifty miles to find one. And then you're having a rodeo too? Bobby can't wait. Well, me either to tell you the truth. Bobby's been wanting to get into the circuit for some time now, but with the farm keeping him busy, he doesn't have the time to go to the ropings on the weekends. And now that it's so close we can come every weekend. Why, I'm so hyped up I could just scream!"

Sabrina smiled benignly and listened to the young woman chatter on and on. Finally, Lula left to find her husband.

"Gee, and I thought I talked fast," Sabrina commented dryly as she watched Lula chatter to everyone she saw as she headed toward the barn.

"She's always been that way," Jenna said with a laugh as she placed a tray of pastries on the table. "From the time she was born. Doc Maynard said he couldn't shut her up then and neither her momma nor her husband has been able to shut her up since."

"Well, at least she's enthusiastic about this. Maybe we could use her to promote the ropings and the rodeo," Sabrina said tongue-in-cheek.

Jenna rolled her eyes as she opened a package of cups and set them in front of the super-sized coffee pot. "Please, that's all we need. If Lula started talking up the rodeo, people would deliberately stay away because she annoyed them so much about it."

The next hour was spent busily selling coffee, juice and pastries to the growing crowd. By the time things slowed down, they were both exhausted, but overjoyed at the morning's sales.

"This was much more than I expected," Jenna said as she counted the money from the sale. "Granted, it's not a fortune, but there's definitely a profit in here."

Sabrina beamed. "I knew it would work. Just wait until lunch." She craned her neck to see the riders heading toward the corral to saddle their horses.

"Go ahead and watch. I've got it under control here," Jenna said as she pulled up a chair and eased into it. "It's slow right now and my feet could use a break. Damn heat is making them swell again. And my back is killing me today."

She was concerned about Jenna. She'd been complaining of her back hurting all morning, and try as she might to get her to go inside, Jenna refused. "Are you sure you don't want to lie down inside? I can watch things here while you rest."

Jenna propped her feet on a milk crate and waved her away. "It's much too beautiful today to lay down inside. Besides, I might miss something. I'm going to have a glass of tea and watch the roping from here."

Sabrina started to object again, but Jenna interrupted. "I'll be fine here, you go ahead."

As she headed to the corral she made a mental note to do a cost comparison of adding some help to the food and drink stands, instead of Jenna doing all the work.

There was a seat still available on one of the metal benches just outside the ring. Perfect timing as a roping was about to begin.

The men on horses were behind the starting line, the nervous calves parallel to them in a separately confined area. The gate opened and a small calf shot out and made a beeline for the opposite end of the long arena. Rider and horse flew past the starting line and took off after the calf at full steam. The cowboy kept one hand firmly on the reins, the other swinging the rope over his head.

It didn't take long for the rider to toss the rope over the calf's head. The cowboy's horse stopped instantly and the rider leaped off and dashed toward the restrained calf. He threw the calf down and tied three of the animal's legs together using a string he was holding in his teeth. As soon as he was done he threw his hands in the air to let the judge know he was finished. Then he remounted his horse and slackened the rope holding the now prone animal.

A few seconds ticked by and the calf struggled mightily but remained tied. The run was over and the rider was scored for his time.

Sabrina was amazed at the quickness and agility of the ropers. The events from start to finish couldn't have taken more than ten to fifteen seconds at most. Murmurs among the crowd indicated it was an average run, leading her to believe that some ropers could do it faster. Incredible. To her it happened so fast it was all a blur.

Several other contestants did the same thing as the first, some faster, some slower than the others. Her heartbeat quickened every time a calf bolted through the gate and the next roper took off after the fast-footed animal. It was exciting to watch. She couldn't quite get over the dexterity and skill one had to have to rope a calf.

After watching at least half the riders do their runs, she reluctantly stood so she could go relieve Jenna. As she turned to leave, her gaze whipped to the next rider in the line. It was Kyle.

Unable to tear her gaze away, she stepped closer to the corral fence, resting her forearms on the top rung.

God he looked sexy. Dressed in faded jeans, weathered boots and a long-sleeved denim shirt, he wore beige chaps over his lean legs and sat his horse like a king. His black cowboy hat rode low over his face, obstructing most of Sabrina's view with the exception of the unshaven beard spread over his strong jaw.

She broke out in a sweat that had nothing to do with the warm weather.

The calf sprang through the gate and before Sabrina could blink Kyle tore out after the animal. He quickly roped the calf and flew off his horse, dropping and tying the bawling animal with lightning speed. The rest of the competitors looked like turtles next to him. She was stunned, her mouth gaping open in shock. She'd never seen anyone move so quickly, with so much precision and agility. The crowd agreed with her as they stood and cheered wildly for Kyle's performance. He scored a time under seven and a half seconds.

Turning to acknowledge the crowd, Kyle swept off his hat and smiled, his gaze scanning the bleachers until his eyes settled over her. Their gazes locked and he fixed her with a look of heated desire that melted her on the spot.

He was sending her a message. And she received it loud and clear. Her cheeks flamed hot and she hoped no one could see the way he was looking at her.

But how could they? Their eyes had met for only a millisecond, but to Sabrina it was an eternity.

Just as fast as he'd spotted her he turned away, waved once more to the crowd and walked from the center of the corral, streams of applause still ringing out at his performance.

She stood at the fence until she couldn't see him any longer, then turned toward the concession area to relieve Jenna.

Sisterly pride rained over Jenna's face.

"Wow," was all Sabrina could say. Jenna nodded.

"Told you he was the best."

"The best is an understatement. That was the most amazing thing I've ever seen. He was so fast, clearly heads above the others."

"I know. Of course these competitors ride the circuit, not professional rodeo like Kyle did. They'd expect him to be better. But I don't think many of them really knew how good he was."

"They know now," Sabrina said.

Jenna grinned. "Yes they do."

"Nothing like a bunch of hungry cowboys to fill the coffers," Jenna said. "The barbecue cost us practically nothing and brought in more money than we thought it would."

Sabrina agreed. If today was any indication of the kind of crowds to expect every weekend, the sale of food and drink would certainly help bring in extra cash.

"We leased a lot of our stock today too," Brady added as he walked up and grabbed fresh lemonade from his sister. "More than I thought. Guess the guys don't want to haul their own horses here, which is much better for us. And they want to start steer wrestling and bull riding too, so the Old Devil will get quite a workout in the upcoming weeks."

Old Devil, Sabrina knew, was the Morgan's Brahman bull, a huge, mean-looking creature that clearly ruled the cattle roost on the ranch. She'd given Old Devil a wide berth when Kyle pointed him out one day. How anyone could ride something as big and fierce as him was beyond her. But she couldn't wait to watch someone try.

"That's great news," Sabrina said.

"Even better, I heard there'd be more ropers coming next weekend, now that the word's getting out we've been authorized to host a circuit event next month."

Jenna rubbed the small of her back as she gathered up the remaining food trays. "I'm so happy this worked out. Kyle's been carrying this burden alone for far too long, and I'm glad we're all doing something to help for a change."

Brady nodded. "Me too. Damn stubborn is what he is. Never once thought about sitting down with us and coming up with ideas to make money. He just thought he could do it the same way as it had always been done, except we were short on cash after…well, after…"

"After Amanda took one-third of what we own you mean?"

The three of them turned at the sound of Kyle's voice.

"Yeah, after she took the money," Brady finished, not contrite in the least he'd been caught talking behind his brother's back.

"Anything else about me the three of you would like to discuss?" An angry tic formed at the corner of Kyle's mouth, twitching rapidly.

"We were just talking about how well everything went today," Sabrina said, hoping to diffuse a potentially explosive Kyle. "You did a wonderful job."

His gaze whipped to her, freezing her on the spot. Wow, was he angry. "I didn't do squat. All of you did."

Jenna touched the sleeve of his shirt. "That's not true, Kyle. You brought these people out here—all of them. Without your reputation, no one would have come."

He stared silently at his sister. Then his shoulders relaxed and he hugged her. "Thanks, Jenn," he said softly as he kissed the top of her head. "Thanks for all the work you did today, too. And shouldn't you be off your feet resting or something?" He glared at Sabrina as if Jenna's presence was somehow her fault.

"I tried to get her to rest, told her I would take over, but—"

"You should have tried harder," Kyle said sharply.

Jenna pushed away from her brother's embrace. "Hey, am I not here or something?"

Kyle looked down as Jenna tapped him in the chest with the point of her finger. "This isn't the dark ages, buddy, and I'm perfectly healthy. And more than capable of deciding when and if I need to lie down. So just butt out and quit trying to blame Sabrina for something that's obviously my choice."

Now Sabrina knew what Kyle meant by the look Jenna gave him sometimes. She was spitting mad at her brother.

"That's my cue to hightail it out of here before my little sister decides to start on *me*." Brady donned his cowboy hat and turned away.

"If it isn't the whole Morgan family, assembled like a herd as usual." Amanda Dent's syrupy voice halted Brady's imminent exit. He turned to face her, as did Kyle and Jenna, a united family front.

"Go away Amanda," Kyle said. "You're not wanted here."

Amanda swept her long brown hair off her shoulders, her jewelry doing the same annoying jingling it had in the grocery store. "I didn't realize this event was invitation only. After all, it's not like the elite of Dreamwater are here. Then again," she added with a dismissing look at the lot of them, "they wouldn't come if they were invited."

"*You're* not invited, Amanda. I thought I made that perfectly clear when we divorced."

"*We* didn't divorce, darling. I divorced you, remember?"

Her sugary voice grated on Sabrina's nerves. It was beyond her how Kyle had stayed married to the shrew as long as he had. Now she understood why he said he traveled so much.

"However, I see you've managed to find a new plaything," Amanda said as she eyed Sabrina and wrinkled her nose. "Lowering your expectations I see."

Sabrina bristled, not about to take any guff from the dime-store, country-club-queen wanna-be. "Now just a minute—"

Kyle cut her off. "As a matter of fact, I think I've upgraded, Amanda," he said as he slipped his arm around Sabrina and pulled her next to him.

Shock kept her from protesting his movements. Shock and the fact Amanda didn't like it one bit that Kyle had his arm possessively around Sabrina's waist. And that suited her just fine. Perhaps she'd see how far she could push the two-timing snob.

Sabrina pressed her left breast further into Kyle's chest as she wrapped her arms around his waist. "Thank you, my love," she said as she turned her best dreamy-eyed look in his direction.

Kyle looked down at her, and suddenly there was no game being played. His emerald eyes darkened, those flecks of yellow shimmering like gold in his heated gaze. She breathed deeply, her nipples awake and aware of the masculine chest they rested against as they rose and pebbled under her thin blue tank top. Her eyes widened at the sensation.

Kyle felt it too because he grinned. "Miss me while I was busy today, babe?"

It was all she could do not to burst into embarrassed flames on the spot. But she'd never let Amanda know this was all a game.

"You know I did," she said in a voice sounding too low and breathy to be her own. She trailed a finger along his chest and smiled like a contented cat. "You belong here, at my side, and when you're not here a part of me is missing."

"I'm here now," he answered and tilted her chin up. He wrapped his arms fully around her and pulled her close, then pressed his lips firmly against hers in a heated kiss that sent Sabrina's desire to dangerous levels. With that one kiss he inflamed her, and she wished with all her might that they were alone. His tongue darted deeply in her mouth before he pulled it back, sliding it gently against her open lips.

Their mouths parted and Kyle held her to him, smiling down at her as she stood rooted to the spot, utterly speechless.

If that was just an act then Kyle Morgan should win an Academy Award.

"This is disgusting," Amanda spit angrily. "We *are* in a public place, you know."

Sabrina tore her gaze away from Kyle and tried not to grin as Amanda looked ready to physically tear the two of them apart.

"Kyle just doesn't care where we are. When he wants to kiss me, he does, don't you, baby," she said to Kyle in a sugary voice that even grated on her own ears. Sabrina couldn't help it. She really wanted to annoy Amanda. The woman was irritating as hell.

Brady coughed. "I can attest to that. Why just the other night I saw the two of them in the barn—"

His words were cut off by a sharp jab in the ribs from Jenna.

Sabrina hoped Brady was making that part up, that he hadn't really seen their kiss in the barn the other night.

"I do what I want on my own property, Amanda. And I choose who can and can't be on it. And since I don't want you here, I'd like you to get your bony butt off the Rocking M. And take that snake of a husband with you, if you can find what rock he slithered under today."

Amanda gasped. Sabrina smirked. Maybe she couldn't punch her lights out, but at least she took satisfaction in Kyle letting his ex-wife have it.

"No rock, Morgan. A Dent doesn't need to hide." Jackson Dent appeared and stood beside his wife. "Hello, darlin', having fun?" he said as he kissed Amanda on the cheek.

She affected a pout. "I was until they ruined it for me. They were all ganging up against me, Jackson. It was awful. Where were you when I needed you to defend my honor?"

Kyle's snort at Amanda's use of the word *honor* almost caused Sabrina to laugh out loud. She couldn't suppress the giggle that escaped her lips as Kyle bent and whispered in her ear.

"I think she lost her virginity in preschool behind the jungle gym with Billy Kirkwood."

Amanda's eyes narrowed as she watched Kyle whisper in Sabrina's ear. Sabrina laughed out loud at the outrageous things Kyle said about his ex-wife.

"Never you mind them, honey," Jackson said in a sickening sweet way that made Sabrina's stomach turn sour.

"You weren't invited either, Dent," Kyle said as he turned from Sabrina's ear. He left his arm dangling over her shoulder, lightly trailing his fingers from her jaw to her neck. Sabrina shivered. "So why don't you and your trampy wife take the road back to your own place and stay the hell off Morgan property."

Amanda started to speak out at the insult, but Dent's hand on her arm silenced her. "Doesn't matter what he or any of them say or do," Dent said with an evil gleam in his weak eyes. "After this useless spectacle today, it's only a matter of time before the ranch is ours."

"You don't have a chance in hell of taking this ranch, Dent, so just give it up," Kyle said.

Dent sniffed. "You think these ropings or the pitiful rodeo you're planning will make any money? Oh, you might have drawn a respectable crowd on your name alone, but that was before I spread the word today."

Sabrina was shocked that Dent knew about the rodeo. No one had mentioned it to him, but of course since he milled around the crowd today word would have gotten out.

A crowd had begun to gather, watching the exchange between the Morgans and the Dents with obvious interest. Neither group seemed affected by the fact they now had a sizeable audience.

Sabrina figured the rumor mill would run rampant for the next week or so as word spread about the altercation between the Morgans and the Dents.

"I don't have time for this, Dent. Spell it out for me." The tic at Kyle's mouth twitched angrily again.

Dent examined his neatly manicured fingernails and turquoise adorned fingers. "Well, it just so happens the same weekend you're holding your pathetic rodeo, I'll be hosting one too."

Kyle was silent. Sabrina worried her lower lip in anticipation of his response.

Finally shrugging as if he didn't care, Kyle answered. "Doesn't matter what you do. We'll still draw better than you."

"I hardly think so, Morgan. Remember, I have a lot more money than you do, so I can draw big names and sponsors to provide more prize money for the winners. You know as well as I do the good competitors will go where the money is."

As soon as Amanda let out the snicker of glee, Sabrina wanted to slap her.

Dent turned his eyes to Sabrina. "Told you, missy. You should have put your money with a winner like me."

That was all Sabrina could take of the two of them. She held on tight to Kyle's arms as she answered Dent. "Frankly, Mr. Dent, I think I already picked a winner in Kyle." Her eyes traveled over Amanda. "Seems to me you just pick up on Kyle's cast-offs. I'm putting my money where the original is."

"That does it." Amanda started toward Sabrina, who was more than ready to go head-to-head with the snobby jezebel and took a step forward to confront her. Kyle had to forcibly hold her back to keep her from attacking the brunette.

Restraining his angry wife, Dent said, "I think we've done enough damage today." Tipping his hat to the ladies, Dent strode away, dragging his cursing wife behind him.

After Dent's departure and Kyle's glare at them all, the crowd dispersed, leaving the four of them alone.

Silence surrounded them as they watched Dent walk away. Kyle still held on to Sabrina's arms as she continued to grumble at

Amanda's retreating form. Several unkind words crossed her mind but she refrained from saying them out loud.

"Damn, Sabrina, you're sure a hellcat when you get riled," Brady said with a grin. "You fit in with the Morgans quite well."

Jenna laughed. "That's for sure. If I weren't so pregnant I'd have stomped that bimbo into the dust. At least Sabrina gave her what for. Brady's right. You fit into this family just fine."

Sabrina finally calmed down enough to realize she was still being held in Kyle's strong arms. "You can let me go now," she said as she turned her head toward him. He tried to straighten his expression but not soon enough. Sabrina caught the smile at the corners of his mouth.

"What's so funny?"

"You are. The way you took off after Amanda like you were defending your own family."

The realization of her actions finally hit her. "Oh. I'm sorry," she said to all of them. "I had no right to fly off like that but that woman irritated me to the point I couldn't hold back any longer."

Once again she had acted without thinking. And in front of a crowd too.

"Hey," Jenna said, grinning. "Nobody's angry at you, Sabrina. We're downright proud of you. You acted like a Morgan today."

"Jenna's right," Kyle added. "You did just fine."

"So now what do we do about Dent and his rodeo?" Brady asked.

The smile left Kyle's face. "I don't know. I want to find out what he's putting on over there, see if he's as big a threat to our rodeo as he thinks he is. Then we'll figure out what to do."

"And if he's right?" Jenna asked the question no one wanted to. "If he can outsell us with big names and big prizes?"

Kyle didn't pull the punch. "Then we're screwed."

ം ം ം

Sabrina thought about the day as she finished cleaning up the kitchen, having sent Jenna home hours ago despite her protests.

It had certainly been an eventful day. First the roping and all its excitement, then Kyle kissing her in a way that didn't feel at all like play-acting. And finally the bombshell dropped by Dent.

The Morgan family worked so hard to keep the Rocking M afloat. She had come to feel a part of their family, and would do anything she could to help them hold on to their land. But what could she do?

Kyle had already refused to take any more of her money, so that just left the ropings and the rodeo, with the key being the rodeo. There had to be a way to beat Dent at his own game.

She thought about it for a few moments, when suddenly an idea came to her. Of course. The perfect solution to draw more contestants to the Rocking M's rodeo lay with Kyle's past in the profession. She'd have to get started on her plan right away.

The back door slammed shut as Kyle walked into the kitchen. She hung the dishtowel and turned to look at him.

"You look exhausted," she said, worried over the drawn expression on his handsome face.

He managed a weak smile. "It's been a long day, but they're all pretty much like that." He grabbed two beers out of the refrigerator and handed one to her. They leaned against the kitchen counter side by side and sipped in silence.

She wanted to talk to him about Dent, but knew he had a short fuse where his neighbor was concerned. She wasn't up to another battle with him. As it was her emotions were a jumble of confusion anyway.

The way he looked at her today, the way he held her and kissed her. Was it just a game he was playing? Or was it real?

He'd made it clear before he wasn't interested in a relationship with her, but then he kissed her like he meant it. The man confused her. Did he want her or didn't he?

Sabrina pondered that thought as they drank their beer. There was no use lying to herself. She felt something for Kyle. Something powerful that had nothing to do with play-acting. Something real. And scary.

She turned to him. "Kyle, about today."

He put his beer down and turned to face her. "Yeah, I've been meaning to talk to you about today. Well, actually, the last damn thing I want to do about it is talk. I'm done talking." Taking the beer from her hand, he placed it on the counter then took her in his arms, his lips crashing down over hers.

Chapter Ten

Sabrina's lips parted and Kyle's tongue swept inside, curling around hers and sliding gently back and forth until she was mindless with wanting.

He pulled her against him, his cock already hard and pressing against the aching center of her sex. She heard her own moans as he rocked against her, pinning her against the counter at the same time his relentless assault on her mouth continued.

She couldn't get close enough. She felt a need she never had before with Mark, a quest for fulfillment she wanted desperately. She searched for exposed skin as she clutched at his shoulders. Frustrated with impeding clothing, she reached for his shirt and tore it from the waistband of his jeans, sliding her hands over his hot flesh.

"Yes," he said through rapid breaths. "This is what I wanted to talk about, what I needed to...oh the hell with talking." He growled as he slid his hands once more over her ass, grasping her thighs and lifting her onto the countertop. He stepped between her legs, cradling her head in his hands as he grabbed a handful of her hair and pulled her mouth toward his.

Instinctively she moved against him until he moaned into her mouth. She reached down to unbutton his pants but his hand stilled her. She looked up at him, hoping not to see denial once again on his face.

Savage desire emanated from his eyes, the emerald orbs so dark they were almost black. He drew a ragged breath. "God, Sabrina I want you."

Relief flooded her very soul at his words. He wasn't turning her down, telling her she was foolish, telling her he didn't really want her. "I...I want you too, Kyle," she managed, so overcome with her newfound passion she could barely get the words out.

"I want to make love to you. But I also have to be honest with you, because I don't want to hurt you."

Not sure where the conversation was heading, she tried to calm her breathing and nodded. "Go ahead."

"I want you. I've wanted you since the first day I laid eyes on you. But there's something you need to know."

He stroked her cheek so gently it brought tears to her eyes. Blinking quickly she said, "I've wanted you too. From the first."

He smiled at her, tenderly, and tasted her lips. Then his expression grew serious. "I want to make love to you, but I can't give you what I think you need."

Now he was confusing her. "What do you mean?"

"I can't have a relationship. I'm not ready for that yet. All I can offer you right now is sex, and I think you're looking for more than that."

She was stunned. Sex. That's all he wanted from her, all he could offer. An angry rush came over her but she quickly tamped it down.

He'd never made any promises to her, never made her think he felt anything for her other than desire. He didn't tease her or chase her or give her any impression he was after her money for any reason. So what right did she have to be angry at his honesty? He wanted her— physically. And that was all. Was it enough for her?

"I don't know what to say." She searched his face. His expression was a mix of emotions, remnants of passion still lurking but tempered somewhat by the seriousness of their discussion. "I appreciate your honesty, I really do. Just like I hope you'll appreciate mine."

He nodded. "Tell me what's on your mind."

Despite their conversation, Kyle continued to caress her arm, her cheek, the tenderness in his touch almost causing her to throw her thoughts out the window and beg Kyle to make love to her. But that wasn't who she was, and it was time he realized it. Maybe it was time she figured out what she really wanted too.

"I've had sex with only one man in my life," she began.

"Your ex-husband."

"Yes. And sex with him was…"

"Unsatisfying?" he finished for her.

She laughed lightly. "Yes, you could say that. But there's more."

Kyle stilled. "He didn't hurt you did he?"

She shook her head. "No, not sexually. Mark was a very controlling man. He liked to be in charge. All the time. And he didn't like to relinquish control. Ever."

Awareness lit his eyes and he nodded. "He had to be master in the bedroom too, then."

Sabrina blew out a breath in relief. "Yes. I was never allowed to…"

The corners of his mouth lifted. "Express yourself?"

"Yes." God this was more embarrassing than she thought it would be. Good thing Kyle knew what she was trying to say and could finish her sentences for her.

"Why don't you just spell it out for me?"

Easier said than done. "I'll try." She looked down at her hands, clasping and unclasping them in her lap. "I've never done anything, was never allowed to do anything sexually other than lie still while my husband did his thing until he was finished." There, she'd gotten it all out.

"In other words, you just had to lay there and take it?" Kyle had an incredulous look on his face that almost made Sabrina laugh.

"More or less. He didn't want me to experiment, make the first move, or ask for anything. He didn't care whether he pleased me or not, only that he was satisfied. Which usually didn't take very long," she added with perverse delight.

That made Kyle laugh. "I see. Sounds like a very unfulfilling sexual experience."

"But the reason I'm telling you this is so you'll understand that my wanting to make love with you is special. It means something to me and I don't take it lightly."

"I kind of figured that, which is why I had to be honest with you. I don't want a relationship."

Sabrina knew she should feel anger at being rejected yet again, but Kyle wasn't really rejecting her. He was rejecting himself, his ability to feel, to give anything to a woman.

"You care about me and you don't want to."

He shook his head. "No, I don't. I'm sorry but I don't."

She smiled at him. "You're lying to yourself and to me, Kyle. No one who kisses me, who touches me like you do, is without feeling."

He stepped away, pacing the length of the kitchen. "You're wrong. That's what I'm trying to tell you. This thing between us is purely physical, and that's all. I want you. Hell yes I want you, but I don't want you to think it will go beyond that."

He looked like a lost little boy. His hair a mess, his clothing in disarray, confusion softening his normally rugged features. Sabrina wanted to wrap her arms around him and hold him, tell him everything would be all right. He needed her—he just didn't realize it yet.

"So now what?" she asked.

"I don't know. I guess it's up to you to decide if you can handle a purely physical relationship, or if we should just forget about it and go back to being business partners only."

A lot to think about. What did she want? Would she be satisfied with having only a sexual relationship with Kyle? And if not, would she be content longing for and wanting a man she couldn't have?

"I don't know what to say," she answered as truthfully as she could. "It's obvious we have an attraction, and one I'd like to pursue. I've spent my entire life being sheltered, being told what I could and couldn't have. Frankly, I'm tired of waiting for what I want."

He approached her, stopping short of stepping between her legs again. Laying his hands on either side of her thighs, he looked into her eyes. "What do you want, Sabrina?"

As she looked into his eyes, the answer was clear. She wanted him. Any way she could have him. For once in her life she wanted to feel, to allow herself the chance to choose her own destiny. It was time to take charge of her life—she was, after all, an independent woman now.

Her decision made, she reached for him. "I want—"

"Oh hell you guys, I'm sorry to interrupt but my water just broke."

Sabrina's gaze shot to the doorway. Jenna leaned against the door to the kitchen, dressed only in her nightgown. Kyle ran over to her immediately and Sabrina jumped down off the counter to accompany him.

"Where's Luke?" Kyle asked as he sat Jenna down in the chair.

"He went with Brady to attend a horse auction tomorrow. By now they're probably halfway to Dallas and I can't reach him on the cell phone. Damn idiot's battery is probably dead again. He can never remember to charge it."

"Are you having any pains?" Sabrina asked.

Jenna nodded. "Yeah. Big ones too." She looked over at Kyle. "I think my labor is going to be like Mom said all hers were. And I thought I had a few more weeks left too."

"Oh great." Kyle straightened his tousled hair and took a deep breath. He looked at Sabrina. "Mom had all of us in record time—never made it to the hospital once." Turning his attention back to his sister, he asked, "How far apart are the contractions?"

"About two minutes," she replied and then clutched Kyle's hand as a contraction overwhelmed her. Sabrina knelt by the side of the chair and held Jenna's other hand until it passed.

Jenna inhaled deeply as the last of the contraction subsided. "This is gonna be tough, I think."

"Let's get her upstairs," Kyle said as he lifted Jenna easily in his arms.

"Shouldn't we go to the hospital instead?" Sabrina asked.

He shook his head. "Not a chance. Hospital's an hour and a half away. She'll have this baby by then." He motioned to the phone. "Try Luke's cell phone again and see if you can raise him. He needs to know he's about to become a father. And call Jenna's doctor—the number is on the pad by the phone—and let him know what's going on. See what he wants us to do."

She nodded and dialed Luke's number as Kyle carried Jenna upstairs. After several attempts she finally reached him, and he told her excitedly that he and Brady would turn around and head back to the ranch. Sabrina assured him she and Kyle had the situation under control.

Right. Like anyone could control when a baby wanted to be born.

She hoped Kyle knew something about birth, because she was completely clueless. She had a rudimentary understanding of the process, of course, but had never seen one up close. She had a feeling that was going to change tonight.

The next step was contacting Jenna's doctor who acted like having a baby at home was as natural as pouring milk from a bottle. Easy for him to say—he already knew how to do it. He gave her instructions and told her he'd be there as soon as he could but they should be prepared to assist Jenna with the birth since it was unlikely he'd make it in time. He said to call him on his cell phone if Jenna started to push, and he'd talk them through it.

Trying not to panic, Sabrina hurried upstairs with the list of instructions and found Kyle had put Jenna in what used to be her childhood bedroom. Creamy wallpaper covered with tiny violets surrounded the room. A queen-size, four-poster bed adorned the middle of the room. Kyle had stripped the fluffy purple comforter off the bed and was placing plain white sheets on it.

"All the years I spent in this room growing up, and I never expected I'd deliver my first child in it."

"Would you like me to carry you to your place?"

Jenna shook her head. "Makes me feel closer to Mom to be in this house, you know?"

Kyle nodded and stroked his sister's hair while they exchanged warm glances in memory of their mother.

Then Jenna got busy as another contraction hit her. She forcefully inhaled and exhaled as she stared ahead, gripping Kyle's hand.

He looked at Sabrina, a calm smile on his face as if he were trying to assure her it would all be okay. She smiled and informed them of her conversations with Luke and the doctor.

"I guess this baby's coming with or without the daddy or the doctor being present," Jenna said as she panted through yet another difficult contraction.

"They tend to have their own minds when they're ready to be born," Kyle said with a smile. "You know how it is, it's just like the cattle. In the middle of a blinding snowstorm they'll drop their calves."

"Oh great," Jenna replied, her sense of humor intact. "Now you're comparing me to a cow."

Kyle and Sabrina both laughed. She wiped Jenna's brow with a wet cloth. She wanted to keep Jenna calm, but inside Sabrina was near panic. She'd never done this before—had never even been around a woman who was pregnant. Despite her assurances to Jenna, she had no idea if things were proceeding smoothly or not.

"You're doing fine, honey," Kyle said with a soft voice as he held Jenna's hand. He pulled up a chair next to the bed and spoke reassuringly to his sister, helping her through the difficult contractions and reminding her to focus on breathing through the pain.

Kyle glanced at Sabrina, his emerald eyes intense and concentrated. They were going to do this together.

She gathered the necessary supplies the doctor told her they'd need and continued to work with Kyle to keep his sister calm. Her labor was proceeding rapidly and soon Jenna was soaked in sweat and preparing to bear down and deliver her child.

Kyle instructed Sabrina to sit next to Jenna while he prepared to deliver the baby. He told her this was old hat to him, having seen his brother and sister born when he was no more than a child himself, as well as hundreds of cattle and horses.

Sabrina wiped Jenna's brow and helped her focus on breathing as instructed by Dr. Maynard. Jenna appeared to be handling everything, talking and laughing in between contractions. Sabrina hoped she could handle it as well as the mother-to-be, and prayed she wouldn't pass out when the time came.

It seemed like they were at it for hours but it was actually less than a half-hour when Jenna announced she had to push. Kyle calmly told Sabrina to get the doctor on the phone and help Jenna sit up so she could press through the contractions.

She relayed the doctor's instructions to Kyle as Jenna strained to push the baby out.

It didn't take long at all before Kyle shouted, "I see the baby's head! Push again at the next contraction, Jenna. Hard."

Sabrina supported Jenna's back as she inhaled and pushed.

"Ok, Jenn, you're doing fine. The baby's head's out. Just one more deep breath and push and we should have a baby."

Jenna took a breath and forced it out as she pushed her child into the world with one hell of a yell of pain.

"Here it is," Kyle said excitedly as he held up a wet, squealing baby in his hands. "It's a boy." Kyle followed the doctor's instructions and laid the baby on Jenna's stomach.

Tears rolled down Jenna's face as she gingerly grasped her baby's tiny fingers. "He's perfect," she said as she laughed and touched her son. He was red and wrinkled and squalling loud and long.

Sabrina had never seen anything so beautiful in her entire life as the screaming bundle of creation before her. Her heart beat so fast she thought she might faint. The sight of new life before her touched her like a magical spell, and she sat in the chair with unabashed tears streaming down her cheeks.

"That he is." Kyle wiped his sister's dampened hair and kissed her forehead. "Good job, sis," he said with a smile.

Jenna held her son, her face beaming with the glow of new motherhood.

Pangs of want and desire hit her with such a force it took her breath away. Seeing Jenna hold a baby in her arms awakened what she had missed all these years, what she would never experience herself. She forced the feelings inside. Nothing was going to spoil Jenna's moment. Now was not the time for her to feel sorry for herself.

Kyle turned his gaze to Sabrina, his face glowing with joy and a hint of moisture in his eyes. She smiled back, feeling closer than ever to him.

Dr. Maynard finally arrived and after inspecting both Jenna and the baby pronounced them fit and healthy.

"Women have babies at home all the time, dear," Doctor Maynard said to Sabrina. A kindly man in his early sixties, he had a full face and a cheerful smile. His bedside manner was definitely more along the lines of a country doctor than a big city one. He laughed and joked with Jenna and Sabrina, tickled the baby's feet and told Kyle he made a damn fine doctor.

No sooner had Dr. Maynard left than the door downstairs slammed open and heavy feet pounded quickly up the stairs. Luke raced into the room and skidded to a halt as he saw his wife holding their newborn son. Brady followed behind but lingered in the doorway, grinning widely at his sister.

"Here's your son," Jenna said proudly as she gently lifted the baby into her husband's waiting hands.

Luke's hands were as big as the rest of him, making the infant look like a tiny ball in his massive arms. Then suddenly the big mountain of a man broke down and cried as he held his child for the first time.

Sabrina and Kyle left the new parents alone to bond with their baby. Brady claimed exhaustion from the day and the whirlwind trip and went to bed since he had to get back on the road early in the morning.

There was no way Sabrina would be able to sleep yet. She was too wound up, adrenaline still pumping through her system.

Kyle must have felt the same way because he followed her downstairs.

She stood in the middle of the kitchen, her arms wrapped around herself, and stared out the window at the moonlight. What a night it had been.

"Thank you," Kyle said as he stopped behind her.

"For what?"

"For helping me tonight. For helping Jenna. You did a great job keeping her calm."

"I had no idea what I was doing up there. Frankly I was scared to death. I'd never seen a baby born before."

"You couldn't tell," he said in a low voice as he laid his hands on her shoulders. "You did great."

"Thanks."

They stood like that for a moment, both of them staring out the large window of the dark kitchen. Kyle's hands continued to rest on her shoulders. She was finally starting to come down from the adrenaline high of Jenna giving birth. Her anxious jitters were replaced by a restlessness she couldn't name, but she knew it had something to do with the warm male standing behind her.

"How about a drive?"

She nodded. "That sounds fine. I could use a little fresh air."

"I'm going to clean up a bit. Meet me outside in about fifteen minutes."

Sabrina freshened up too, then they got in the truck and Kyle headed down the dirt road leading further onto the Rocking M property.

During the past few weeks she'd seen much of the Rocking M, but not all. Although typically ranchers drove their trucks to the outlying areas of their properties, Kyle wanted Sabrina to grow more comfortable riding a horse so he had been limiting their excursions around the property to areas they could reach on horseback.

In the darkness she was disoriented. The full moon shone brightly in the sky, but no other light was available as they headed further and further into the woody area of the ranch. Tall oak trees lined the side of the road, obstructing any view of what lay behind them.

"Where are we going?" They had driven in silence for almost thirty minutes, Sabrina assuming Kyle was as deep in thought about the events of the day as she.

"There's a place I've been wanting to show you, but it's not reachable by horse so I haven't had a chance yet." He glanced at her. "You don't mind the ride, do you?"

She shook her head. "Not at all." The night was beautiful, the moon full, the weather quite warm. The truck's windows were rolled down and the leisurely pace blew a balmy breeze against her hair and face. Sabrina inhaled the scent of night, of dirt and wooded forest. Cicadas hummed their songs of the evening, their rhythmic pulses hypnotic. She finally began to release the tensions of the day.

"So what kind of place are we going to?" she asked.

He smiled. "You'll see. It's kind of special and I think you'll like it."

They came to an off road and Kyle turned the truck and headed over dirt and rocks. The road was full of severe jolting bumps and sharp curves. It couldn't even be called a road, in her opinion—really little more than a narrow path in the heavily forested woods. She hoped Kyle knew the way back because she didn't see him throwing breadcrumbs out the truck windows to map their trail.

He halted the truck at the end of the road, turned off the lights and opened his door. He grabbed a bag from behind his seat and came around to her side of the truck.

"It's pretty dark out here. Take my hand so you don't fall."

She grasped his hand and he led her from the truck down a narrow pathway between a crop of trees so tall they momentarily obstructed the moon overhead, plunging them into total darkness. She held on tight to Kyle's hand, knowing if she let go she'd be lost.

They finally reached the end of the long row of trees, and she couldn't suppress her gasp as the forest opened up before her.

The moon was so full it shone like midday, its light casting a luminescent sheen over the expansive lake centered in the middle of a clearing. Majestic oak trees surrounded them on all sides, and grass grew from the edge of the trees to the bank of the lake. Scattered throughout the grassy areas were hundreds upon hundreds of lavender wildflowers, popping up like silver-tinged rainbows across the valley of green.

Sabrina laid her hand on her heart, emotionally struck at the raw beauty of this secluded Eden. The trees stood so tall it seemed as if she and Kyle were completely isolated. The rich, thick grass felt lush under her tennis shoes, and she longed to kick them off and feel the cool blades tickle her feet. Not a sound could be heard except for the trees rustling in the slight warm breeze.

"What do you think?" Kyle whispered behind her.

She turned to look at him. "I've never seen anything so spectacular. Doesn't it take your breath away?"

He shook his head. "No, you take my breath away. You should see your face."

She tilted her head. "What's wrong with my face?"

"Nothing," he said as he laughed. He picked up a curl of hair that had come loose from her ponytail and played with it, sliding it over his fingers. "It glows in the moonlight. You have a child's wonder in your eyes, like you've never seen anything like this before."

"I haven't. I've never seen a place so beautiful."

"And I've never seen a woman so beautiful."

Her heart soared and her breath hitched at his words. "Thank you."

"I thought we'd spread a blanket out, have a drink and look at the moon. If that's okay with you."

Wow. Now this she hadn't expected. It was almost like a...date. "I'd love to."

He opened the bag he brought from the truck and spread the blanket near the water's edge. Then he produced a bottle of wine, an opener, and two plastic cups. She giggled at the disposable plastic glasses. Mark would have had an apoplectic fit if she'd tried to serve wine in anything less than fine crystal.

"What's so funny?" Kyle asked as he fit the corkscrew into the bottle, popping the cork out easily.

"I was just thinking how different my life is now compared to a year ago."

He handed a glass of white wine to her, and she sipped it as she sat on the blanket.

"How different?"

She kicked off her tennis shoes and wiggled her toes in the thick carpet of grass, sighing as the cool blades caressed the bottom of her feet. "Just different," she said. "I don't know. Like this impromptu picnic. Mark never would have thought of something like this. Everything was planned, each day had an agenda. In his world, spontaneity was nonexistent."

"Too bad for him," Kyle replied as he sipped his wine. He sat on the blanket next to her, one leg stretched out in front of him. "Spontaneity makes life exciting, don't you think?"

"I wouldn't know," she replied absently. The reflection of the moon over the lake looked like a woman's waving silver hair undulating on the surface of the water. "Is the water warm?" she asked as she turned to Kyle.

He shrugged as he sipped his wine, the hint of a smile hidden behind the cup. "Don't know. Why don't you go stick your toes in it and find out?"

"Okay." She rose, glass in hand, and walked the few steps to the water's edge. Although summer was fast approaching, she knew there hadn't been enough days of warm weather to heat the water yet, so Sabrina expected it to be ice cold. Sliding one big toe gingerly in the lake, she turned to Kyle and exclaimed, "It's warm!"

He nodded and grinned. "Lake's fed by hot springs underground. That's part of the attraction of this place. A big warm bathtub."

She dipped her whole foot in the water, wetting the bottom edge of her jeans. She longed to float on the water's surface, swim a few laps, and relax in the oversized hot tub.

"Want to take a dip?"

She whirled and almost lost her balance as Kyle spoke behind her. He grabbed her arms to keep her from falling.

"How do you do that?" she asked as she steadied herself in his grasp.

"Do what?"

"Sneak up on me all the time. I never hear you."

"I think it's because you're so often lost in thought, like you were just then." He turned her to face him. "What were you thinking about?"

She looked again at the water. "I was thinking of this lake as a big hot tub and had this sudden urge to take a dip."

"Let's do it then." He let her go and walked toward the blanket, slipping off his boots and socks.

"Do what?"

"Take a swim in the lake." He started to unbutton his shirt.

Sabrina's eyes widened. "What are you doing?"

He reached the last button and pulled the shirt off his shoulders. His naked torso glistened in the moonlight, the dark burnished curls on his chest glowing bronze. "I'm going with your suggestion, Sabrina."

"What suggestion?"

"To go skinny dipping." He stood there waiting for her. "Are you going to take your clothes off or are you planning to swim in jeans and a T-shirt?"

Skinny dipping? That would mean... Good Lord he was unbuttoning his pants. He expected her to swim naked with him!

Chapter Eleven

Kyle laughed at the shocked expression on Sabrina's face. "What? You've never gone skinny dipping before?"

She shook her head furiously. "No."

"You wanted new experiences didn't you?"

She nodded mutely.

"Independence, freedom, make your own choices? That kind of thing?"

"Yeah, I guess."

He stepped toward her, placed his finger under her chin and lifted her face to his. God her eyes were beautiful. So full of wonder, so much innocence reflected in their amber depths.

"Sabrina, what do you want to do?" She opened her mouth to speak but his finger on her lips stilled her. "Don't think about the way your life used to be, think about what you want now. From your heart, what do you want to do?"

She pondered and he watched her expression change from uncertainty to determination. "I want to go swimming in the moonlight. With you."

He sighed deeply. Her answer fired his blood like nothing ever had. Trying to quell his baser thoughts, Kyle turned his back on Sabrina. "Go ahead and undress, then get in the water and I'll follow you."

171

He waited but didn't hear anything.

"Sabrina?"

"Yeah?"

He half-turned to look at her. She was still standing there, completely clothed. And contemplating. "You don't have to do this if you don't want to."

She stared at him, fierce determination spreading across her features. "Turn your back to me, Kyle, while I undress."

He did as he was told, trying not to imagine her lifting the T-shirt over her head, wondering what she was wearing underneath. A sensible cotton bra? Or something wicked and lacy? How would her soft skin look bathed in moonlight, her breasts exposed, jeans unzipped, half-clothed and half-naked. God, why did he do this to himself?

"I'm almost ready," she said in a shaky breath.

He was beyond ready. He already felt the tightness in his jeans, and wondered how he was going to get undressed and into the water without Sabrina becoming aware of his growing desire for her.

He flinched as he heard the zipper drawing down, then the rustling as she slipped out of them. Hearing her, knowing what she was doing, but unable to see, conjured up vivid images in his mind. Whose idea was this anyway? He must be insane.

He heard the movement of the water as she stepped into the lake. Now it was his turn.

"I'm in the water, Kyle."

"I'll be right there," he replied, trying mightily for control. She'd probably be too shy to look anyway. He quickly shed the remainder of his clothes and turned around.

Obviously she wasn't *that* shy. She stood in water up to her collarbone and watched him, her eyes assessing, wide-eyed and appreciative. Damn. It would have been easier if she hadn't looked. The woman was a constant surprise.

"You peeked," he said as he entered the water and stopped inches away from her.

She smiled, a slight blush staining her cheeks. "I couldn't help it. You're beautiful you know."

He shook his head. "No, not me. You." He reached out and pulled the ponytail holder from her hair, sweeping the now-wet, bottom half of her hair over her shoulders. She looked like a siren standing there. Calling to him, beckoning him near. The closer he got, the deeper her intake of breath, the top swell of her breasts rising teasingly from the water with every inhalation.

"I didn't peek at you when you undressed."

She shrugged. "That's your own fault for being a gentleman. You could have."

Damn, she surprised him.

"So, do you want to swim or something?" she asked, biting her lower lip in that way Kyle found so incredibly arousing.

Or something. What he wanted was to taste her sweet mouth again, but instead he took the high road and pushed off the bottom of the lake with his feet. "Let's go."

She swam after him, both their strokes light and easy. They stopped in the middle of the lake, treading water as they caught their breath.

There was something so sexy about knowing you were swimming next to a naked woman, yet not being able to really see her. Knowing she wore nothing, but unable to make anything out other than shadows under the rippling water, was driving Kyle out of his mind.

They alternated swimming and treading, talking easily about the ranch, Jenna's baby and the upcoming rodeo, but always circumventing any conversation about the two of them. Kyle was going crazy being so near her and not touching her.

"Ready to get out?" he asked. They had swum back to their point of entry in the water and stood, their feet buried in the sandy bottom below.

"I don't think so. Not yet."

She didn't look nervous, just contemplative. Kyle wondered if she was afraid what would happen when they both exited naked from the water. He had a pretty good idea what he'd like to have happen, but that was up to her.

Her hair was wet and slicked back from her face, making her eyes more radiant than usual. Perhaps it was the reflection of the moonlight, but Kyle swore he saw flickers of raw desire cross her features every time they changed positions and her face was bathed in the light.

"Kyle."

"Yeah?"

"I've decided I'd like you to make love to me."

He blinked. "What?"

"Don't make me repeat it," she said in a soft voice, innocence and embarrassment showing on her face. "You heard me the first time."

"Are you sure? You know what we talked about. I don't want to force you."

"You're not forcing me. I want to." Those warm whiskey eyes darkened with passion. "I don't think I've ever wanted anything more in my entire life."

He didn't need to be any more convinced. He couldn't believe she had come right out and said it. Her innocence and honesty were incredibly refreshing after so many years of living with Amanda's double talk and insincerity. There were no games with Sabrina. She always meant what she said.

"If you want to, that is," she added. "It's not required, I mean if you'd rather not—"

He cut off her words by pulling her toward him and sliding his lips over hers. She tasted like sweet wine and sugar, her mouth warm and inviting as he kissed her deeply.

She twined her arms around his neck and moved closer, her breasts pushing against his chest. The contact of her naked body against his was electrifying. His cock lurched upward, pressing into her belly and he could no longer hide his need from her. He ran his hands over her back, feeling the softness of her skin from her neck to the cleft at the end of her back. He grasped her ass, squeezing and caressing the soft, firm globes, eliciting a moan of pleasure from her.

"I've never felt this way before," she gasped as Kyle tore his mouth away from her lips to rain soft, wet kisses along her neck and shoulder. "Is it always like this?"

Every touch of his lips and hands on Sabrina's body sent his desire for her to unbearable levels. "No, it's not always like this." And it was true. He'd never felt this way before, so joined, so complete, as he did when he touched her. Everything felt right.

Warning bells sounded in his head as his thoughts jolted him. It felt right. It shouldn't. He didn't want this. This attachment, this need for her. But he pushed the thoughts aside. He'd think about them later. Not now, not when he held her in his arms, so willing, so honest in her emotions and needs he almost couldn't bear it.

She grabbed his head with both hands and tilted her mouth over his, pressing her lips firmly against his open mouth and sliding her tongue inside, twining ever so seductively with his.

He had to get closer. There wasn't a part of her body he didn't want to touch, taste and see. The need to be a part of her overpowered him until he ached from it. He grabbed her butt and lifted her up to carry her out of the water, but as he did she wrapped her legs around his waist, pressing her pussy against his shaft.

Then she surged against him, ever so slightly, and shredded whatever chivalrous thoughts he had left.

He stood still and groaned in agony and bliss, tortured by the feel and taste of her. Her breasts bobbed teasingly in and out of the water, and he laid her back, needing to see her. She arched for him, allowing him access as he held her with one hand and stroked her breasts with the other. He watched with growing desire as her nipples pebbled and rose against his questing fingers.

Bending over her, he licked one dusky pink nipple, feeling Sabrina shudder under him as his mouth seared her soft flesh. He could still smell peaches, an ever-familiar scent whenever she was around.

He had to get her out of the water soon or the sheer pleasure of touching and tasting her would weaken him until he drowned them both.

Sabrina couldn't think with all the feelings coursing through her at once. Kyle's hands and mouth were everywhere, touching and tasting, eliciting sensations she'd never experienced before.

Deep in her heart regret crept in. She had missed the glorious thrill of lovemaking for so many years. But how could she miss what she hadn't known existed? And now that Kyle had opened her eyes and her body to what she could have, she wanted more.

His hands brushed over her throbbing breasts, her nipples tightening in anticipation of his touch. She sighed as his callused hand lightly scraped over her sensitive nipples, sending jolts of desire through her.

She raised up and kissed him, running her palms over his rough beard as she pulled his mouth toward hers. The muscles of his shoulders and arms bunched under her gliding hands as she held him, his groans of delight driving her to slide her hips seductively against his cock. The ache was almost unbearable and she gasped as she instinctively sought relief for the pulsing need inside her.

The freedom to explore, to rock against him, was an incredible delight. Kyle let her play, let her move, let her experience the simple pleasure of rocking her pussy against his shaft. It was a shattering experience. Her clit was hard, pulsing, a tight knot of exquisite pleasure. It was torture. It was heaven.

Kyle whispered to her, telling her she was beautiful, how much he wanted her. His gritty voice in the night poured over her in a sensuous rush of passion and resonating desire. His cock slid against her aching sex, pushing her past the point of sanity as he poised at the entrance to her pussy, teasing and testing until she couldn't stand it any longer.

"Kyle, please," she murmured. Her words were no more than a panting gasp as she opened herself to him. Unable to bear the anticipation any longer, she pressed against his turgid flesh until the tip of his arousal slid inside her moist heat. A pure groan of delight escaped her parted lips.

His eyes flew open. "Sabrina, we can't, oh God, wait, we need to—"

Oh no. Not this time. No more waiting. "No, Kyle, I've waited long enough." She gasped as she tightened her legs around his waist and lowered herself onto his swollen flesh until he was buried deep within her. This time she knew what she wanted, and she didn't want his misguided attempts at chivalry to distract her.

She whimpered at the sheer pleasure of having him inside her. He filled and delighted her, both physically and emotionally, as his touch and murmurs overwhelmed her senses. His shaft pulsated rapidly and she felt her body instinctively accommodate him, tightening and contracting as he slowly rocked his hips against her.

"God Sabrina, you feel so damn good," he rasped against her ear as he held her close, her sensitive nipples scraping against the crisp hairs of his chest, searing her with an almost unbearable delight.

She arched back, allowing him access to her breasts, and he took advantage, sliding his work-roughened hands over her nipples, turning them in his fingers as he thrust against her aching flesh.

This was the wonder and joy of two people making love. The way it was supposed to be, both partners taking and giving completely, enhancing their pleasure and delighting in the responses of the other. Sabrina reveled in every groan, every thrust, every rush of whispered desire from Kyle.

He gave back what she gave to him, both of them feeding a primal need to please and be pleased, to satisfy and be satisfied.

His rocking motion intensified as the water lapped around them, splashing onto their chests and shoulders as he quickened the pace of his thrusts.

She gasped, the building tidal wave inside almost making her weep as she sought the unfamiliar, craved a fulfillment she knew existed but had never felt with a man before.

In response to her cries of pleasure, Kyle adjusted his rhythm so his strokes were long and measured, his movement fluid and intensifying until she was clutching at him, her head thrown back in abandon and her hips rising to meet each thrust.

She was panting now, moaning wildly as the pressure built to the boiling point.

"Kyle. Oh God, Kyle," she gasped into his mouth as he seared her lips with a hot kiss, his tongue thrusting in rhythm to their joining.

She felt the first overwhelming contractions pulse within her, tightening around Kyle's swollen cock until she cried out his name, floods of incredible sensation coursing through her, relentlessly squeezing every ounce of pleasure she could bear.

He tore his mouth away and clutched her as he groaned long and low, shuddering with an incredible climax she could feel deep within her. She laid her head on his shoulder and rode out the waves of ecstasy with him, taking in his moans of pleasure, his ragged gasps as he held them both in the aftermath of their lovemaking.

They stood in the water, still joined, their lips tasting each other's delight as they struggled to regain normal breathing.

"We need to get out of the water," Kyle said as he kissed her neck.

"Mmm," was all Sabrina was capable of. It was the first time she had truly made love and she wanted to savor the moment in time and memory forever.

He changed positions and Sabrina felt a sudden loss as he withdrew from her. He swept her up in his arms and carried her to their blanket, both of them dripping wet. He laid her down and curled up next to her, scanning her body as he drew lazy circles over her stomach with his fingers.

His eyes blazed dark as he looked her over from head to toe. She cringed under his assessment and tried to turn away but he held her in place.

"A little late for modesty, don't you think?" His eyebrows arched and the corners of his mouth lifted in a lazy smile.

"I can't help it. You're looking at me."

He nodded, a gleam shining in his emerald eyes. "Yes, I am. This is the first time I've seen you naked, you know."

"Oh." He was right. They had just shared the most intimate of acts, and yet he hadn't really seen all of her, since she had been almost completely covered by water.

"You have an incredible body, Sabrina," he said as he circled one pink nipple with his index finger, grinning as it crinkled and stood up as if reaching for his fingertip, craving that touch once again.

"My hips are too big."

He shook his head and slid his hand from her breasts to her waist and hip. "No, they're perfect. You look like a woman."

"Men like their women skinny," she countered.

His eyes narrowed. "Who told you that?"

"Mark. He watched everything I ate, told me when I gained even a pound, and made sure I stuck to the menu he designed for me." One of the first things she'd done after leaving Mark was eat every single forbidden item she couldn't have while they were married. Subsequently, she gained five pounds almost immediately.

"He lied to you. Your body is perfect. You're a beautiful, desirable woman, Sabrina. And you have a woman's body, all curvy in the right places. Which is what most men want. Your ex was wrong."

Kyle made her feel good about herself, an unknown commodity with Mark, who'd spent years doing the opposite. Sabrina trailed her fingers over his roughened jaw, focusing on his mesmerizing eyes as she threaded her hand into his hair and pulled him down for a kiss.

She sighed contentedly into his mouth as he caressed her lips, touching the tip of his tongue with hers, teasing her, pulling away and smiling before dipping his head again and covering her mouth in a tender assault.

Sabrina reached for him, loving the contrasting feel of his skin, so incredibly soft in some places, hard worked and callused in others. The differing textures thrilled her senses, eliciting jolts of tactile pleasure.

"When I touch you it excites me," she said as he pulled his lips from hers, his intense green eyes magnetic as he studied her.

He shook his head. "You amaze me with your honesty." His hand blazed a hot trail over her collarbone, circling her breasts and curving over her stomach and hips.

Sabrina arched her hips instinctively, beckoning his hands to move lower. "I'm just telling you how I feel," she answered between rapid breaths, his hands performing magic on her body. "I can't help but be honest with you."

His hand stilled on her hip, gently flexing and releasing against her soft flesh. "Speaking of honesty, Sabrina, we need to talk."

He turned away and sat up. Sabrina rose and positioned herself next to him, her knees drawn up to her chest.

"About what?"

"About what we just did." He was looking at the water but turned to face her. "I didn't protect you just now. And I'm so sorry."

She stared at him, confusion muddling her mind. "What do you mean?"

"When we made love, in the water. I didn't use protection." He sighed and pulled both hands through his damp hair as he turned his eyes once more toward the rippling moonlit water. "I've never put a woman in a position like that before. I've always used protection. I don't know what I was thinking."

Protection. Now she understood. "Kyle, it's all right," she said as she touched his shoulder.

"No, it's not. I had it here in my jeans."

"It's all right, really. I understand about diseases, but if you've always used protection before you don't need to worry about it. And as far as me, there was only Mark and he was unnaturally antiseptic about things. I can assure you we're both okay."

His head whipped around, his green eyes full of regret. "I could get you pregnant."

She felt the loss as soon as he spoke the words. The tears threatened and she forced herself to look away. "No, you couldn't."

"You're taking some form of birth control?"

She shook her head.

"Then I don't understand."

Try as she might to avoid it, she was going to have to tell him. "I can't get pregnant, Kyle," she said, trying to keep the misery out of her shaky voice. "I'm incapable of it."

He scanned her face as if he were trying to understand what she had just said. Then the realization hit. "Oh. Damn. Sabrina I'm so sorry," he said as he pulled her toward him, wrapping his arms around her.

He held her like that for a while, both of them silent.

"How do you know you can't?"

Sabrina sighed. "Mark wanted to get me pregnant. And when he couldn't he made me go to the doctor with him. They ran some tests and Mark told me I couldn't have children." She grimaced at the memory. "He was so angry with me about that."

She felt Kyle tense. "He got angry because you were unable to have a baby?"

She nodded.

"What an ass."

She nodded again. "I know. That was the last straw. Him blaming me for my inability to give him a child."

"And what you went through tonight, with Jenna. Knowing..."

"It's okay," she said as she stroked his damp hair. "I've known about this for a long time. And just because someone has a baby doesn't mean I'm going to fall apart."

"It hurt you though, didn't it? I saw it in your eyes, something there, but I didn't know then."

"I said I don't fall apart, I didn't say it doesn't hurt. It will always hurt. I really wanted children, Kyle, more than anything. More than breathing."

He stroked her hair and held her, giving her the solace she had desperately wanted for so long but never got from either Mark or her own mother.

"Thank you," she said as she pulled back and smiled at him.

"For what?"

"For tonight." She motioned toward the lake. "For this, for making love to me, showing me how it could be between a man and a woman."

"My pleasure," he said, his voice deepening as he lay back and pulled her against him, their bodies fitting together intimately, perfectly. "I'll be happy to show you anything you'd like," he added, a wicked gleam in his emerald eyes.

Sabrina laughed as she bent to kiss his full lips. "I think there are many things I'd like to learn about," she said. "I have so many questions, and so much lost time to make up for. Do you think you can spare the time?"

He flipped her over on her back, drawing squeals of laughter from her as he covered her body and kissed her senseless. "You can take the rest of the night, babe."

And she did.

Chapter Twelve

The ropings had paid off. There were more and more participants each week and an equal increase in spectators. And the money they made was phenomenal, as every weekend their income increased until the ranch had banked a considerable amount of money. Enough, in fact, to exist the entire summer without having to raise another dime.

With the money they'd make from the rodeo, the Rocking M would once again be profitable.

Sabrina had more than enough work to handle. Not only was she still learning ranching, she had also taken over the concessions for the ropings since Jenna wasn't quite up to jumping back in yet.

Little Matthew was only four weeks old, but already a ladies man. She had to laugh every time the women fussed over him. Jenna always brought him outside during the ropings and she and the baby would be immediately swamped by auntie and grannie wanna-be's.

Okay, she had to admit she did a little bit of fussing over baby Matthew, too. Who wouldn't? With his round cheeks and big blue eyes he looked like an angel. And she couldn't get enough of him.

"I can't tell you how much I appreciate the break," Jenna said with a delighted sigh as she rested on the front porch swing while Sabrina held Matthew in her arms. "Where would we be without Auntie Sabrina?"

"Are you kidding? I love it." She cuddled the baby close to her, unable to resist pressing a kiss to his chubby little cheeks. He smelled like baby powder and lotion, so sweet it brought tears to her eyes whenever she held him.

"You're not gonna cry *again*, are you?" Jenna rolled her eyes and laughed. "I swear if you tear up every time you hold Matthew I'm not going to let you near him anymore."

She cast Jenna a weepy grin as the baby gurgled at her, blowing spit bubbles from his cherubic lips. "I can't help it. He smells so good—like purity and innocence." She looked up at Jenna. "He's beautiful, Jenna."

Jenna beamed a new mother's grin. "Yeah, he is, isn't he?"

Petunia snorted her agreement, making both the women laugh.

"Ah yes, there's my baby," Sabrina said with a smile as she watched her pig patrol the front porch. Okay, maybe it was a pig, but Sabrina had grown to love her like any pet. Petunia was a constant companion, fairly clean considering she was a pig, and always stayed near Sabrina. Plus she was housebroken—what more could a pet owner ask for? If she couldn't have a baby, then at least she had her pig.

No one knew Sabrina wasn't able to have children. No one except Kyle and he swore he'd never tell. He said she had a right to her privacy and it was her choice who to tell or not.

"You two aren't ogling that kid again, are you?" Kyle walked up behind Sabrina and looked over her shoulder. "You'd think the newness would have worn off by now."

Oh sure, he'd like them to think he wasn't as loopy over the new baby as they were. But he wasn't fooling her. She caught the goofy face he made at the baby over her shoulder.

"Right, Uncle Kyle. Like you have no use for him at all," Jenna said with a laugh as he took the baby from Sabrina.

"Hey, I wasn't finished yet." Sabrina protested Kyle's theft of the baby.

"You're never finished holding him," he answered. "If I don't steal him away from you I'll never get a chance." He turned to her, smiling in a way that said he knew why holding Matthew meant so much to her. She returned the smile, touched by his tender gaze.

The past few weeks had been amazing. Her knowledge of ranching was growing by leaps and bounds, and she was thrilled at the abilities she now possessed. Her confidence soared as her skills increased.

But it wasn't only ranching that had her glowing. It was her relationship with Kyle. They couldn't get enough of each other, stealing away every chance they could to be alone.

Despite his protestations of no involvement, he was as involved with her as she was with him. If they found themselves alone in the barn, he'd grab a quick kiss as soon as he made sure no one was looking. In the kitchen, the family room, out on the trail, anywhere they were by themselves he'd pull her into his arms, kiss her, and if time permitted, make wild, passionate love to her.

They kept their relationship to themselves, not wanting to broadcast it to anyone. The last thing they wanted was for people to think there was something going on between them. Because once her time on the ranch was over, what was happening between them would be over, too. Less messy this way. They'd have nothing to explain to anyone. Plus, Sabrina liked just keeping it between the two of them. More...intimate. A secret romantic relationship. Kind of thrilling, actually.

Okay, maybe for Kyle it was just sex. But for her it was something else. The thrill of a romance, of tender looks and passionate kisses. To her it was love.

She was having the time of her life. And falling hopelessly in love with Kyle in the process. A huge mistake since they had no future together, but she couldn't help herself. What she was going to do when the time came to leave she had no idea, but she wouldn't trade the past couple months with Kyle for anything. She'd leave when it was time—she'd have to, both for her and for him. But she'd leave without regret for having loved him.

Falling in love had been unexpected. After all, he'd made it perfectly clear he was only looking for a sexual relationship with her, and to that she had agreed. But every day they spent together convinced Sabrina her feelings for Kyle were genuine.

Yes, he was grouchy sometimes, and even yelled at her on occasion. Even she was surprised to realize she could hold her own with him and yell right back. Something she'd never have done with Mark. But Kyle allowed it—expected it from her, even. He wasn't outward about it, and never said anything directly, but in his own way he was teaching her to stand up for herself, to never let a man push her around. Including him.

And he could also be tender, loving, romantic, making all her dreams come true. She felt her heart opening moment by moment and couldn't do a damn thing to stop it. Nor did she want to. She'd gone into this with her eyes wide open, and planned to keep them that way.

In the meantime, it was thoroughly enjoyable to be in love.

Now that the rodeo was coming up in less than a week, her excitement level was growing. She had put her plan for the rodeo's success into action. Jenna loved the idea after Sabrina confided in her, and they agreed to keep it a secret from Kyle. Both of them were aware if he knew what Sabrina wanted to do, he'd have said no.

And that would be detrimental to the success of the rodeo.

Entries were already pouring in, and she could see the turnout was going to be much better than she expected. Fortunately, Kyle was too busy preparing the ranch and working with Brady and Luke on the stock to pay much attention to the other details, relying on Sabrina to handle it. She was pleased he put so much confidence in her abilities, considering she'd never done anything like this before.

No one mentioned Jackson Dent's rodeo, and Kyle wanted it that way. He said worrying about it would only distract them from their own event, and there wasn't much they could do about it anyway.

"Are you getting excited about the rodeo?" Jenna asked.

They sat on the swing and watched Kyle walk the length of the long white enclosure holding baby Matthew in his arms, Petunia following closely behind him as he paced back and forth. Apparently the pig had also bonded with Kyle.

"Very. I can't wait, actually," she whispered so Kyle couldn't hear. "Not only for the rodeo itself, but to see his face when he finds out what I did."

Jenna smiled. "You did a great job. Have you seen the list of entrants lately?"

"I did. Much better than I thought. Kyle was very well liked in rodeo, wasn't he?"

"Yes he was. He made a lot of friends when he competed. Nice to see they're all still around."

"What are you two whispering about?" Kyle strode up, crying infant in hand, and handed him over to Jenna. "Matthew is wet. He stinks too." He wrinkled his nose to accentuate the information.

Jenna laughed at his screwed up face. "Oh I see how it is. He's fine as long as he's fed, dry and smells good. But the minute he does anything that requires changing, you get all *single guy* on me."

Kyle nodded and gratefully gave up the smelly baby to Jenna. "You got that right."

Jenna went inside to change Matthew. Kyle sat on the porch swing next to Sabrina, his long legs stretched out in front of him. They both stared ahead at the activity near the corral.

Preparations for the rodeo were creating a bustle of activity at the ranch, much more than usual business. The extra horses and cattle that had been purchased were being brought in, along with the Rocking M's bulls.

"I'd love to fuck you right now," Kyle said quietly without looking at her.

Sabrina's body heated, the flush of arousal instantaneous. "That would be nice," she replied without glancing in his direction. "Think you could get around to that sometime soon?"

"Oh, I'm sure I can break free at some point today."

He rested his hand on the seat of the swing, his fingers lightly touching hers. She inhaled sharply, the slightest touch of his body to hers causing tingling sensations all the way to her toes. "I want you, Kyle."

He sighed heavily. "You drive me crazy, do you know that? I'm hard."

She risked a glance in his direction, watching the rise and fall of his chest as he circled her fingers. A glance further south showed his growing erection. He laid his other hand in his lap. She grinned. "I hope so. I hope I make you want me as much as I want you."

"You're slowly killing me is what you're doing," he replied as he turned his head toward her.

His eyes were dark with desire, a look she was getting used to seeing. She couldn't get enough of him. No matter how many times they touched, or kissed, or made love, it wasn't enough.

"Then I'll make sure you die happy." She slipped her hand out from under his and rose from the swing. "I have something in mind for

189

later, if you can manage to catch up with me," she said with a half-smile.

"You can bet I'll manage," he said, the intimate promise reflected in his intense gaze heating through her. "Now get out of here. I have to sit and do some cattle counting or something until I'm fit to join the others."

Snorting, she headed into the office to busy herself with preparations for the rodeo. She needed to stay focused, stay active, until she could be alone with Kyle.

ço   ço   ço

What a long day. He was tired, sore and sweaty. And needed a shower badly.

As he stepped inside the house, the cool air conditioning gave a welcome relief from the oppressive heat he'd worked in all day.

Ignoring the disappointment he felt when he didn't find Sabrina waiting for him, he headed to the refrigerator for a cold drink. Over the past few weeks they'd developed a routine. At the end of each day he'd head into the house and would always find her waiting for him in the kitchen, something cold for him to drink in her hand. They'd move to the family room, curl up together on the sofa and talk about the day. One thing would lead into another, and soon they'd be making love.

Brady must be aware of what was going on between them, because he rarely spent the night in the house anymore. Although he never mentioned it to Kyle, and Kyle certainly didn't volunteer that he and Sabrina were lovers. Brady claimed his absence from the house was due to being busy with the horses, or some hot poker tournament going on in the clubhouse, but Kyle knew better. He was giving them time alone.

Either way, he was grateful. There wasn't enough time in the day to be alone with Sabrina.

He fixed a glass of iced tea, then started turning out the lights downstairs. Sabrina must have gone to bed early. Trying to force the disappointment from his mind, he headed up the stairs.

She did look kind of pale and tired today, and he wondered if she was working herself too hard. Not only had she taken over Jenna's duties at the ropings, but she was also knee-deep involved in the rodeo, and wouldn't let anyone help her with the paperwork and dealing with the entries.

Kyle was so busy practicing for the rodeo events while still trying to run the ranch he hadn't had time to argue with her about taking on too much. Maybe after he took a shower he'd knock on her door and they could talk.

Talk. Yeah right. Like he really wanted to talk to her. What he really wanted to do was walk through her door, strip her clothes off and kiss every inch of her beautiful body. Then lose himself in her until they were both so exhausted they passed out, wrapped in each other's arms.

But what he should do is let her rest tonight. She looked like she needed it.

Once in his room he immediately stripped off his grimy clothes. He was so deep in thought when he entered the room he hadn't heard the noise coming from the bathroom. That was odd—his shower was running.

As he opened the door to his bathroom he was greeted by a cloud of steam so thick he couldn't see more than a few inches in front of his face. And not only was his shower running, but the closer he got to the oversized glass door the more he realized there was someone inside the shower.

And that someone was humming in a decidedly feminine voice.

Kyle opened the door and his most vivid fantasy came to life. An incredibly beautiful naked woman with streaming blonde hair turned to face him, a sultry smile and invitation spread over her face. Warm amber eyes gleamed brightly with desire as she beckoned to him with her crooked finger.

"Need a shower?" she asked with a devilish wink and an arched brow as she looked him over appreciatively from head to toe. Her blatant appraisal of his body started adrenaline pumping through Kyle's body. He stepped inside the tile and glass enclosure and shut the door.

"As a matter of fact I do. I'm filthy, sweaty, and sore."

Sabrina pursed her lips. "Aww, poor baby. Let me help you wash the dirt and sweat off." Rather than grabbing a washcloth or nearby sponge, she poured liquid soap into her hands and rubbed them together until a thick lather formed. "Turn around," she commanded.

His balls began to throb. Kyle did as he was told, presenting her with his back as he leaned his hands against the cool tile wall. He sighed deeply at the first touch of her slick, soapy hands. She spread the lather from the top of his shoulders to the lower part of his back, kneading his tired muscles in the process. Kyle groaned as she worked out the tougher kinks with her thumbs and fingers.

After she finished with his back, she soaped her hands again and moved down his body. He shuddered at the feel of her silky hands on his ass. Her murmurs of delight only made standing there, unmoving, harder. And that wasn't the only thing that was hard. His cock stood up, clamoring for the feel of her sweet hands.

"Now face me," she said in a throaty voice that sent thrills of anticipation through him.

He turned and smiled as her eyes gravitated over his chest, stomach, and lower, then quickly flew up to meet his. She grinned but didn't say a word, pouring more soap onto her hands.

She laid her hands on his shoulders, spreading the soap over his upper body from chest to stomach in agonizingly thorough circular motions. Her fingertips were light and gentle, weaving feathery trails through the soapy lather. She threaded her fingers in the curling hair on his chest, lightly scraping his skin with her nails. His breath caught and he inhaled sharply as jolts of desire traveled through him.

He prayed this torture would end soon so he could pull her close, kiss her mindless, then carry her out of the shower and make love to her.

He was wrong. The torment continued.

Her eyes never left his as she took the shower nozzle off the wall and rinsed his chest. Then she grabbed the soap and dropped to her knees in front of him.

He hissed as she soaped the most intimate parts of him, gently and thoroughly until he was pulsing in her hands. Bracing his palms on the wall of the shower, he gritted his teeth and mentally prayed for mercy. The look of delight on her face was agony to him as he struggled to maintain composure while this sensuous nymph worked magic with her hands, stroking forward, then back, her fists priming his balls every time she touched them. He could come so easily, could shoot a hot load right there. But he wanted it inside her, wanted to feel her sweet pussy gripping him when he came.

"Oh God babe, please." He didn't even know what to beg for other than sweet release.

"Your wish is my command," she said with a husky voice as she rinsed him. But instead of rising and stepping into his arms, she placed her hands on his hips and placed a kiss at the juncture of his thighs.

He was speechless. He could only watch as she lowered her mouth over him. His breath rasped raggedly as she teased him, tasted him, tortured him, her movements slow and thorough until he was certain his knees would buckle. Watching her lips slide over his shaft, the way her tongue darted out licking the drops of pre-come off his cockhead. She cradled his balls in her hands and squeezed, then engulfed his shaft with her mouth. The heat and moisture burned him alive.

He couldn't take any more. He turned off the shower, reached down to pull her up and swooped her into his arms, stepping out. Grabbing an oversized towel he carried her to his bed.

"The sheets will get soaked," she protested as he laid her on the bed.

"I don't give a shit," he replied as he lowered himself on top of her.

She kissed him with such open desire it was almost painful. Never before had a woman opened herself up to him, letting him in completely. She pleased him in ways no woman before her ever had. Undoubtedly no one ever would again.

He roamed aimlessly over her body, driven to explore. At times like this he wished he had ten hands because he didn't know what part of her to touch next, and hated leaving an inch of her undiscovered. His hands and mouth covered her as he trailed his fingers over her swollen breasts and nipples, rolling them between his fingers until they hardened and she was gasping with desire.

"Please, oh God, please," she begged.

His mouth formed a half smile. "Not yet." He had more exploration to do. He teased her erect nipples with his tongue, alternating between both until she turned her head from side to side, delirious with pleasure.

"Now, Kyle," she demanded again.

"Soon. I'm not finished here." He wanted to please her like she pleased him. Or did he just want to return the torture?

Trailing a line of soft kisses over her stomach, he paused when he reached her thighs. She raised her head and watched him, curiosity and desire mixing on her heated face. He smiled at her, then bent his head and kissed the soft curls nestled between her thighs.

Her mouth opened in a loud moan as she grasped his head, throwing her head back as he licked her clit, lapping the bud with rhythmic strokes until she was writhing beneath him.

When he was certain she was ready to explode, he sat back on his haunches and grasped her hands, pulling her astride him. She twined her arms around his neck and kissed him deeply as he slowly entered her. She pulled her mouth away from his, her gaze locked on him as he slid his cock to the hilt inside her. Her eyes were pools of liquid amber, on fire with her arousal.

God, he loved seeing her turned on like this. The innocence fled, replaced instead with a hot woman demanding her pleasure.

"Fuck me, Sabrina. Take what you want."

The tempo was swift as she rode him, not once stopping to catch her breath as she sought her release. Her breath came out in short, gasping pants as she rocked her pussy, grinding against his pelvis. He let her have her way, let her take them both where she needed to go. When she climaxed, her eyes widened and teared up. She cried out her ecstasy, then dragged her lips over his for a passionate kiss that tore him apart. Unable to hold back, he surged forward and let go, groaning against her mouth and spilling inside her with a forceful shudder.

She made him shake, damn her. The things this woman did to him scared the shit out of him.

Sometimes he had to remind himself he was just in it for the sex and nothing more. But Sabrina made it damned difficult to remember that.

He lay back on the bed, pulling her next to him, her head on his shoulder. He caressed her back and damp hair, kissing her forehead.

"Always wanted to find a beautiful woman in my shower," he whispered against her ear.

Sabrina giggled. "To be honest, I had that fantasy my first night at the ranch."

"You did?" Kyle pulled back and looked at her, her easy smile relaxing him like nothing ever could. In her arms, he had found a peace and contentment he hadn't known existed.

"Yes I did. Of course I was embarrassed by it then, since I'd never had a fantasy in my life, and here I was, having just met you, and experiencing this full-blown, vivid, sexual daydream about lathering your body up in the shower."

"You never had a fantasy before?"

She stroked his chest while she spoke, winding her fingers in the curling hairs. "No. Silly, huh? But like I told you there was no one before Mark, and with him—well, he wasn't the kind of guy a woman would fantasize about." She laughed. "At least not *this* woman." She turned and leaned on her elbows, kissing his neck, rekindled desire evident in her blazing amber eyes. "You, on the other hand, are every woman's fantasy. Especially this woman."

"Hmm," he said as he pulled her on top of him, drawing her face to his for a kiss. "Perhaps we should explore some of your other fantasies."

Wicked delight shooting from her eyes, she nodded. "Perhaps we should."

It was some time later that Kyle lay awake, holding a slumbering Sabrina in his arms.

She was a constant surprise to him. Such innocence, so naïve, and yet so incredibly expressive—no holds barred, honest passion. She couldn't be coy or insincere if her life depended on it. What you saw was what you got.

And he liked what he saw. And he knew he was damn lucky to have her, even for a while.

He pulled the covers over her bare shoulders as she shivered and scooted closer against his body for warmth. He wrapped both arms around her and never wanted to let go.

He loved her.

God, what a revelation to have at three o'clock in the morning. He was in love with Sabrina. Truth be told, who wouldn't be? She was beautiful and intelligent, full of compassion and warmth and it was clear she had a wealth of love to give the right person.

But Kyle wasn't the right person. Not for her—maybe not for anybody. He'd failed to make his marriage to Amanda work, and so far he hadn't done a great job making the Rocking M successful either. He had too many scars and regrets, too much anger and frustration inside him to make a good husband to Sabrina. Because of what she went through with her first husband, she deserved the right one next time.

Besides, she was excited about starting her new life. She craved independence—wanted to do it her way, and all alone. They'd talked a lot about that in the past couple months. Sabrina had something to prove, at least to herself. That she could stand on her own two feet and make a success of her life without anyone's help.

And there was no way Kyle would interfere in that. He may love her, but she didn't need to know that. And it may kill him when she left, but he'd never let her see it. When it was time for her to leave, strike out on her own and start her new life, he wouldn't stand in her way.

In the meantime, with the time they had left, he'd love her with all he had.

After she was gone, he'd pick up the pieces and go back to the way he was before she got here.

Miserable, frustrated, and alone.

Chapter Thirteen

Sabrina was certain the nausea overwhelming her for the past few days was due to her excitement about the rodeo. It absolutely couldn't be some kind of flu bug because she didn't have time to be sick. Today was the rodeo.

After pressing a cold washcloth to her sweating face and neck, she started into her bedroom to dress but was overcome by a wave of dizziness that threatened to drop her to her knees. Fortunately she made it to the bed before she completely lost it.

"Sabrina? Can I come in?" Jenna whispered on the other side of the door. Sabrina looked at the clock and saw it was only six thirty in the morning, so she wasn't late yet.

"Sure," she managed weakly, unable to stand and open the door for her friend.

Jenna walked in with a big smile. "Hey. You're not ready yet? Let's get going, you lazy bum," she said as she rounded the bed and stood in front of Sabrina. "Oh my, you look pale. Are you all right?" Her smile faded to one of concern as she felt Sabrina's forehead.

"I'm fine. Just a bout of nervousness I think."

Jenna assessed her with furrowed brows. "Looks like more than nervousness if you ask me."

She groaned and dropped her head to her hands. Just what she didn't need today.

"Please tell me there's no flu going around. This can't be happening to me."

"How long have you been feeling like this?" Jenna asked as she sat on the bed next to Sabrina.

"About a week, I think."

"Hmm. Have you been throwing up?"

"A little."

"I see."

After a moment of silence, Sabrina lifted her head and looked at Jenna. "The flu you think?"

A slight smile curved the corners of Jenna's mouth. "Maybe. When are you throwing up?"

"In the mornings, mostly. Then I feel better for a while until late afternoon when the nausea hits again. But mostly I'm just dead tired lately. No matter how much sleep I get I can't seem to get ahead of it."

Jenna took the washcloth from her hands. "I need to ask you a question," she said from the bathroom.

"Shoot," Sabrina said, grateful the nausea was beginning to subside.

Jenna returned to the bedroom and instructed Sabrina to drop her head to her chest. Then she placed the cold cloth over the back of Sabrina's neck.

"When was your last period?"

"I don't know." She'd never been good at tracking them anyway, and was so busy the past few months she didn't keep track at all. "It's been a while. I think."

"How long a while?"

Sabrina tried to gather her scattered thoughts and remember. The last time she had one was...well longer than usual, that's for sure. "I think it was at the end of April, not too long after I got here." Removing the cloth from the back of her neck, she looked up. "Why?"

Jenna crossed her arms in front of her. "You don't have a fever and you feel bad then good then bad again so it can't be the flu because you'd feel bad all the time for a couple days and then it would be over. And you're tired all the time. Are your breasts sore?

Come to think of it they had been sore. Probably because her period was all screwed up. "Yes, they have been."

"It's pretty obvious don't you think?"

Not to her. "What's pretty obvious?"

Jenna rolled her eyes. "Sabrina, you're pregnant."

Boy, Jenna was way off base on that one. "No, I'm not." How many times over the years had she wished for it, hoped for it? Only to break her heart over and over again when she realized it wasn't going to happen. Ever.

"You can deny it all you want, but the signs are there. It's been about six weeks since your last period, you have morning sickness and you're drop dead tired. Sounds like first trimester of pregnancy— believe me, I know. I just lived it, remember?"

If only it were true. But it wasn't, could never be. "I can't be pregnant, Jenna."

A smug smile crossed her features. "Why is that?"

She took a huge breath to clear her head. "Because I'm unable to conceive."

The smile left Jenna's face, replaced by a curious frown. "Are you sure?"

She nodded. "My ex-husband took me for tests and we found out I would never be able to have children."

"Fertility tests?"

"Yes. All of them."

"Did you get a second opinion?"

"It wasn't necessary. We went to the best fertility specialist in the country. We were certain, believe me."

Jenna thought for a moment. "Hang out here for a minute. I'll be right back."

"I'm fine now, really. You don't need to come back."

"Indulge me, okay? I'll be back in less than five minutes."

Sabrina managed to dress and comb her hair in the time Jenna was gone. She felt better already, and almost laughed at Jenna's absurd assumption she was pregnant. It was obviously some kind of bug or just an extreme case of nerves. Which would also explain the delayed period.

True to her word, Jenna was back in less than five minutes, carrying a box with her. "I had this at home because I bought an extra when I wasn't sure. It hasn't expired yet, so I want you to take this test."

She handed the blue and white box to Sabrina, who examined the label, her eyes widening as she read the box.

"This is a pregnancy test."

"As a matter of fact it is."

"Jenna, I already told you I can't—"

"I know what you told me, but I want you to take it anyway. Even if you think it's a waste of time, do it for me. Please?"

If she'd learned one thing in the past couple months, it was not to argue with Jenna when she had "that look". Nobody won an argument with her when she stared you down that way.

And if she planned on arguing, they'd both be late and today was not a day to be late. Her mind was already full of things she had to do before everyone arrived.

"Fine. I'll be right back. But this is stupid."

She went into the bathroom and read the box wistfully, foolishly hoping the test would come out positive. But she'd long ago given up hoping for miracles. She thought about just telling Jenna she took the test, but then shrugged and did it anyway.

Sabrina walked out with the stick held out in front of her. She hadn't even bothered to look at the results, since she already knew what it would say.

"Here," she said as she handed it to Jenna. "I told you so."

Jenna looked down at the test and then up at Sabrina, a smug look on her face. "No, honey, I told *you* so." Jenna returned the test to Sabrina.

She blinked as she looked at it. Once. Twice. There, as clear as day, was a plus sign. Positive. Her eyes met Jenna's. "This isn't right. It's a mistake."

"Those things are ninety-nine percent accurate. They don't make mistakes. Sabrina, you're pregnant."

You're pregnant. The very words she was convinced she'd never hear sent chills coursing through her body. Suddenly it all made sense. The sickness in the morning, the tiredness. The soreness in her breasts she had been feeling but hadn't paid much attention to. All were clearly signs of pregnancy.

Her legs shook and she struggled to breathe normally as tears blinded her. She plopped down on the bed before she collapsed. "I can't believe this."

Jenna held her hand. "Whoever said you couldn't conceive lied, Sabrina. Or your fertility test results got mixed up somehow. Because you sure as hell are pregnant."

The truth slammed into her like a charging bull. Mark. He'd lied to her. She'd bet her last dime Mark was the one who wasn't able to produce children, and he had turned it around to make her at fault. Anger like she had never felt before flooded through her veins.

"My ex-husband told me I couldn't have children. No wonder he went to the doctor alone to get the results. He wouldn't let me go with him. That rotten bastard lied to me." She looked up at Jenna through the tears. "How could he do this to me? How could he tell me something so devastating, something that hurt me so much for so many years? Do you know how much I wanted to have children?"

Jenna nodded. "I've seen you with Matthew. I know what he means to you." She stroked Sabrina's hair. "Don't think about him, Sabrina. You can't do anything to change what he did to you."

Easy to say, hard to do. Fury bubbled up inside her, a hatred so deep for her ex-husband it threatened to blind her. He'd done many things to her during their marriage. Things she had chalked up to her own stupidity for allowing them. But this. This was the worst. No one had the right to hurt her like he had.

"You're mad as hell aren't you?"

She tried to focus on Jenna through the rage. "That's an understatement. I've never been this pissed off, or felt more powerless. He hurt me more with this than he ever had before. And the worst thing is, there's nothing I can do about it now."

"Isn't there?" Jenna smiled triumphantly. "Don't you think this is the ultimate revenge? You've already gotten back at him, Sabrina. You've created a child. That's something he'll never be able to do."

She pondered what Jenna said. As she wiped the tears away, her world suddenly brightened. "You're right. I'm going to have a child— something that's a part of me. He can't take that away from me, he can't diminish it in any way. This baby is mine, half of everything I am. And he'll never, ever know that feeling." She suddenly felt a lot better, the deep hurt and anger fading somewhat, but not completely. She made a mental note to make sure some how, some way, Mark found out she conceived a child.

"Now that we've settled that, I'm guessing the other half of that baby you're carrying is my future niece or nephew?"

Sabrina's eyes widened as her hand flew to her mouth. "Oh my God, you're right. This is Kyle's baby—Jenna I'm having Kyle's baby." The chills she felt earlier returned as she thought of the child she carried, a result of her love for Kyle.

"That's not a surprise to me, or anyone else around here," Jenna said with a teasing smile. "You two have been mooning over each other for more than a month now."

"You noticed? We tried to keep it a secret."

Jenna snorted. "Right. A secret? Come on, Sabrina. It was so obvious to everyone the two of you couldn't take your eyes off each other. Or your hands and other body parts obviously," she said with a wink and a nudge of her shoulder.

Try as she might to be embarrassed, Sabrina couldn't muster even the slightest blush. "Well, so much for being low key," she said with a satisfied smile and a shrug.

"So. Now what?"

Now what indeed. A little later she headed downstairs to begin her duties for the eventful day. Her head was spinning in so many directions she didn't know where to start.

Just dealing with the fact she was pregnant would have filled a normal day. Couple that with needing to tell Kyle they were going to have a baby, and finding the right time to tell him amidst the chaos that would surely arrive in less than a half hour and she was more than overwhelmed.

After grabbing a glass of juice she walked outside to determine where to start. The day had dawned with a bright orange sun, the blue skies clear and without a single cloud. And it was already warm. The temperature was sure to bake the participants in the rodeo today. The dusty ground already felt heated under her feet. Temperatures hadn't cooled down much overnight, a sure sign it was going to be a blistering hot day.

Better to wait until after the rodeo to tell him. She wanted to set the scene, make sure they were alone so she would have his complete attention. She couldn't wait to see the look in his eyes when she told him he was going to be a father. That they had made a baby together. But not before the rodeo. There were already people arriving on the ranch, and she didn't want Kyle distracted with that not-so-little piece of news while he was trying to compete. Besides, she already had one surprise lined up for him today, in fact a few of those surprises would be showing up any minute now. She'd let the really big news wait until later tonight.

Damn. It was hot already and the sun had barely risen. Kyle wiped the sweat from his brow as he prepared the horses and tack for the day's events.

It was hard as hell to pull away from Sabrina's warmth well before dawn, but he forced himself to choose the rodeo over pulling her naked body under him and waking her with a soft kiss and some gentle lovemaking.

She'd be mad at him for not waking her, but she really needed some sleep. He noticed she hadn't been feeling well the past few days, and he wanted her to get some rest before the day started. She was overworking herself, and with it being so hot lately he didn't want her to suffer heat exhaustion in the middle of the rodeo.

As he dressed and went downstairs to brew a pot of coffee, he wondered exactly when he had fallen in love with his partner. The first time they argued, that mixture of never before expressed indignation and pure innocence on her face? When he massaged her beautiful body after her first riding lesson? Or when they argued in the barn and he kissed her. Maybe it was when they made love in the warm lake water.

No. He knew when it was. When he first saw her, he was mesmerized by her beauty, her nervousness, and her guts. He remembered then thinking she was trouble. He was right. Since that first day everything about her had troubled him. Despite his upfront honesty about keeping things purely physical between them, he had gone ahead and lost his heart to her. And his mind in the process.

Today was the rodeo, he had a million things to do, and absolutely no time to stand around mooning over Sabrina.

"So who are the cow eyes for, wild man?"

Kyle whirled at the familiar voice. His eyes widened as he recognized Joey Lantin, one of his former rodeo buddies from the professional days. "What the hell are you doing here?"

Joey grinned, clear blue eyes glittering brightly in the morning sun. "Getting ready to kick your butt in your own rodeo. What do you think I'm doing here?"

"I don't think so, Lantin. If there's any butt kicking to be done, it'll be done by me." Another professional rider, Marsh Sampson's booming voice was unmistakable. Thick and muscular, he looked more like a wrestler than a cowboy. "Damn, Morgan, ranch life looks to be about killing you. You look old and worn out," he said with a wink.

"Yeah. Hard to believe he's lost the boyish looks that used to draw the ladies." A third of the top competing rodeo stars in the business stood next to the other two. Rod Thomas was short and wiry, and could ride a bull like nobody's business.

"I can't believe you're all here," Kyle said as he shook hands with his friends. "Damn, it's been years, hasn't it?"

"Sure has," Joey said. "We thought you'd be back after you got things settled here. Must have found something to keep you at the ranch."

Yeah. Near bankruptcy almost costing his family their ranch. "Just been busy," he said as he looked over his friends. "Are you all really going to compete here today?"

"Sure," Marsh said with a smile, a piece of straw tucked neatly between the top and bottom row of teeth. "Should be easy money for us, considering there's no competition here."

Kyle didn't know how or why three of the best competitors in professional rodeo were competing in a small circuit event on the Rocking M, but he was damn glad to see them. He grinned at all three as his long lost competitive spirit resurfaced with a vengeance. "We'll see about that, guys. We'll see."

The crowds in attendance exceeded everyone's expectations. The additional bleachers they'd brought in for the rodeo were full, every available space was occupied, and anyone who didn't get a seat was milling around trying to seek out a viewable location.

Sabrina milled through the crowds, smiling at people she already knew and introducing herself to those she didn't. From the conversations she'd had this morning, people had come from over a hundred miles away to either participate in or watch the rodeo. And they told her it was because some of the big names in rodeo were here, both past and present.

How they'd managed to keep that information from Kyle was beyond her capacity to understand. She chalked it up to him being busy and preoccupied both with the rodeo and with her, and silently thanked the heavens for divine intervention. Kyle hadn't found out what she'd done.

She couldn't help but grin like a Cheshire cat. Her plan had worked, beyond anything she had dreamed. Not only had professional rodeo cowboys come through and shown up, but some pretty big corporate sponsors had put up prizes for the winners once they discovered some of their spokesmen were coming to this little rodeo in the middle of nowhere.

And one thing she learned was that word got out fast around rodeo. Once they started spreading the news, it blew through Oklahoma and the surrounding states like a brushfire in a drought-ridden forest.

Not only could amateur riders compete alongside the best in professional rodeo, but people coming to watch could see the cream of the crop for less than half the price of a ticket to a big professional event.

It was going to be a great day. With the best yet to come tonight. When she had the father of her child alone at last.

The father of her child. The hairs rose on the back of her neck. In some ways the fact she really was pregnant hadn't soaked in yet—she couldn't really believe it was true. But it was.

She was dying to tell Kyle. But like she told Jenna this morning, she wanted to wait until the time was right to tell him. Jenna swore she wouldn't breathe a word of it to anyone until Sabrina told her that Kyle knew.

Speaking of Jenna, she was in her element, supervising a couple of the local high school girls they employed to run the food and drink stands. A line ten people deep kept the girls busy, and Jenna looked pleased as she could be while giving instructions and smiling at the patrons.

"Where's Matthew?" Sabrina asked as she walked behind the counter.

"In the house. Maylene Davis is sitting with him while he naps. Good thing too, since it's way too hot out here today for him." Jenna wiped sweat from the back of her neck as she opened another box of cups to place under the counter. "We're selling drinks as fast as Ashley and Megan can put them out there."

"That's good news," Sabrina answered as she bent to help Jenna. "Everything seems to be going well so far."

"Yeah. Thanks to you and your great ideas. I don't know how we could have done all this without you. You have such wonderful organizational skills." Jenna leaned back and stretched. "You put all of this together in such a short period of time. I could never have done it all."

Sabrina grinned. "You were a little too busy doing other things to think about all this, don't you think?"

"Maybe you're right about that. But still—take a bow. You deserve it. And my family will be forever in your debt. With the word out about the stock available for lease at the Rocking M, we'll make plenty of money to keep this ranch afloat for many years."

Sabrina breathed deeply to quell the threatening tears. All she wanted was to help the Morgan family save the ranch. If things worked out like she hoped, she could leave knowing she had done the best she could to insure their future.

Leave. She'd be leaving soon. Or would she? Thoughts about leaving, about her pregnancy and what it would mean for her and Kyle, ran rampant through her mind despite her best efforts to put them aside for now.

Yes, she had a million questions. But until she and Kyle could talk, there would be no answers. Now was the time to think about the rodeo.

"I think I'll head over to the arena and see what's going on. Will you be all right here or would you like me to stay and help?"

Jenna shooed her away. "I've seen hundreds of rodeos, and I'll take some time to peek when I can. The girls and I have it covered here. Go. Enjoy."

She didn't need to be told twice. She was itching with excitement to grab a spot where she could see and watch the rodeo. Her heart raced in anticipation of fulfilling yet another one of her dreams. Another realization of something she had always wanted, but had been denied.

"Need me to help you find a spot so you can see?" Brady nudged his horse alongside her as she walked. A beautiful caramel and white Paint, Sabrina had named the horse Crazy, more so for his owner, she thought, than the horse himself.

"I don't think there's a spot left," Sabrina said with a smile, disappointed she wouldn't get a ringside seat, but thrilled nonetheless at the size of the crowd. "I might have to grab a pair of binoculars and climb up on the roof."

Brady laughed at her. "No you won't, honey." He held out his hand as he had with Emma not too long ago. "Climb aboard—I'll find you a spot."

As she grabbed Brady's hand and climbed up on his lap in the saddle, Sabrina remembered a few short months ago she had never even seen a horse up close, let alone ridden one. Now she rode almost daily, with confidence and a never-ending feeling of joy and freedom as soon as she mounted one of the beautiful creatures owned by the Rocking M. How much her life had changed.

Brady rode behind the seating area reserved for the competitors. He held Crazy still as she dismounted. "Have a seat over there—you'll be closer to the action than any of the people who paid for their tickets. I gotta run and get ready for my event. Kyle and I have to seriously whoop some ass in team roping." He winked at her and rode away.

She hadn't met any of the men she invited to attend the rodeo, but she knew them from their pictures on the professional rodeo website she searched while looking for competitors for the Rocking M's event.

"Come on up here, darlin', we'll make room for you." A big bear of a man held out his hand and helped her onto the bleachers, yelling at the young cowboys sitting in the first row. "Lady here, you lazy good for nothing cowpokes. Scoot yer as...er...rear ends over and let her take a seat." After she settled in, he sat his massive frame next to her. "It's about time I had something to look at around here besides a bunch of ugly, smelly cowboys." He tipped his hat and introduced himself as Marsh Sampson.

"So you're the girl with the pretty voice who invited us all here," he said with a grin. He introduced her to the rest of professional rodeo's finest. Almost everyone she'd invited had shown up. She was overwhelmed by the friendship these men felt for Kyle. When she told them he needed them here, not one of them hesitated before saying they'd come.

She met both professional and amateur rodeo cowboys, a nicer group of men she'd never met before. Sabrina thought with some satisfaction that despite the education and money all of Mark's friends and associates had, she had never been as comfortable with any of them as she immediately was with this down-to-earth group of horse and bull riders.

She had never been happier in her life.

One by one the events took place. She cheered and gasped along with the crowd as participants rode like a gusting wind, threw a rope like an arc of lightning, maintained their balance on a bucking horse or angry bull, and sometimes fell with a thud, raising a cloud of dust so thick you had to wait for it to clear to see if the rider would get up or not.

Every time an event came up in which Kyle participated, she watched in total amazement as he mastered it. He won almost every event in which he competed. Somehow she wasn't surprised.

His friends won a few events too, as did some of the circuit competitors, which made for a very exciting rodeo. No one came away disappointed as prizes and prize money were handed out at the end.

With a contented sigh, Sabrina rose from the bleachers. The dust had long settled and the crowd spilled out of the bleachers in search of a last drink or hot dog before the long ride home. The sun had begun to descend toward the treetops, its fiery hot glow shimmering like laser beams through the thick branches.

It had been an incredible day, and not one she'd soon forget. Now she had to wrap things up so she could spend some time with Kyle. Between catching up with his old friends and participating in the rodeo, they hadn't done more than glance and smile at each other the entire day. She was anxious to get to him, but first there was work to be done.

In a minute. As soon as the sun sank below the trees, as soon as she visually inhaled once more the picturesque beauty of a dusty golden sunset over the Rocking M's first rodeo.

"I've missed you."

She turned her head and smiled at the man she loved. "I've missed you too. You were wonderful today."

He smiled back, his full lips curving in genuine pleasure. "I had a good time. It was a great day, and the Rocking M made a ton of money. I can't believe how it turned out."

"I can. I told you people would come, Kyle. I told you this rodeo would be a success. I can't imagine there's a soul within a hundred miles who went to Jackson Dent's rodeo today."

"We're about to find out," he said as his eyes narrowed at the approach of his nemesis.

Dent stormed up to them, hands fisted at his sides. Kyle smiled benignly. "Aren't you supposed to be busy at your own rodeo today?"

"You know damn well almost no one showed up at my rodeo," Dent said. "You invited all your professional pals to yours, and everyone wanted to come here to see them instead. Do you know how much money I lost today because of you?"

Kyle affected a look of mock regret. "Gee, that breaks my heart. Guess that means you won't be trying to buy the Rocking M, then, doesn't it?"

"I'll still get this ranch, you'll see."

Kyle brushed dirt off the sleeve of his shirt, shrugging off Dent's warning. "Your threats don't mean a damn thing to me anymore, Dent. You're nothing more than a blowing tumbleweed across my property. So why don't you just blow back on out the same way you came in?"

"I'll beat you yet, Morgan. I took your wife and a third of your money along with her. Soon enough I'll have your ranch too."

Sabrina watched the interplay, noticing the tic forming at the side of Kyle's mouth. She hoped they wouldn't come to blows and end up spoiling what so far had been a perfect day.

Kyle advanced on Dent, causing the man to back up a few steps. He grabbed hold of Dent's shirtfront and held on with his fist. "Let me make this as clear as I can. You didn't take my wife, I let her go. As soon as you put your hands on her she was worthless to me. Actually even before then, and you can feel free to tell her that. And if it took some of our money to get her off my hands and into yours, that's fine with me."

Sabrina smiled as she listened to Kyle give Dent what she knew was well deserved. The man had been a prickly thorn as long as she'd been on the Rocking M. Frankly, she didn't know what kept Kyle from knocking the man out.

"And another thing," Kyle added. "You didn't best me today like you thought you would. You've never been able to. Not when we were kids, not when we entered rodeo competitions, and sure as hell not now."

Dent paled at Kyle's words. "I will, Morgan. Someday, somehow, I'll take this ranch from you."

She shook her head, almost pitying Jackson Dent. He was one of those people who would never be happy, never be satisfied. Always comparing himself to someone else and coming up short. And of course since the object of his comparison was Kyle, in her opinion he'd never win.

Kyle released his hold on Dent's shirt and pushed him away with the palm of his hand. "I'm tired of playing this game with you, Dent. Get off my property now or I will personally throw you off. And if you come back again, I'll take out my shotgun and shoot you as a trespasser."

The tone of his last statement carried a threat no sane man would ignore. Apparently Dent had some sanity within him because he straightened his shirt, turned quickly on one booted heel and stomped away.

"About time you shut that slime ball up," she said as she threw her arms around him.

Kyle's face changed instantly from anger to a smile as he pressed a kiss to her forehead. "He's all talk and no action. Always has been, always will be."

"You're certainly not," she said with a grin.

He removed his cowboy hat, his hair and face soaked with sweat, dirt streaks like painted stripes smudged along his tanned face. He'd never looked more appealing to her.

"I need a shower. Care to join me?" His eyes held a promise of more than just cleanliness if she took him up on his offer.

"Mmm, I'd be delighted to scrub your back for you."

"Good." He dipped his head for a light kiss. "I've been thinking about your hands all day," he said as he pulled a wisp of hair from her ponytail. "And your mouth, and your—"

The sound of a clearing throat interrupted Kyle's next words. They both turned to see Kyle's friends with gear in hand and grins bigger than their faces could hold.

"I see we interrupted," Joey said without apology. "You didn't tell us this lovely lady was yours," he said motioning to Sabrina.

"Now we're all so devastated she's taken we'll have to leave and drown our sorrows in town." Rod threw his arms around the men on either side of him. "I, of course, will get lucky tonight, as usual."

Kyle laughed. "You usually do," he said with a grin. "You're more than welcome to stay the night if you'd like."

"Nah, we gotta get on the road," Marsh replied. "Have to be in Denver by Tuesday." He held out his hand to Sabrina. "Glad to meet you, ma'am," he said.

"Same here," she replied. "I'm so glad all of you could come."

"How could we not come, considering your request was so sweet, and your SOS about Kyle needing our help so convincing," Marsh added.

Joey and Rod shook her hand as well and thanked her for inviting them to the Rocking M's rodeo.

"If you do it again next year, let us know. We had a hell of a time."

They said their goodbyes and walked away. Contented and happy, she turned to the man she loved.

And came face to face with the angriest man she had ever set eyes on. His face changed before her eyes—the loving looks replaced by a mask of rage and fury.

"Just what do you think gives you the right to manipulate my life like this? Who the hell do you think you are?"

Chapter Fourteen

Uh-oh. Sabrina had seen that look all too often the past few months.

"*You* invited them here." His eyes blazed with anger as he advanced on her.

She wiped her hands on her denim shorts, prepared for an argument she really didn't want to have with him. "Yes, I did but—"

"You asked my friends to come save my ranch? To save me? Who the hell gave you the authority to do that?"

"I was trying to help." She'd never seen him this angry. Not even at Jackson Dent. She backed away, not wanting to confront this side of him, not prepared for his reaction.

"Do you know how embarrassing that was for me? To find out you called my friends and begged them to help me?"

"I hardly had to beg them, Kyle. When I explained you were in trouble and needed them, they were happy to help."

The glint in his emerald eyes was harsh. His cynical laugh made her cringe. "Oh, that's even better. You tell people I used to compete with that I can't make it on my own here and I need their help. That's priceless. Perfect. God, Sabrina, how could you do this to me?"

This wasn't at all the response she was expecting. She expected him to be a little miffed that she'd gone behind his back to invite his friends, but then after it was a success he'd agree she'd done the right thing. She didn't expect this raging temper. Who was this man before her? He was like a stranger—so full of venom it practically oozed from every pore. She could feel the tidal wave of fury as he blasted it in her direction.

"I knew you wouldn't be happy about this, but please let me explain. I asked your friends to help, and they were more than happy to. It's not like I handed over the ranch financial statements. You don't need to get angry with me about this. It worked out great. The rodeo was a success."

"No, *you* think it worked out," he said pointing a finger at her. "I say this is a disaster. I'll never be able to show my face around professional rodeo again. Not only did I have to leave competing, but now my former competitors had to ride to my rescue to save a ranch I'm obviously incapable of running myself."

"You're not incapable at all," she explained. "I just thought the rodeo would do so much better if we brought in some of the big names to compete." He leveled a look so murderous it made her cringe. "I was only trying to help."

"You didn't. Once again, you stuck your nose in where it doesn't belong. How many times do I have to tell you I don't need your help? I can handle things fine on my own here, and I don't need you to rescue me."

"I thought..."

"No," he interrupted. "You didn't think. That's the problem. You think because you have money and a short-term investment in the Rocking M that gives you the right to make decisions about it. It doesn't."

She hated feeling this way. Having to explain, apologize. Just like she used to with Mark. Wasn't their relationship different? "Kyle, it was an idea I came up with to help. The feelings I have for you...what's been going on between you and me..."

He grabbed her by the arms and she gasped as she looked in his eyes and saw how cold they were. Where was her lover, the man whose passion and warmth had brought her a new life, new dreams, even the miracle of a child?

"What's been going on between you and me is just sex, Sabrina. Nothing more than that. And it certainly doesn't entitle you to go off on your own with a stupid plan you think will help."

She tried to still the trembling in her limbs as the full impact of his words hit her harder than if he'd slapped her across the face.

Just sex. That's all it was to him, that's all she was to him, a convenience. Any real feeling was on her side only. Her heart tore in two as her dream shattered.

She could feel her own anger rising along with her voice. "This is all about your pride, Kyle Morgan. Just like it always has been. I've done nothing but try to help since the day I got here, and you've done everything you can to make me feel guilty for trying. Maybe I shouldn't have come here after all."

His lips tightened as he spit out the words. "Maybe you shouldn't have. Since the first day you got here you've done nothing but meddle in my family's business, and frankly I'll be glad when you're gone so you stop interfering in my life."

How much more could she take? His words stabbed at her, each sentence drawing more blood until it was almost unbearable.

"I've had just about enough," she managed on a shaky breath. "No matter what I do, no matter how good my intentions, I will never be able to satisfy you. I'll never be able to help."

"I never asked for your help," he said roughly as he turned and started to walk away. "I never wanted it."

She grabbed his arm and turned him to face her. He wasn't going to leave with the last word. "Yes, you did ask for it. Maybe you didn't want it, but at first you needed me. Or at least I thought you did. I was quite obviously wrong in that assumption." She returned his icy stare, using her anger as a shield to protect her from the raw pain threatening to tear her apart.

He just stared at her, through her, as if she wasn't speaking.

She took a trembling breath and wiped away the tears. She would not allow him to hurt her any more than he already had. "I'll be leaving soon anyway, so none of this matters. For the remaining time I'm here, I'll stay out of your way."

He didn't respond for a moment, then nodded. "Fine. You do that." Then he gathered up his saddle and walked toward the barn.

She stood rooted, unable to make her feet move as she watched Kyle's retreating form. She forced a ragged breath, her shoulders heaving in the effort. It was stupid to stand here, watching him, hoping he'd turn around and come running back to her, take her in his arms and tell her he was wrong.

He didn't care about her at all. This wasn't even a partnership, let alone a relationship. Like Mark, it would always be about his way, and no matter what she tried to do to help he wouldn't let her. Pride wouldn't let him.

Damn him and his pride.

Forcing her feet to move, she made the short walk to the ranch house, but couldn't bring herself to go inside and face Kyle's family. She stood on the porch watching the setting sun bank along the horizon, sinking slowly until the flame went out completely, leaving her alone in the gathering darkness.

Kyle threw the saddle down as he entered the barn. The sun had set, casting shadows through the old wooden building. But he didn't turn the light on, preferring the darkness to match his mood.

If he lived to be a hundred he'd never understand how she could have done this to him.

When his friends showed up this morning, he was elated, assuming they'd heard about the rodeo through the grapevine and came out to give him their support out of friendship.

Their appearance at the rodeo did wonders for the success of the event too. Maybe it would have done as well without them, but Kyle doubted they would have had the turnout they experienced today without Joey, Marsh and Rod's presence. Any rodeo fan would be hard pressed to pass up an opportunity to see the top three competitors in the profession.

And then, to find out the reason they came was in answer to Sabrina's distress call was almost more than he could bear. Not her distress of course. Oh no, she had to go and tell them that he was incompetent and incapable of running his family's ranch successfully, and then beg their help.

Rescue him. That's what she'd been trying to do since the day she stepped foot on the Rocking M. A rescue he never wanted, and didn't need.

A bridle sailed across the barn, followed by ropes, a pair of boots, and a screwdriver. When there were no more loose items to throw, he felt a little better.

Blowing a quick breath, Kyle picked up the discarded saddle and placed it on the rack in the tack room, then tried to keep his hands busy by tidying up the barn. Before he started throwing more things and making a bigger mess out of the place than he already had.

He could have done it all himself. He could have asked his friends to come, but he didn't. Because he didn't need their help, and even if he did, not in a million years would he have asked for it.

Men didn't ask for help. They solved their own problems, without begging for aid. His father had run the Rocking M from the time he was old enough to manage the business until the day he died. And he ran the ranch expertly, profitably, and efficiently.

Kyle should have been able to do the same thing. Only he couldn't. He failed. Even Sabrina recognized that, or she wouldn't have asked his friends to come to the rodeo.

How pathetic he must seem to them—to everyone who knew about it, and he was certain more people than just his three friends knew what Sabrina had done.

God he was angry with her.

When there was nothing left to put away, he picked a bale of hay and sat on it, brooding. He had every right to be angry with her. She had stepped out of line, beyond the boundaries they set, and gone over his head and made him look like a fool in the process.

So he'd hurt her feelings. Big deal. He pushed aside the memory of her amber eyes pooling with tears, the pain he inflicted shadowing her face as she paled at his insults and shouts. He ignored the way her whole body trembled when he shouted at her. This was her fault and she deserved his anger, and he'd be damned if he'd let himself feel guilty for it.

He pushed aside the comparison of his tirade to that of what she might have experienced at the hands of her ex-husband. It wasn't the same thing at all. It wasn't.

They were business partners, that's all. They'd had fun, shared some great sex, but that was it. This whole idea he was in love with her was ludicrous from the start. He had no idea how that notion had settled in his brain, and chalked it up to foolish desire, making his libido lead his heart down the garden path.

No more. It was time he took charge of his life again, and got things back to normal around here. In no time at all she'd be leaving, and that would be the best thing for him, as well as for her.

Then neither one of them would mistake their relationship for anything deeper than what it was—a mutual physical attraction. A hot spark ignited into a flame that would burn bright as long as they were together, but like flame and oxygen, slowly fade out and extinguish as soon as they parted.

He wasn't wrong about this, and he wasn't wrong about how he reacted to Sabrina's scheme today. The stabbing ache he felt all over had more to do with sore muscles than guilt and regret. He didn't love her.

He wouldn't love her.

ର ର ର

The next few days Sabrina spent as much time as she could hidden in her room. She couldn't face Kyle again, and didn't want to explain to his family what happened between them.

She still had things to do, otherwise she'd have packed up the night of the rodeo and left the ranch. But she wasn't a quitter, and she made promises that she planned to keep. No matter how hard it was to stay here, no matter how much it hurt to see Kyle every day.

Jenna tried to cajole her into talking, but Sabrina feigned morning sickness and exhaustion, avoiding her. But Jenna was pretty sharp and knew something had changed between Sabrina and Kyle. Jenna asked if Sabrina told Kyle about the baby. The timing wasn't right, she explained to Jenna. But she wasn't going to tell him.

Kyle was all about independence. He wanted his freedom and she was going to make sure he got it. There was no way they'd be able to work things out now, and she wouldn't subject her child to growing up in a family devoid of love. She'd been through that and knew how it felt, and her baby wasn't going to grow up that way. If she had to raise the child alone, she'd do it, and give it enough love so he or she would never doubt they were wanted and cherished.

All she wanted to do was help the Morgans, help Kyle. And every time she tried he turned it around so that she felt she'd done something wrong. Just like Mark used to do.

No, not quite. The situations were completely different. The men were different. Try as she might to lump Kyle in with Mark, they were completely different.

Maybe she should have handled things differently. Maybe she should have approached Kyle about her idea for the rodeo, and let him decide if it was the right thing to do.

She wasn't a man, and didn't have those pride issues to deal with. Had she simply run amok with her newfound freedom and independence? Had she even considered how Kyle would feel about the situation? No, she hadn't.

He had made his feelings for her quite clear the other night. He hated her business interference, and reiterated the relationship they had was purely physical. There were no emotional attachments on his end, so when she left he'd be able to move on with no lingering feelings.

But she wouldn't. Not only had she fallen in love with the Rocking M, she had completely lost her heart to Kyle. She'd take away wonderful memories, despite his anger toward her the other night. And she'd take something else with her when she left.

His child.

She stretched her legs and placed a hand on her lower abdomen, caressing the new life that grew within her. No matter what, she'd never regret the time she'd spent here. She had learned so much, not only about ranching but her own abilities.

And when she bought her own ranch and settled in, she'd be able to use her newfound knowledge to make a success of it.

For her, and for her child.

It wasn't going to be easy raising this baby by herself, but she could do it. She had money, and she was smart. She'd hire good people to help her, and they would be fine.

If her heart ached at the thought of leaving the Rocking M, it was only because of the way she felt about the people here. She'd miss Jenna and Luke and Brady. And of course little Matthew. They were like family to her.

The more time she had to think, the more she realized that in many ways Kyle was right. She had no right to be upset when he told her their relationship was purely physical. He'd been honest with her from the start. He told her a sexual relationship was all he was capable of, and she'd accepted his terms. Just because she fell in love with him didn't mean he owed her his love in return.

She had a lot yet to learn about love and relationships. And as long as she lived, she'd never be able to understand men.

ॐ ॐ ॐ

"You are an idiot of epic proportions," Jenna said with hands on hips as she confronted Kyle near the horse corral.

"Now what did I do?" He turned to look at his sister.

"I don't know. But I've been watching you and Sabrina the past few days. You hardly stay in the same room together for more than a few seconds, and neither of you says a word to the other. What happened?"

He turned away and went back to work on the saddle. "That's none of your business, Jenn. Stay out of my affairs."

She walked around until she stood in front of the saddle. "Is that what she is to you? An affair?"

He didn't answer. He wasn't in the mood to deal with her prying questions. "Not now. I'm busy."

"You're just going to have to unbusy yourself and talk to me because I'm not leaving until you do."

He glanced up and saw her fold her arms across her chest and glare at him. "I don't want to talk about Sabrina."

"Why not? Obviously there's something wrong with you two. She won't talk to me either."

"Did it ever occur to you that maybe neither of us wants to discuss it?"

"You need to talk to her, Kyle. I don't know what happened, but trust me. You need to settle it before she leaves."

"Leave it alone, Jenna. We're dealing with it just fine."

"No, you're not," she replied as she stepped toward him and brushed his forearm, a mixture of anger and concern on her petite face. "And you need to. You'll regret it if you don't."

"Would you please stay out of my business? God," he said as he pulled a hand through his hair, "you're just like Sabrina. Always interfering."

Jenna paused for a moment. "This is about the rodeo, isn't it? The fact she called on your friends and asked them to come."

"It's about more than that," he replied as he resumed work on the saddle.

She jerked on his arm until he looked at her. Her eyes narrowed in anger. "No, it isn't. I bet you're pissed because she went over your head and did something that ultimately saved this ranch's butt, and you just can't handle the fact that you didn't think of it yourself."

"Jenna, I'm warning you. I don't want to discuss this with you."

"Tough. We're discussing it whether you like it or not. I can't believe you would be angry with her for that. She did a wonderful job and worked hard to insure the rodeo's success. How could you be mad about that?"

"It's more than that. It's her interference in our lives, the fact she just goes along and does whatever she wants to without thinking of the ramifications."

"Oh, please. That's not it at all. Do you know how excited she was when she came up with this idea?"

He focused on his sister. "You knew about this?"

The corners of her mouth lifted. "Of course I did."

"Why in the hell didn't you tell me then?"

"Because you'd have said no."

He nodded. "Damn right I would have. You had no business making those kinds of decisions without involving me. This is a family partnership, and none of us make choices without the other." He straightened and leaned against the saddle. "As I recall, I wasn't in favor of letting Sabrina work here, but since this is a family business we put it to a vote and I lost."

Jenna opened her mouth to speak, then paused for a few seconds. "You've got me there," she said with a frown. "You're right in that respect. We probably should have decided as a family. For that I'm sorry."

How could he stay mad at her when she was so upfront and honest about everything? If she was right she stood firm in her beliefs. But if she was wrong she admitted it and moved on.

"Thanks," he said as he hugged her to him.

"But Kyle, you really need to talk to her."

He sighed. "We don't have anything left to talk about."

"How about the fact you two love each other? Isn't that enough to talk about?"

He shook his head. "It's not love. It was just physical, and now it's over."

"You are so pigheaded!" Jenna pushed him. "When are you going to open your eyes to reality? Sabrina's the best thing that ever happened to you, and if you'd ever get down off your macho male horse you'd realize that everything she's done is because she loves you."

Jenna stomped off muttering something about idiots and morons.

As usual Jenna didn't know what she was talking about. She thought just because she and Luke were happy together, every couple should be.

Later that night as he sat in the office doing paperwork, Kyle recalled that conversation with his sister. In some ways she was right.

Despite his best efforts to place himself in the position of the one who'd been wronged, he failed. He'd been overly hard on Sabrina. Yes, she was wrong in going behind his back and calling his friends. He stood firm in his belief that a ranch's partners made decisions together. But then he let emotion get the better of him and lashed out at her.

His pride got in the way all the time. When would he learn to push it aside and do whatever's best for the ranch? If he'd done that years ago maybe they wouldn't have fallen on such hard financial times.

It would have been easy to ask his friends to come to the rodeo. They would have done it in a heartbeat, no questions asked. And maybe part of the reason he was so damn angry at Sabrina was because he didn't think of it first.

He rose from the desk and looked out the window of the office. Dusk had settled over purple skies, the almost full moon casting a glow over the hills in front of the ranch.

So now he'd alienated a woman he cared about, causing irreparable damage to their relationship. And she was about to leave the ranch forever. So what did he want to do about that? What could he do? Ask her to stay?

No, that wouldn't work at all. Sabrina wanted to own a ranch. Something she'd dreamed of her entire life. Despite what he might want, it was time to put her first.

She deserved better than a man who couldn't decide what he wanted. He knew she made him happy, even when he was spitting mad at her. But she also frustrated him and drove him crazy with desire at the same time. He'd gotten used to seeing her every day, being near her all the time. And suddenly she wasn't there anymore. Sleeping alone again the past several nights had been a rude awakening.

He missed having her warm body next to his every night. Drifting off to sleep after making love, his nose buried against her hair inhaling her fresh peach scent, his arms wrapped around her silken body. And he'd slept better with Sabrina in his bed than he had in years.

He leaned against the wall next to the window, his eyes drifting upward to the second floor where Sabrina had hightailed it as soon as dinner was over. And as was typical the last few days, without a word or a look in his direction.

What did he expect? He had used her, took advantage of her vulnerability, and then when she tried to help him he turned around and threw it back at her. He cringed when he remembered the words he'd spoken to her in anger.

I'll be glad when you're gone so you can stop interfering in my life.

He remembered the look on her face when he said it. She had paled immediately, and tears fell over her cheeks as she stood there, shaking like a leaf. God, he felt awful. What was wrong with him? Why did she bring out the best and the worst in him at the same time?

And more importantly, now that it was said he couldn't take it back, couldn't change what he'd done. Did he even want to? And what about Sabrina? What did she want? Was it fair for him to pull and push her back and forth like a yo-yo?

If he had a shred of decency in him, he'd stop tormenting her and let her start a new life.

She had a right to the independence she craved so desperately. She had a right to get out there and buy her own place and run it herself. She'd no doubt be successful at it. Sabrina had a sharp head for business and a great deal of common sense, the perfect combination for running a ranch. She had a right to try. She'd earned that right.

And she had a right to find someone who'd love her the way she deserved to be loved.

Kyle wasn't going to stand in her way.

Because no matter what he thought, no matter how hard he tried to convince himself, he really did love her.

And because he loved her, he was going to let her go.

Chapter Fifteen

The past few days had been miserable.

Sabrina walked around on eggshells, steering clear of Kyle as much as possible while still trying to learn as much as she could in the short time remaining.

And today she had to pack. Tomorrow she would leave.

Things were still unsettled between her and Kyle. She thought about approaching him to apologize, but he seemed to be avoiding her as much as she'd been avoiding him. Anyway, she wouldn't know where to start.

Even Jenna was mad at her. She explained she couldn't tell Kyle about the baby, and gave her all the reasons why, none of which seemed sound to her friend. Jenna argued that Kyle had every right to know he was going to be a father. She didn't agree and they ended it with an awkward stalemate. Jenna promised she wouldn't tell him, which was a relief.

The last thing she needed right now was a confrontation with Kyle about her pregnancy. Things were shaky at best with battling morning sickness along with the despair she felt about leaving.

If she told him about the baby he'd make her stay. But out of a sense of honor, not out of love. He'd probably even marry her, an idea that should excite her, but didn't. She'd rather be a single mother than force him into a marriage he clearly didn't want.

Yes, she could tell him about the baby and ask for support, even give him visitation. But that would mean they'd stay connected forever. And that was something Sabrina couldn't bear. She thought long and hard about the disservice she may be doing her child by not allowing it to see its father, but that was her decision to make. Right or wrong, it was her choice.

He made it clear he didn't love her. He didn't get her pregnant on purpose because she was the one who assured him she couldn't conceive. Why did he have to be burdened with a child? Some day maybe he'd marry again and have children. A wife he chose for himself, a child he wanted.

But he wasn't going to have this one. Selfish, she knew, but she didn't care. This was her child, and she had the right to make the decisions.

She was in her room packing when a knock sounded at the door.

"Come in," she said, thinking it was Jenna ready to go another round in trying to convince her to tell Kyle about the baby.

But it wasn't Jenna. Sabrina turned around to find Kyle standing in the middle of her bedroom. Her heart started its familiar racing at the sight of him.

God, she missed him. So much the ache was physical. Her whole body hurt.

His faded jeans clung to his lean body, the tight navy T-shirt outlining his strong shoulders and chest. And those enigmatic eyes that both thrilled her and touched her heart. If she lived to be a hundred she'd never forget the way his eyes glittered with passion when he made love to her.

No matter how many times she saw him, how intimate they had been, how familiar every line and angle of his face was to her, the sight of him still made her pulse pound like a teenager with a crush on a rock star.

"Hi," she said with a half-smile.

"Hey." His smile was just as tentative. He glanced at her bed to see luggage spread out and some of her clothes neatly tucked inside. "Packing already?"

She nodded. "I didn't want to wait until tomorrow. I thought it best to get moving on it as soon as possible."

"I see."

This was so uncomfortable. This silence, this barrier that stretched between them. And Sabrina had no idea how to breach it, how to get things back to the way they were before. Did she even want to? What would be the point? Either way she was leaving tomorrow, so maybe it would be better to leave things the way they were.

His gaze shifted to the things she had piled everywhere. He walked to her dresser and picked up her bottle of perfume. She watched as he closed his eyes and held the bottle to his nose, inhaling deeply. Her heart rose to her throat as she remembered the feel of his lips against her neck, the sound of his breath as he inhaled her scent.

"I wanted to talk to you before you left," he said after he put the bottle down. His voice was deep and arousing to her senses.

"Sure." She motioned to the loveseat and sat, waiting for him to sit next to her.

He sat but didn't shift close or touch her in any way. She sighed with regret, knowing how much she already missed the feel of him next to her in bed at night. Knowing after tomorrow she wouldn't see him anymore caused knots in her stomach and her heart to ache with a pain that had become all too familiar over the past few days.

As they sat together in silence, she thought of all the reasons he would want to talk to her today. Her fairy tale mind conjured up images of him getting down on his knees and begging her forgiveness, asking her to stay and marry him. She would, of course, smile indulgently, caress his cheek and tell him there was nothing to forgive, declare her love and wait for him to take her in his arms.

She smiled thinking of that scenario, wishing for it to be real. But she was also a realist. She may wish for it to happen, but chances were it wasn't going to.

She was an adult now and had long since outgrown fairy tales, had learned long ago that those were the stuff of fantasy. Reality was much harsher. Fairy tales didn't exist.

"There's something I've been wanting to do for the past few days, but you and I haven't been able to connect."

She turned to look at him. He stared at his boots, surveying her room, glancing outside. Anything but looking her in the eyes. That didn't bode well for her dream scenario.

"What is it that you've wanted to do?" Wishing what he wanted was to kiss her and hold her wasn't making things any easier.

"I wanted to give you something."

He stood and turned to face her, causing her heart to beat a frantic rhythm in her chest. She was certain Kyle could hear the loud thumping because she certainly felt it pulsating through her.

He reached into his back pocket and pulled something out of it. "I wanted you to have this before you go," he said as he handed an envelope to her.

Sabrina took the envelope and opened it. Inside was a check for a considerable amount of money. "What is this?" she asked as she looked up at him.

"That represents the amount of money you invested, plus three months of interest."

She shook her head and tried to hand the envelope back to him, ignoring the disappointment flowing through her. "This isn't what we agreed on. I was only supposed to get a percentage back, not the entire sum plus interest."

"I know. But the ranch is doing fine now—much better than we thought it would. And I wanted you to have it so you can use it for the ranch you buy. It'll be like you never even invested your money here. Like it never happened."

Like them, she thought miserably. More like *they* never happened. It was obvious. Kyle wanted to erase her presence on the Rocking M, eliminate any reference to her, even monetarily. He really thought so little of her, even less than she imagined.

"Thanks," she said quietly as she clenched the envelope in both hands in an effort to stop them from shaking. *Please leave, Kyle. Leave before you see me cry again.* "Is there anything else, because I'm kind of busy here."

She waited but he didn't respond. She couldn't look up, couldn't meet his eyes or she knew she'd lose it. At best she had a very tenuous hold on her emotions. If he blinked she'd probably burst into tears.

"I guess not," he finally answered. "I'll see myself out."

Sabrina breathed on a shaky sigh as he closed the door behind him.

That was it. A final, impersonal goodbye. *Here's your check, nice knowing you, see you later.* For all intents and purposes that was pretty much what Kyle just said.

How stupid could she be to think he'd rush in and declare his love for her before she left? Love like that only happened in fairy tales and romance novels. Reality was harsh, bitter, devoid of the depth of emotion found in fiction. There was no such thing as finding your soul mate, meeting the man of your dreams, or having a love that surmounted all obstacles.

Standing on wobbly legs, Sabrina walked over to the bed and began to fold the clothes she'd placed there to pack.

Time was running out, and her time on the Rocking M was over. Instead of being asked to stay, she'd just been given her walking papers.

ৎ ৎ ৎ

The last of her things were finally loaded into her car. Several of the hands had been kind enough to bring her luggage down and pack it in the car for her. There was nothing left to do except say her goodbyes.

The hard part. The hardest thing she'd ever have to do.

Petunia snorted at her feet as Sabrina held the leash. She smiled down at her pig, wondering what in the world she was going to do with it until she found a ranch.

Well, she'd just have to find a place that would allow her to include Petunia. She'd already contacted her attorney to let her know she was returning to Dallas, prepared to look over potential ranches for sale. Pamela said she'd get right on it.

"You're really leaving." Brady walked up to her, sliding an arm around her shoulders. "I wish you weren't. I feel like I'm losing a sister," he said as he kissed her cheek.

"Me too," Jenna added as she stepped next to her brother. She held baby Matthew who was growing steadily every day.

Swallowing the lump in her throat that threatened to bring on the tears, Sabrina smiled at both of them. "I know. I'll miss you both so much. But I'll call, and I'll write. Maybe I'll even visit sometime," she said, knowing she would never step foot on the Rocking M again.

"Well, I'm not very good at emotional goodbyes, so I'll just say 'see ya' and get on to my work here," Brady said with more emotion than Sabrina had ever seen. He smiled down at her, his blue-green eyes sad and without their normal twinkling light. "So, see ya," he whispered against her ear as he kissed her cheek, turned and walked away.

"Don't go, Sabrina," Jenna said as Sabrina watched Brady walk briskly toward the barn.

"I have to," she said as she gathered Matthew in her arms, holding him close and pressing a soft kiss against his fine black hair. She inhaled Matthew's sweet scent one last time before handing him back to Jenna.

"No, you don't have to. You can talk to him, tell him about the baby."

Since the *him* in question had yet to make an appearance, Sabrina shook her head. "It's better this way, for me as well as Kyle. We both need to move on with our lives."

"I can't help but feel the two of you belong together, if only you weren't both so stubborn." Jenna patted Matthew's back as he began to whimper.

"You need to go feed Matthew, and I have to get going if I want to make Dallas before dark." She had to make an exit and fast, before she completely fell apart. If she did that, she'd never leave.

"I'll always be here for you, Sabrina, as your friend," Jenna said with tears in her eyes. "And as one of the owners of this ranch, you'll always be welcome."

They hugged, and Jenna ran off toward her small white house, leaving Sabrina standing in front of the main ranch house alone.

She couldn't help but glance around, hoping despite herself that Kyle would show up and at least say goodbye.

Feeling ridiculous standing there alone, and knowing he wouldn't come, she situated Petunia in the car. Sabrina took one last look at the place she had come to think of as home, heaved a deep, quaking sigh and finally let the tears fall as she started the car and drove away from the Rocking M.

From his position at the side of the barn, Kyle watched as Sabrina said her goodbyes to Brady and Jenna. Even at this distance he felt her pain, felt it stab through him like a knife. It tore at his heart as she obviously watched and waited for him to appear, and it took every ounce of willpower he had to keep from running after her and begging her to stay.

But he swore he wouldn't. He was giving her what she wanted, even if it wasn't what she thought she wanted right now. In time it would be, and she'd be grateful she left. Once she found the right man.

Brady stopped in front of him as he passed the side of the barn. He looked Kyle in the eyes, disappointment clearly showing in his blue-green gaze.

"Coward," was all Brady said to him as he continued past Kyle toward the corral.

Brady was wrong. Letting Sabrina leave took every ounce of bravery he had. Ignoring the emptiness in his chest where his heart used to be, Kyle threw himself into working the Rocking M.

He avoided his brother and sister for the next week, hoping he wouldn't have to face them after Sabrina's departure. It was hard enough walking through the empty house at night, feeling Sabrina's presence but knowing she wouldn't be there to welcome him, hold him, love him. After the first night she was gone he avoided his bed like the plague.

Kyle knew it was going to be bad when she left, but he hadn't expected this despair, the empty feeling and utter loneliness. Before, his work had always kept him busy, kept his mind off feeling alone.

So he worked from before dawn to after sunset, driving himself until he was completely exhausted. Because he didn't want to face Brady and Jenna, or sleep in his bed alone, he decided to work on the outer acreage of the property so he'd have to spend nights in the one room cabin on the outskirts of their land.

But at night, when he lay down on the small bed in complete exhaustion, sleep wouldn't come. Images of flowing blonde hair and innocent amber eyes haunted him. He could still smell her, that fresh peach scent that was so much a part of her. It was embedded in his senses and he couldn't make it go away. Neither could he rid himself of the feel of her silky skin against his work-roughened hands.

Even when Amanda had done her worst to him, left him for Dent, took a third of the ranch with her, it hadn't hurt this much. Hell, it hadn't hurt at all. And she had been his wife.

Sabrina had been—well, what exactly had she been to him? They never had a formal relationship, and yet she had gotten under his skin and became so much a part of him even he didn't realize how much until after she was gone.

And all his thoughts of how noble he was being by letting her go were a crock of shit. He loved her desperately, missed her painfully, and wanted her back with a need so fierce it threatened to drive him insane.

"You going to hide out here forever?"

Kyle whipped around to see Jenna standing before him. He'd been focusing on repairing the torn fence and hadn't heard her drive up.

"What are you doing here?"

She stood, hands on hips, giving him "the look". "I've come to bring you home, where you belong."

He shook his head. "I'm busy here."

She looked at the fence and back at him, her left brow lifting in disbelief. "You are not. There's nothing wrong with the fence and you know it. You're hiding."

"I'm not hiding," he lied. "I told you, I've been neglecting this section for too long and before we move the herd up here in the fall I need to make sure the fence is secure."

"You're missing Sabrina and you don't want to admit it."

He turned away then, not wanting his sister to see the pain in his eyes. "No, I'm not missing Sabrina. She's gone and that's that."

"Not quite."

He sighed, not wanting to go down this road again. "Look, Jenn, I appreciate your matchmaking efforts, but it's too little too late. Sabrina and I had nothing together, so it's time to give it up."

"I never took you for a coward, Kyle Morgan."

He stood then, walking over to her. "I am not a coward."

She stared straight faced at him. "Then you're a liar."

He sighed heavily. She was baiting him. "I'm too busy for this, Jenn." He started to walk away but she stepped in front of him.

"Kyle, how do you feel about Sabrina?"

He wanted to ignore the question, wanted to go back to work and work until his brain was too tired to think about anything at all, least of all Sabrina. But as he looked at the face of his sister, for a second it was his own mother standing there. He wondered how she would feel about the way he was acting.

"Tell me, Kyle," she said as she placed her hands on his arms. "Tell me the truth."

He couldn't ignore her any longer, any more than he could ignore the gut-wrenching pain in his heart. "I love Sabrina."

Jenna's eyes welled with tears at his admission. "I know that." She stepped into his arms and he held her close, thanking God that at least one of the Morgan's had the gift of common sense. She stepped back and looked at him. "So tell me what happened between the two of you."

Kyle dropped his head. "I really screwed up. I let my pride and anger take control, and I know better. Especially considering what she went through with her ex-husband. God, Jenn," he said as he leaned against the truck and pulled both hands through his hair. "It was bad."

"So I gathered. How bad?"

"Really bad," he said, thoroughly ashamed at the way he'd treated Sabrina. "I told her I'd be glad when she was gone so she'd stop interfering in my life."

Jenna took a deep breath. "Kyle, sometimes your stupidity amazes me."

He laughed at her insult. "Sometimes it amazes me too."

"So, what about Sabrina?"

"I want her back."

Jenna cocked her head and raised her eyebrows in question. "Why?"

Why did it take him so long to realize the answer? It was so simple. "Because I love her and want to marry her."

Then she gave him a loving smile that shot straight through Kyle's heart. When she smiled like that she reminded him of their mother.

"Good reason. So what are you going to do about getting her back?"

Kyle hugged his sister. "I have no idea. First I have to find her, then I'll figure out how to convince her to come back to me."

ॐ ॐ ॐ

Two weeks and nothing. Sabrina flipped through another pile of listings, yet not a single ranch for sale appealed to her.

She needed to find something soon, because housing Petunia in their temporary apartment was irritating the landlord to the point no matter how much more rent she paid him, she'd soon find herself a fairly wealthy homeless person.

"Nothing?" Her attorney Pamela Morris opened the door ahead of her secretary, who was bearing tea for both of them.

Sabrina shook her head as Louise poured the tea. "Nothing," she replied as she thanked Louise.

"Are you sure you're not being too picky?" Pam was not only her attorney, but also one of Sabrina's few friends in Dallas, most everyone she knew having sided with Mark during the divorce. Pam had steadfastly stood by her despite Mark's threats to ruin her practice. Sabrina remembered Pam laughing in Mark's face outside the courtroom and daring him to try. That day she'd earned Sabrina's loyalty for life.

"Of course I'm not too picky," she said as she discarded the current pile along with the other rejects. "They're just not what I'm looking for."

"They're just not the Rocking M, you mean," Pam said with a wise smile.

"I don't know what you mean," Sabrina lied. "Surely you're not suggesting that I'm comparing every property against the Morgan's ranch?"

Pam leaned back in her leather chair, twining her hands together on the desk. "That's exactly what I'm suggesting."

"That's ridiculous," Sabrina said as she fiddled with her shoe, looked through her purse for a mint, and straightened the magazines on the table next to her. "I most certainly am not. Why the Rocking M was an average ranch at best, and I can afford much more than that."

"Uh huh. You're a terrible liar, Sabrina," Pam said with a grin.

That was the problem with having friends. They knew you too well. "Okay, so maybe I haven't adjusted to having left yet. But I'm getting there." That was also a lie. There wasn't a moment since she'd driven away from the Rocking M she hadn't thought about the ranch, about Brady and Jenna, Luke and baby Matthew.

She also thought about Kyle, but not that often. No more than twenty-five hours a day. When she went to bed at night, she remembered the feel of his strong body pulling her against him. When she woke up, she remembered sharing breakfast with him, working along side him every day. Remembered his looks, his touch, the way he smelled, and the funny way his hair spiked up in twenty different directions when he first got out of bed. Most of all she remembered the way he kissed her, the way he loved her.

She remembered the way she loved him. And her heart broke every single time a picture of him entered her mind.

"Why don't you just go back there?"

"I can't, and you know very well why."

"Because you're afraid."

Sabrina shook her head. "Because of many reasons that I don't want to go over again, Pam. My mind is made up."

"Your friend Jenna was right, you know. He does deserve to know."

Sabrina had filled Pam in on the details, including the surprise she felt when she learned she was pregnant, and how Mark had told her she'd be unable to conceive. Pam's eyes lit up first in fury, then in delight as she pondered ways they could squeeze more money out of Sabrina's ex-husband as recompense for having lied about her inability to get pregnant. But Sabrina wanted no more contact with Mark. That part of her life was over and forgotten.

"By the way, I ran into Mark at the club the other day," Pam said in an offhand way that clued Sabrina in to the fact there were more than just pleasantries exchanged.

"And?"

Pam pondered her well-manicured nails, and pulled her chin-length blonde hair behind her ears. "Oh, nothing. I just casually mentioned that I had recently seen you and you were doing quite well."

"And?" Sabrina had played this game before with Pam. She knew there was more.

"Oh, not much really. I just may have mentioned that you positively glowed, and pregnancy was definitely agreeing with you."

Sabrina laughed out loud. Leave it to Pam to dig the knife into Mark whenever and wherever she could. "I take it he was surprised to hear that?"

Pam leaned forward, her blue eyes sharp and glinting with delight. "He positively paled. Sputtered and mumbled, it was pathetic really," she said without an ounce of remorse. "Frankly, I was afraid I was going to have to call one of the club attendants to carry him off, he looked so weak."

"You are so bad," Sabrina said, but she had to admit a certain sense of satisfaction at Mark finding out about her pregnancy. "And thank you," she added.

"Oh, you're welcome. Truly, it was my pleasure."

Sabrina didn't doubt that in the least. "What do you have for me to look at today?" Another round of reviews of ranch properties for sale. The search was getting tedious, and Sabrina knew she was going to have to settle on one and fairly soon. Otherwise she'd be too far along in her pregnancy to start up an operation and would have to wait until after the baby was born. And that she didn't want to do.

"There are a few interesting ones," Pam said as she handed several papers across the desk to Sabrina. Then she sat back sipping her tea, smiling like a child with a secret she couldn't wait to spill.

"What?" Sabrina asked suspiciously. She knew that look. Pam had something she was dying to tell her. Probably more gossip about Mark.

"Nothing. Just read the listings."

She perused the properties. The first couple were in Texas, and too close to Dallas for Sabrina's comfort. She didn't want to locate that close to Mark. Two were in Oklahoma, one a fairly sizeable and quite profitable operation, the other somewhat smaller but in a prosperous area. Both definitely had potential and she informed Pam she'd be interested in those.

"Read the last one before I start making calls," Pam said, the grin never leaving her face.

Sabrina shook her head at her friend and glanced down at the paper in front of her. Her jaw dropped.

There, staring back at her from the page, was Kyle, standing in front of the entrance to the Rocking M. A paragraph in bold letters proclaimed *Rancher For Sale.* Not *Ranch For Sale,* but *Rancher.* Sabrina looked up at Pam, unable to hide the shock on her face.

"Is this some kind of joke?" Sabrina felt chilled despite the comfortable temperature in the room.

"No," she said. "Read it."

She lowered her eyes again to the page, wanting to run her fingers over the picture of the man she loved. Instead she read the advertisement underneath it.

Ranch in Dreamwater, Oklahoma. Thirty-Five Hundred plus acres capable of sustaining hundreds of head of cattle and horses. Large ranch house with multiple work buildings and corrals. Incredibly secluded and very romantic, hot, spring-fed lake.

Currently owned and run by one incredibly stupid man with too much pride and not enough common sense to hold on to the best thing that ever walked into his life. Needs immediate rescue by beautiful blonde with eyes the color of warm whiskey and hair like spun gold.

Potential investor must go by the name Sabrina Daniels. Said investor needed here urgently. Owner willing to subject himself to

many humiliations in order to get the woman he loves to come back to
him.

She read it over and over until her eyes blurred so that she could no longer read the passage again. She looked up at Pam as she wiped the tears with the back of her hand. "He loves me," she said in a giddy, hiccupping voice.

"Undoubtedly," Pam said dryly. "He'd have to in order to make a complete ass of himself like that."

Sabrina read the listing again. And again. And again. He loved her. He wanted her back.

"Well?"

She finally tore her eyes away from the picture of Kyle's face and looked up at Pam. "Well, what?"

"What are you waiting for? Grab that feisty little pig of yours and hightail it back to the Rocking M, where you belong."

Chapter Sixteen

"I'm here to rescue you."

Kyle's heart stuttered at the familiar and oh-so-welcome voice. He craned his neck from under the pickup to see trim ankles and the pink painted toenails he'd grown to know and love so well. But this time alongside the two-footed woman of his dreams, four pink hoofed feet stood next to her, and a discernable snort was heard next to the sultry voice.

He slid out from under the truck, squinting in the bright hot sun. Once again, a vision blinded him. He grabbed his T-shirt and wiped his hands and face, then stood, ready to face the angel standing before him.

She looked so different today than the first day he'd met her. Before she was perfectly coiffed, dressed in silk and heeled sandals. Today she wore jean shorts and a basic T-shirt, plain sandals, little makeup and her hair piled high in a ponytail. And she looked more beautiful to him today than she ever had before.

"Care to run that by me again?" Kyle ached to grab her and pull her to him. He wanted to feel her body, her life force pulsing against him, and kiss her until their lips were raw.

"I said I'm here to rescue you," she repeated, a smile lifting the corners of her mouth despite her attempts to give him her most serious look.

Petunia added her two cents worth with a resounding snort at Kyle's feet. He bent down and scooped up the bundle, kissing her soundly on her big pink snout. "Petunia, I've missed you so. Thank God you've come back to me."

Sabrina giggled. "I see I have a rival for your affections."

"Oh no you don't," he said as he stepped toward her, cradling Petunia under his arms like a football. "I want to kiss you, I need to touch you, but damn if I'm not covered in Dreamwater dirt and blasted motor oil."

"I could care less," Sabrina answered as she moved to his free side, twining her arm around his waist. "Kiss me before I die."

That was all the permission he needed. He placed Petunia on the ground, then grabbed Sabrina to him and pressed his mouth hard against hers, pouring all the regret, apology and longing he had into that one kiss. Her lips parted and welcomed him, her soft mouth kissing him back with as much passion and fervor as he had within him.

"Are you two going to get a room or will there be a spectacle occurring right in our front yard? And if so, can you hang on a few minutes while I sell tickets? We could use the extra cash."

Sabrina tore her mouth from Kyle's and peered over his shoulder at Brady standing against the front steps, arms crossed in front of him and leaning casually against the banister. "Hi Brady," she said with a grin, no longer embarrassed to be caught in the arms of the Rocking M's senior partner. Kyle turned also, his arm remaining around Sabrina's waist.

"Hi yourself," he said, that devilish smile making her feel more at home than she ever had before. "And welcome back. Or should I say, welcome home."

"Thanks. It's good to be back." This *was* home. It had been since the first day she stepped foot on the ranch.

"It's about time you got back here. I've had about enough of Kyle moping about, dragging his feet, head down, like a lost puppy without you. It was pathetic," Brady said with a wink.

"Hey," Kyle interrupted. "I wasn't that bad."

"Yes, you were." Jenna opened the front door and came down the stairs. "Actually you were worse. You should have seen him, Sabrina. He's completely lost without you. Can't function, can't work the computer, can hardly even ride a horse any more." Throwing her arms around Sabrina, she hugged her tightly. "Welcome home, my sister."

Sabrina had to suck in her emotions, otherwise she'd be a blubbering mess of tears. "Thank you," she said in a shaky voice to Jenna. "I missed you."

"Same here. Now please forgive my brother and tell him you love him so we can get back to normal around here. I've got to relieve Luke and take care of Matthew so he can help Brady tend to the horses before the rain hits." She squeezed Sabrina's hand. "We'll talk later."

After Jenna left, Sabrina turned to Brady. He was leaning against the truck, the grin plastered to his face as if it were permanent. Her gaze shifted to Kyle, whose impatient stare should have clued Brady in immediately.

Finally, Kyle cleared his throat and got Brady's attention.

"Oh, yeah," he said with a shrug. "Horses. That's right. I'm in charge of the horses aren't I?" He shifted his hat over his eyes and tipped it with his finger toward Sabrina. "Later, partner." He walked away whistling.

Finally, they were alone and Kyle turned to her, once again wrapping her in his arms.

"We have a lot to talk about," he said.

"Yes, we do."

Kyle took her hand and led her up the white wooden stairs to the porch. He sat on the porch swing and pulled her down beside him, not once letting go of her hand. Sabrina calmed at the feel of his warm strength touching her. "First, I want to say something to you."

"Okay." She turned her head to look into his eyes.

"Forgive me," he said as he grasped both her hands. "I can be incredibly bullheaded at times. Hell most of the time. I never meant to hurt you. Sometimes I talk without thinking, and I end up hurting the people I love the most. God knows I've done it to Jenna and Brady so many times they simply ignore me now. You'll have to learn to do the same thing."

"I'll try."

He was opening his heart to her, confessing his weaknesses, and not making empty promises. It was everything she needed to hear.

"And now for the second thing."

"Go ahead."

"I love you, Sabrina."

No, that was the *only* thing she needed to hear.

"I love you too, Kyle."

His eyes welled then, surprising her. She caressed his cheek, feeling the familiar and welcome roughness of his beard against her palm. It sent tingles of pleasure through her and she shuddered.

"I want to marry you."

Her hand froze on his cheek as she looked at him. "You do?"

He nodded. "Yes, I do. But before you say yes, there are a few things you need to know about me."

Sabrina doubted there was much about Kyle she didn't already know, but nodded. "Go ahead."

"I'm a mean, prideful, surly, grouchy pain in the ass."

She tried not to smile. "Tell me something I don't know."

"I'll hurt you. Say things in anger I don't really mean. More times than I want to."

"Yes, I know that too."

"But I'm not Mark. I might say something stupid, then I'll spend a week showering you with my love and apologizing over and over until you forgive me."

Now she did smile. "I'm counting on it."

"And when I yell at you, I expect you to yell back."

"That seems to come fairly easily to me."

He grinned. "Life with me won't be easy."

"That's an understatement."

"But I'll love you with all my heart, every single day for the rest of our lives."

She squeezed his hand. "Yes."

He looked at her quizzically. "Yes what?"

"Yes, I'll marry you. Despite your stupid, bullheaded, moronic pride. I love you, Kyle Morgan. I want to work this ranch with you, raise a bunch of children with you, and be your wife, your lover, your friend, and your partner. I will spend every day of the rest of my life trying to make all your dreams come true."

He paused, tilting his head sideways.

"What?"

"You said children." He looked confused. "I'd love to adopt some if that's what you're saying."

She shook her head, a sly smile on her face. "I don't want to adopt any. Well, not right away. Maybe down the road."

"Okay, so you want to wait before we adopt kids. That's fine. I can do that."

"You don't understand, Kyle. I want children right away."

"Okay, now I'm really confused."

She took a deep breath and let it out. "I'm pregnant."

He looked as if she were speaking a language he didn't understand. "Huh?"

"You heard me," she said with a grin she could no longer suppress. "I'm pregnant. With *our* child."

"Our—I don't understand. You can't get pregnant. You told me."

"That's what I thought too. But it turns out Mark lied about my inability to get pregnant. It was him, not me, who couldn't have children."

Kyle stood and paced in front of the porch swing. Then stopped and turned to look at her, shock evident on his face. "You?"

She nodded.

He pointed to himself. "And me?"

She nodded again. "Yes. You and me. A baby." She rose and walked toward him, laying her hand on his arm. "Our baby."

He pondered her for a moment, until his eyes welled up. "When?" he asked in a husky whisper.

"About six and a half months."

"How long have you known?"

"Since the day of the rodeo." She prepared herself for his anger.

"You didn't tell me."

"I know. The timing never seemed right. First, we had that big fight after the rodeo, and then we never talked much after that. I figured you weren't interested in me, and I didn't want to force you to keep me around just because I was pregnant."

Kyle dropped his chin to his chest and shook his head. When he lifted it and looked at her, misery shone in his eyes. "I was an idiot. I'm amazed you came back to me after the way I treated you." He picked up her hands, but seemed almost afraid to touch her.

"I had to come back," she said with a smile. "I told you, I have to make all your dreams come true."

"You already have. You rescued me from a life of loneliness. I love you, Sabrina Daniels. I will be the happiest man in the world when you become my wife. And thank you."

She tilted her head. "For what?"

"For giving me a child. And all the love I will ever need." He pulled her against him until her head rested on his chest.

Sabrina listened to the comforting, steady beating of the heart the man she loved had just entrusted to her.

He tipped his finger under her chin, and pressed a passionate kiss to her lips.

She sighed and rested against him, watching as the ranch bustled with the morning's activities. A storm was coming, and there was work to be done. But for now, she was content to be held by the man she loved.

Sabrina thought she wanted independence, and assumed that's what Kyle wanted too. But she discovered true independence was won when you were free to choose.

Both of them were free.

And they chose the love that rescued them both.

Jaci Burton

To learn more about Jaci Burton, please visit
http://www.jaciburton.com. Send an email to Jaci Burton at
jaci@jaciburton.com or join her Yahoo! group at
http://groups.yahoo.com/group/<jaciburtonsparadise to join in the fun
with other readers as well as her newsletter at
http://groups.yahoo.com/group/<jaciburtonjournal for updates about
future releases.

What happens when a bounty hunter finds his prey only to discover she's his mate?

The Bounty
By Beth Williamson
1-59998-047-9

Nicky Malloy is on the run--from guilt, fear, and a murder charge. After three years, the notorious bounty hunter Tyler Calhoun catches up with the elusive lady outlaw. The intensity of their dislike for each other is only matched by the growing passion they cannot seem to control.

A loner by nature, a cold hard hunter by choice, Tyler fights his feelings for his prisoner the only way he knows how--by denying them. He's not prepared for how deeply his feelings will run, or how hard it will be to hold her life in his hands.

Pursued by two hapless cowboys bent on taking Nicky in themselves, Nicky and Tyler are forced to turn to each other for aid, trust, and comfort as their journey progresses on its rocky road. Caught in a web of lies and murder, they hold on to each other as they travel to Wyoming to confront the man that brought them together. Tyler has to decide if his love for her is worth more than the bounty he was sent to find.

This book has been previously published, but substantially revised and reedited.

Warning, this title contains the following: explicit sex, graphic language, some violence.

Available NOW in ebook from www.samhainpublishing.com

Sometimes the only way to find your way home is to leave.

Leaving Mama
By Bobbie Cole
1-59998-032-0

Smoking weed while perched on top of her grandmother's coffin in the middle of a downpour was not how Jillian had seen the trip from Oklahoma to Minnesota as happening. With flights canceled and the airline employees striking, she had no choice but to improvise and use her rock band's hearse. And when Gran exits the hearse after the tires skid on a rain slick highway and the back door flies open, Jillian decides to make the best of the moment.

Things only get worse when they arrive in Minnesota and her oldest sister, Shari, has a stroke at the memorial service. Toss in the fact that their grandmother had led two lives—there was a whole other family they'd known nothing about waiting for them in Minnesota— and life suddenly becomes more complicated.

Available May 30 in ebook from www.samhainpublishing.com

Samhain Publishing, Ltd.

It's all about the story...

Action/Adventure
Fantasy
Historical
Horror
Mainstream
Mystery/Suspense
Non-Fiction
Paranormal
Romance
Science Fiction
Western
Young Adult

http://www.samhainpublishing.com